DEAD OF NIGHT

"That you, Goodnight?" The voice came from the second floor of the dark, abandoned house.

It was McSween's voice, Frank knew, the voice of the man who had left his sister to die. "Come out of there," he said as he climbed the stairs slowly. He reached the second floor and heard McSween's breathing and the whine of the floorboards.

Goodnight pulled his gun, pointed at the sound, fired. He heard the bullet smash into wood and brick, and heard McSween shift direction. He fired again—four times—and heard McSween cry out and fall to the floor. The only sound that remained was the shallow, slow guttering of his breath.

As his body twisted against the rickety floor, the dying man caught his breath enough to ask, "Ever kill a man before, Goodnight?"

"No, but I've got no regrets over this."

"You'll be in hell, then, a long time before you die," said McSween, and stopped stirring on the floor.

D0037069

ERNEST HAYCOX

THE WILD BUNCH

PINNACLE BOOKS
WINDSOR PUBLISHING CORP.

CONTENTS

ONE

THE OWLHORNS

Goodnight crossed the river at a ford whose bottom sands were scarcely covered by water and made noon camp under the shade of a lonely willow. Heat was a burning pressure upon the gray and burnt-brown desert and heat rolled back from the punished earth to make a thin, unseen turbulence all around him. The smell of the day was a rendered-out compound of baked grass and sage and bitter-strong dust.

He lay belly-flat and drank on the upstream side of his horse; he let the horse drift to graze while he built a smoke and stretched out in the willow's spotty shade with his hat drawn over his eyes. Suddenly the sun came around the willow and burned against his skin and he sat upright and knew he had been asleep. He rose up then, a limber man with gray eyes half-hidden behind the drop of his lids. He had a rider's looseness about him and the sun had scorched its layers of tan smoothly over his face. All his features were solid and his shape was the flat and angularly heavy shape of a man who made his living by horse and rope.

When he stepped to the saddle he turned east, as he had been doing for many days — all the way out of Oregon's high range. The Idaho desert lay behind him, and the black lava gorges of the Snake, and the Tetons, and

7

Jackson Hole and the Absarokas. Looking rearward across the leagues of rolling grass and flinty soil, he saw the shadow of great hills lying vague behind the heat haze; forward stood the darker and closer bulk of the Owlhorns. Sundown, he figured, ought to put him into Sherman City at the base of those hills.

Once during the last week he had met a rider and they had said six words apiece and departed on their separate ways. Otherwise travelers were to be seen only as fragments of dust-smoke in the great distance and ranch quarters were small-shaped blurs, like ships hull-down on the horizon. There was such a ranch headquarters now before him, directly upon his route to the Owlhorns; and there was also a pattern of dust on his right, signal of one or more riders moving. He watched that dust for half an hour before he decided it was a single rider heading for the same ranch toward which he pointed.

When a man had long distances to cover, the best way was the slow way; and therefore Goodnight let the horse pick its own gait. He sat easy in the saddle for his own comfort, and even-balanced to save the horse. As he rode, his eyes three quarters lidded to shield off the glare, he saw all there was to be seen and he speculated long upon the course of a creek or the shape of a vagrant track upon the earth, or the distance from point to point; and sometimes he whistled a little and sometimes he sang a song, and sometimes he rode many miles in steady silence — drawn inward to those strange thoughts which ride close to a man alone. At twenty-nine, these thoughts had tempered him, had fashioned a private world with its images and its long thoughts and its hopes of what might be.

The rider south of him made a sweep through the early afternoon, and curved in until he was directly ahead, two or three miles away. In another half hour the man had reached the ranch house toward which Goodnight also moved at a steady pace. The middle-down sun burned like an open flame on his back and the horizons turned blue-yellow. He crossed the bottom of a bone-dry creek, he saw the flash of bright tin reaching out from the ranch-house windmill. He thought of something funny Niles Brand had once said and he smiled; and he remembered a woman's voice he had heard at some strange place back in the mountains. He had never seen her face; it was only her voice coming out of a house — sleepy and low — and it stayed with him, like one short piece of music whose name he wished he knew.

House and barn and yard came into view and when he got nearer he spotted two men on the porch, face to face with ten feet between them. The nearest man was chalked with alkali dust and his florid face puffed with heat; therefore he was the rider who had just come off the desert. He was quite tall and had a heavy, high-bridged nose and sharp blue eyes which now came around and fastened a coolly inhospitable glance on Goodnight. The other man likewise turned his attention and for an instant Goodnight thought he noticed strain and the distant show of fear on that one's face. Meanwhile he waited for an invitation to dismount.

It was a considerable time in coming. The second man looked back at the tall rider and seemed to speculate upon him. Afterwards he swung his glance to Goodnight again and said, "Get down, man, and come out of the sun."

Goodnight dismounted. He stood at the base of the porch and rolled himself a smoke and he thought: "The small fellow is glad I'm here — I wonder why." He had seen an expression of relief noticeably show on the man's mouth. He finished his cigarette and licked it. But his mouth was dry and so he held the cigarette unlighted, watching the tall man with a greater degree of interest. He had, Goodnight thought, a maverick smell about him. He was painted the same dusty color as were all men in this country but the paint came from another brush. This was Goodnight's quick judgment. It was

9

subject to revision, but he always placed weight on his first impressions.

The tall one said with unconscious arrogance: "If you've got business here, get it done with and be on your way."

The man's words were too sharp and distinct, the tone too clear. A Western man had a looser and easier way of speaking. Goodnight said: "Your outfit?"

"Hardly," said the big-nosed man. "But does that matter?"

"Always like to get my walking papers from the boss," said Goodnight.

The big man smiled in a wintery, indifferent way. He didn't bother to answer. It was the other one who said: — "Water's in the back of the house."

Goodnight nodded. He led his horse around the house to a big trough in the rear. He let the horse drink a little. Then he pulled the horse back and himself drank the small trickle of water coming out of the pipe; then he gave the horse another short drink, and moved back to the front yard. It was not as much as he wanted and not as much as the horse wanted, but they still had the worst of the day to ride through and it was better to make a dry march than to sweat out a lot of water. He stopped at the porch steps, before the two men. He still had his cigarette and now took time to light it. He thought he saw relief once more break over the small man's cheeks. He looked at the tall rider and met the steady onset of the latter's impatient glance.

"Now you can dust along," said the tall one.

The shorter man said: "Cut that out, Bill."

The big-nosed Bill showed an amused grin. "This man's no recruit for you, Harry. He's another bum, another fugitive in a land full of fugitives. There's probably a charge against him somewhere and he's running from it. Just one more crook trying to reach the shelter of the Owlhorns before a bullet catches up with him." He gave Goodnight a stiff jolt with his glance, now losing his idle

10

amusement. "You can make timber by night. Go on, move."

Goodnight dragged in the cigarette's strong sweet smoke and blew it out. He dropped the cigarette and ground it under his boot. He lifted his head on Bill, meeting the man's pushing glance. He said to Bill in the softest voice: "You talk too much."

Bill gave him a prolonged study. The remark seemed to interest him more than to anger him; and that was a reaction to which Goodnight was not accustomed. It quickened his attention and he watched the tall man's face steadily for a sign of change.

Bill said in a half-interested manner: "Have I misjudged you, friend, or are you simply making a demonstration for the sake of your pride?"

"Put in your chips and find out," said Goodnight.

Suddenly the high-nosed Bill laughed. "That's typical," he commented, turning to the smaller man. "An arrival, a word, a threat and a showdown. It never varies. There's damned little originality in this country."

"Is that another speech?" asked Goodnight.

"Don't be proud of your ultimatum," said Bill. "Now I shall surprise you very much. I am going to leave you standing right there, high and dry with your gallant attitude."

"That's one way of saying it," said Goodnight.

Bill left the porch and walked to his horse. He stepped to the saddle and laid his hands on the horn. He gave Goodnight a short smile. "Don't be proud. If I felt like fighting I should certainly fight you. But why should I spend that energy and take that risk on a man who means nothing to me, and probably means less to himself?"

"Let me give you some advice," said Goodnight. "Don't make statements you have to crawl out of."

But it didn't touch the tall man. The tall man's smile simply pushed it aside. He lifted his reins, and nodded at the smaller one on the porch. "He's no good for you as a recruit, Harry. None of these stray riders are. You'll hire him, but all he'll ever do is run for a hole when somebody strange comes up. I'll see you later."

By habit he set his horse into a run, through the blasting heat of this day; and kept up the run for a hundred yards or more. The arid dust boiled around him and hung motionless in the air and laid its suffocating smell across the yard. The sky was overcast with heat fog, like the smoke of a forest fire. Eastward, the Owlhorns showed dim. Goodnight turned his glance back to the man on the porch.

"What was his name again?"

"Bill—Boston Bill Royal."

"So," murmured Goodnight.

"Don't let the words fool you." The man on the porch rested back on his chair and let his arms hang loose across his thighs. He relaxed as though he had been under strain. He patted his shirt pocket and found a cigar. He lighted it and closed his eyes a moment; he was small and dark and his shoulders had begun to fatten up. He looked harmless in the chair and Goodnight turned half away to study Boston Bill, now in the distance. When he swung around again, the little man's eyes were open and watching him, keenly and sharply.

"You want a job?"

"Riding or fighting?"

"Less of one thing and more of the other."

"Where's Sherman City?"

"Over there," said the man, and waved a hand toward the Owlhorns. "My name's Harry Ide. I owe you a favor."

"Maybe I missed something," said Goodnight.

"He caught me alone," said Ide.

"He was gettin' set to talk you to death?" drawled Goodnight.

Harry Ide removed his hat and wiped its sweat band. A small bald spot showed at his scalp lock and the edges of his hair were turning from coal-black to gray. He had

12

the beginnings of a bay window and he seemed to have no danger in him. Still, now and then something seemed to spring out of his eyes at Goodnight, very bright and very calculating. "I wouldn't jump at conclusions," Harry Ide said. "The man's better than he sounds."

"Thanks for the drink," said Goodnight and stepped to his saddle.

"About that job—"

"Maybe I'll be back," said Goodnight and rode off.

Boston Bill had reached Harry Ide's ranch house half an hour before Goodnight arrived. He stepped quickly to the ground and got to the porch and stood with a shoulder against the wall. He said, "Harry," and waited. Somebody moved from the back room slowly and came across the front room. Boston Bill held himself still, and so caught Ide by surprise as the latter stepped through the door. Ide saw him a little too late to put himself on the alert. Therefore he stopped still, facing Boston Bill. His face hardened as he waited and he held Bill's eyes with his own guarded glance.

"You see," said Bill, "I have you on the hip."

"So," said Harry Ide, very dry.

"This is just to show you that you can't always be surrounded and safe. If I want to reach you I can always do it. You didn't even see me coming. Or if you did see me, you never thought I'd be fool enough to walk straight at you."

"Was unexpected," agreed Ide. He was listening to Boston Bill with the gravest kind of care. He remained motionless.

"Your head is full of quick ideas," pointed out Bill, now amused. "You're trying to think of some way to protect yourself. You've got no gun. Very careless."

"That's right."

"It ought to occur to you," pointed out Boston Bill,

"that no man is ever safe."

"It occurs to me now," said Ide.

"Then," said Boston Bill, "it should further occur to you that a bargain is better than a burial."

Harry Ide slowly reached up with a hand and scratched the end of his nose. He held Boston Bill's complete attention. Suddenly he turned and walked ten feet away, and turned back to face Bill again.

Bill said: "Why did you do that?"

Harry Ide shrugged his shoulders. He said, "What's this bargain or burial business?"

"You're doing no good fighting me. You may get killed at it. In any event you're getting poorer at it."

"You're a bright lad," said Harry Ide. "What's the idea you're bringin' me so kindly?"

"Why should we fight at all?"

Harry Ide gave out his dry answer. "I like to keep my beef. I guess I always will fight to keep it."

"I can raid you any time I please. I have done so. Fighting does you no good."

"Show me somethin' better," said Ide. He had been standing. Now he sat down, still making his motions slow.

"Why did you do that?" asked Boston Bill, again curious.

"I was tired of standin'," said Ide.

"No," said Bill, "you did it for another reason. You figure it would be harder for me to shoot a man sitting down."

"Wouldn't it?"

"No," said Boston Bill. "But I'm not thinking of that right now. Listen to me. I'll leave you alone. I'll never come near your range, if you'll stay out of my way."

"You're hurtin' a lot of my friends. I'll stick with them."

"Never mind your friends. Here's another idea. You want a chunk of the hills for summer grass. Go ahead and take it. Just tell me when and where you intend to

14

move in and I'll stay out of your road."

"You are offerin' to sell out your friends if I sell out mine," said Harry Ide. "Now why?"

"Your friends expect you to hunt me down and get rid of me. My friends expect me to dispose of you. That's silly, isn't it? We can both do better."

"I see," said Ide. "You're wantin' more safety than you got."

"Exactly," said Bill.

"I will think of it," said Ide.

"Do so," said Bill. "It is always better to be reasonable. It is also much more profitable." He turned to meet Goodnight as the latter crossed the yard.

The afternoon was half gone and the heat had reached its piled-up intensity as Goodnight rode east. Nothing relieved it. Long as he had followed the trail in all its climates, this day was punishment to him, making breath a labor, turning him nervous. "Hundred and twenty out here," he thought. The edges of his saddle were too hot for comfort and the metal pieces of the bridle sent painful flashes against his eyes. Two miles ahead, Boston Bill kicked up a dust that clung to the air and got into Goodnight's nostrils. He reversed and raised his neckpiece over his nose.

At five o'clock the country lifted from its flatness into rolling dunes of sand and clay gulches; here and there a pine tree stood as advance sentinel to the hills. The hills were before him, black and bulky and high, with the yellow streak of a road running upward in crisscross fashion and vanishing inside the timber. He crossed a shallow creek, pausing long enough to let his horse have a short drink; he reached the road and started the roundabout climb into the benchlands.

His shadow ran before him longer and longer as the sun dipped; five hundred feet from the desert floor he turned to catch the last great burst of flame as the sun dropped below the rim, like unto the explosion of a distant world. After that the land was another land, blue and still and a-brim with the smell of the hills. Coolness flowed against Goodnight, taking the sting of the day's heat from him, and he murmured, "Promised land," and whistled into the forming shadows. The horse increased its gait and at dusk Goodnight rounded a bend and came upon Sherman City, whose main street was this road running through.

The town sat upon a bench, facing the desert but facing the hills as well — a double row of buildings on either side of the road and other buildings scattered through the water-blue dusk. Beyond these buildings, the road met a canyon and vanished into the swift rise of the Owlhorns, the shadows of which lay hard upon the town. A plank bridge carried him over a creek. He rode beside single-story houses squatted side by side, their lights blooming through open doorways, through windows coated with dust. Half down the street another road cut out of the hills to form an intersection. On the four corners thus formed sat a hotel, a store, and two saloons diagonally facing each other. One was "The Trail"; the other's faded sign said: "Texican." Beyond the Texican was a stable into which he rode.

A man drifted out of the stable's rear darkness and looked closely at him, and said, "Third stall back." Goodnight gave his horse a small drink at the street trough, removed his gear and hung it up. He stood a moment in the stall, his hand lying on the sweat-gummed back of the horse, and afterwards walked to the street. Here he paused, rolling up a cigarette. The smoke had no flavor in his parched mouth and suddenly he felt the rank need of his dried-out tissues, and bent down over the drinking trough's feed pipe and let the water roll into his throat and fill up his belly until it would hold no more. Presently he strolled to the Texican and went in.

This was supper hour and slack time. He stood at the

bar with no company except the barkeep, and took his whisky quick and returned to the street; and once again he stopped and rolled a smoke. He had no need of the cigarette but it served to cover his idleness as he looked upon this small town crowded against the bulky, night-blackened Owlhorns. A cooler current flowed out of that darkness and the smell was a different smell, stiffening him and sharpening his senses. He thought: "This may be the end of the journey."

He caught a sudden odor of food from the hotel across the street, its effect on him so sharp that a pain started in the corners of his jaws. Men moved idly in and out of the hotel, bound to and from supper, and men strolled by him, each and all of them giving him a quick glance as they passed; it was a noticeable thing. Three men came from the second saloon diagonally over the four-cornered heart of the town — from the Trail — and moved together toward the hotel. One of them was Boston Bill. Boston Bill saw him and Boston Bill's face showed a small grin as he went on into the hotel with his two partners.

One more man moved out of the upper darkness of the town, his body alternately clear and dull as he passed through the lamplight beams shining from the houses. He was a tall one with sharp edges to his shoulders and a hard-brimmed Stetson sitting aft on his head. When he reached the town's center he paused and looked idly around him and his glance moved to Goodnight, and moved away. He teetered on the edge of the walk, like a man undecided, and at last cut over the dust toward him. He had yellow hair and a light skin blistered by the sun and when he came by Goodnight the light of the saloon hit his eyes and showed the bright-green glint in them. He passed Goodnight within arm's reach. He murmured: "Eat your supper and meet me at the foot of this street."

Goodnight tarried until the other man had swung into the Texican; then he crossed the dust to the hotel

17

and signed the register and climbed a set of squealing stairs to an upper room. He took off his shirt and filled the washbowl from the pitcher; when he washed he felt the sudden cracking of the mask of alkali dust on his face and tough as his skin was the soap burned its freshly scorched surface. It had been that hot a day.

He shook the dust from his shirt and put it on and he upended the water pitcher and drank all he could hold, still unable to slake the thirst in him; he was, he thought, like a board that had lain out in the sun too long, brittle and warped. He passed the open door of another bedroom, inside which six men sat packed around a poker table, and saw Boston Bill there. He cruised down the stairs and found a place in the dining room and ordered his meal; he sat back with all his muscles loose, fully enjoying the laziness and the luxury that followed a long day's ride. He ate his meal when it came and afterwards he remained at the table, a strange thing for him, and built himself a cigarette. He had been tired. Now the energy of his supper was a stimulant that lifted him, and the goodness of being alive made him smile and brought his eyelids together until shrewd lines appeared below his temples. Restlessness bubbled up and little things out of the past weeks came into his mind, little pictures and little sounds, the feeling evoked by starlight, the smell of rain against the hot ashes of his campfire, the sing of wind through the high peaks of the continental divide — and the sound of that unseen woman's voice again.

Maybe the urges of a lone man always at last moved like the needle of a compass to the thought of a woman, or maybe it was because of the woman who came into the dining room at the moment he rose to leave; at any rate, all his attention closed upon her as she paused at the door and looked around her. She was still young, with black hair and a roundness to her upper body, with a filled-out completeness that sang over the room at him and excited all his male interests. Her lips lay together,

18

almost willful, and her eyes were cool and her manner indifferent.

She had found a table when he went by. She was behind him, but the thought of her stopped him at the doorway and he swung to look at her, and he saw that her glance had risen to him. She didn't look away; she caught his glance and held it, as direct as he had been, as though she challenged him to break that composure on her face, or as though, weary of indifference, she wanted to be lifted from it. Her eyes were black-gray and her hands small and square as they rested on the table. She knew she was beautiful and she knew she was a picture framed before his hungry glance. Her assurance said as much as she watched him. He was a man like other men, with all the old impulses. Her manner said that too, but she continued to watch him and he thought he saw a break of interest in her eyes as he turned away.

He returned to the stable to water his horse; then he went into the saloon and bought a cigar, and stood with an elbow hooked to the bar, watching the crowd drift in. Presently he left the saloon and walked idly past the lighted houses on into the darkness at the foot of the street. There was the sagged image of a shed before him. He paused here and he turned as though to go back. Niles Brand's voice came out of the shed's shadows.

"Been waiting a week for you."

"Any news?"

"Ain't picked up any trail of him yet."

"I'm guessin' he's here somewhere. These Owlhorns seem to be where they all hide."

Two

Voice of Hate

Goodnight made a slow swing to search the round-about shadows. The nearest house was two hundred feet away, showing no light. Farther toward the center of town a pair of men stood momentarily on a corner and then walked into the Trail, leaving the street empty. Goodnight stepped behind the shed, coming close by Niles Brand. Starlight and a thin slice of a moon sent down a glow upon the sharp, small smile of his partner and the ruddy face with its pleasant irony.

"How long you been here, Niles?"

"A week. Just layin' around, watchin' men come and go. Keepin' my ears open. This is a hell of a town, Frank."

"He's around here somewhere," repeated Goodnight. "A man will only run so far. Then he stops runnin', like a stampeded steer with no more steam to run on. These Owlhorns have got a reputation for shelterin' wild ones. He's probably here."

"If he didn't stop somewhere else before he got here."

"I raised a smell of him back on the other edge of this desert. He had put up at a line camp, nursing a bad leg. Man described him—young and gray at the edges of his hair. He pulled out after two days, headed east across the desert."

"That sounds like him," said Niles.

"If he started over the desert," pointed out Goodnight, "he wouldn't stop until he got to the next set of mountains. That's here."

"These hills," said Niles, "are two hundred miles long and fifty miles deep. How you goin' to cover all that?"

"Pretty soon he'll get awful tired of living alone. Then he'll come into town for a bust. We'll stick around and wait."

Niles said again: "This is a hell of a town, Frank." He searched for his tobacco and he rolled a smoke blind, and struck and cupped a match to his face. His skin was of the florid kind, burned to a violent red. His eyebrows were bleached to the shade of sand. Momentarily the match light danced frosty and bright in his eyes. He breathed deeply on the cigarette. "Everybody walkin' around, watchin' for somebody else to make a false move. Never saw anything like it."

"Why?"

"The big outfits in the desert summer-graze their beef up in the hills. Last few years smaller outfits have started in the hills, cutting in on the range the desert bunch used to have. Been some battles on that. Then these hills are full of crooks hidin' out, and they been nibblin' away at the desert stuff, drivin' it into the timber and sellin' it to the hill people. As I get it there's a fellow named Boston Bill who's got a dozen wild ones together. They're in the business. Talk seems to be that this Bill delivers the desert beef to a hill ranch run by a man named Hugh Overman. There's a lot of these small hill ranches and they all stick tight, figurin' the desert crowd to be legal game."

"We'll just stay around here and wait," said Goodnight.

"Move easy," said Niles Brand. "All strangers comin' in here are watched. A man's on one side or he's on the other and they'll peck at you and me until they

21

find out. Every time I walk down the road I wonder when somethin' is goin' to bust."

"If we have to meet to talk," said Goodnight, "make it here at night."

"I been offered a job," said Niles. "Chambermaid in the stable."

"Take it," said Goodnight. "That gives you a reason for staying here."

"Oh, my God," groaned Niles. "Me doin' that. What'll you do?"

"I'll find something."

"Be careful who you mix with," said Niles. "Awful easy to get with the wrong crowd."

"All we want is a man," said Goodnight.

"If I ever get a decent bead on him I'll shoot him—and that's the end of it."

"No," said Goodnight, soft and final. "Not that easy for him, Niles." He stepped aside from the shed and gave the street a careful study. A sudden shout came from the heart of town and two or three riders appeared, lifting the deep dust around them; they halted at the saloon on the far corner. Goodnight stepped forward, moving idly back toward the hotel. He passed two dark houses and he passed a third with a light shining out of an open door; he looked through the doorway and saw a woman inside, her back turned to him. Her dress was brown, edged with some kind of metal thread that struck up a sharp shining; and then he remembered the girl who had been in the hotel's dining room. It was the same dress, the same girl.

Beyond her house stood the back side of the hotel, with a narrow alley between. A man sat on a box in the alley's mouth, an old man with white whiskers short-cropped and a narrow goatee. He had his legs crossed, one leg swinging on the other with a quick up-and-down rhythm, and his glance slanted up at Goodnight from beneath the tilted brim of his hat. Goodnight went by him, but a sharp warning struck

22

through him and he turned back to face the old man. He watched the old fellow and wondered how much the latter had seen.

The old man's head came up. He had a sly humor on his face, a bright and beady wisdom in his eyes. He said: "You know why I sit here in the alley? There's always more wind comin' down an alley on a hot night. That's why I sit here."

"Good place to see a lot," said Goodnight.

"I see a lot and I know a lot," said the old one. "I know more'n I ever tell. If I told what I knew I wouldn't be an old man. I'd be a dead one. I guess I'm the only one in town that ain't lined up."

"Lined up how?"

"Lined up," said the old one with a touch of impatience. "On one side or the other side. I'm so old nobody cares where I am. But if they knew how much I knew, they'd care. So I keep still. You ain't lined up, either?"

He made it as a hopeful question, a magpie curiosity glittering in his eyes. His leg stopped teetering and he bent forward and waited for the answer.

"No," said Goodnight. "I'm not lined up," and moved away. He heard the old one's odd chuckle, half wise and half foolish, and he thought: "He saw Niles and me." That was something to remember. He reached the hotel and put his back to its corner and rolled a smoke to demonstrate his idleness. The Trail saloon was before him. The other saloon, the Texican, stood over the dust to his right; before it the newly arrived riders now stood. He lighted the smoke, his interest lifting little by little, prompted by things which he could feel but could not see; and he noticed a man ride out of the hills on a huge bay horse—a little man with a pock-marked face and a set of elbows flopping up and down to the horse's gait. The little man reached the hotel and dropped off, and then he looked around him in all four directions and his glance

23

stopped longest on the men posted in front of the Texican. They were watching him with an equal interest and after he vanished through the hotel's doorway they disappeared into the Texican. In a few moments they returned with three others and all of them stood in a close group, softly speaking; then the group broke and the various men spread into the shadows, one man remaining in front of the saloon.

He had about finished his smoke. He dropped it and ground it out, hearing quick steps behind him. The girl who had been in the hotel's restaurant passed him and looked at him, and went on. He crossed the dust to the Trail, feeling the effect of her nearness, and looked around as he shoved the saloon's door before him; she had reached the front of a store and she had stopped, her glance on him.

He stepped into the Trail. He lifted one finger and laid his elbows on the bar and put his weight on them; and suddenly he felt fine, with a fresh current of interest running through him as he thought of the girl's face and the steady expression in her eyes. The barkeep was a little slow in the way he brought the bottle and glass. The barkeep gave him a head-on glance. "You drank your last drink at the Texican, didn't you?"

"That's right."

"Bob," said the barkeep, calling down the room. "He drank his last drink at the Texican."

Four other men were in this saloon. One of them stood at a small window and looked out toward the Texican; the other three stood by, silent and attentive. The man at the window turned about, solid of shoulder and wearing a bristle-sharp mustache. He came forward, the other three immediately following him. He got directly in front of Goodnight, who had made a turn-about from the bar. Suspicion lay in the room. Tension held the men tight.

Bob said: "Don't you know enough to keep in your

24

own back yard?"

"Whose yard is this?"

One of the others said: "He rode into town before supper."

"Maybe you're strange," said Bob. "Where you from?"

"That's my business, Bob."

"Is it?" said Bob, very soft. "Now maybe." He searched Goodnight with a glance that believed nothing. "And maybe you're not strange. Maybe you know what you're doin'."

"Let's all have a drink and find out what I'm doing," suggested Goodnight.

"Easy won't do it," said Bob. "If you've come over from the Texican to pull a stunt . . ." He stopped and he gave that idea some thought. He walked to the door and slightly opened it, looking toward the Texican. He came back. "You go back there and say we'll meet anything they start."

"You go tell them," said Goodnight. He had this Bob in front of him, with the three others on his flank; they boxed him in and he saw the growing thought of action in Bob's eyes. He made a quarter turn toward the others and he noticed the instant hardening of Bob's face. "Bob," he said, "back up . . ."

A man outside yelled, long and full, and immediately afterwards a gun shouted. Bob dropped his hand toward his gun and made half a pull before Goodnight's right hand came off the bar with the whisky bottle standing there. He aimed it high, grazing it across the top of Bob's skull. Bob's knees buckled and he dropped on his hands. Goodnight jumped past him, to face the others.

But the others were rushing for the street, no longer thinking of him. He gave a quick look at Bob, who rested on his hands and knees and tried to shake the fog out of his head. He reached down and seized Bob's gun lying near the bar; he bent and hooked an arm

25

under Bob and hauled him to his feet. Sense came swiftly back to Bob. He battled down Goodnight's arm and stepped away. "Hell with you."

"If you want a fight there's one on the street. Let's both go look at it." He returned Bob's gun muzzle first and ran for the door, Bob behind him. He pushed through and stopped on the edge of the walk so abruptly that Bob ran into him and pushed him aside. Then Bob's voice called over the dust to a man — to the pock-marked man who had recently arrived in town — now slowly backing away from the Texican and away from a little group of men standing hard by the Texican. "Come here, Slab." Bob ran past Goodnight into the dust, reached Slab and took stand with him, backing away as Slab backed away.

The old ways of violence, never changing, never different, slowly worked through this town and this little stretch of time. The group now forming at the Texican had been patiently building a trap for Slab and now were about to spring it. He saw two other men deep down the north end of the street sitting a-saddle, as though waiting a signal; he discovered Niles Brand posted at the hotel corner, looking on at all of this with his half-smiling interest, and he saw the girl come out of the store which adjoined the hotel. She walked forward to the hotel corner, glanced quickly at the men face to face over the dust, and deliberately cut between them on her way to the diagonal corner.

Bob and Slab had retreated very slowly, one reluctant pace at a time, until they were within twenty feet of the Trail. There had been three others waiting here, but now, out of one dark corner and another of this town, more men had come to place themselves in support of Bob and Slab until there were half a dozen waiting. A voice anonymous and unlocated, yelled "Hep," and suddenly the two horsemen far down the street shot forward on the dead run, headed for the intersection.

26

Goodnight shouldered through the men grouped together and ran for the girl who still was in the street. The pair of horsemen rushed forward. Bob's voice cut cold and confident through the night: "Run us down and you'll never live!" The sound of those two riders was dull and heavy and seemed to grow out of all proportion, and then Goodnight lifted his glance beyond the girl, to the black end of the cross street, and saw a line of men spill out of the timbered canyon into town. He thought: "Somebody laid this trap—and somebody's going to get fooled."

He reached the girl and seized her arm and hurried her on, across the dust to the far walk. He pushed her against the wall of a building and held her there, feeling the even strike of her heart against his arm. She looked up at him and her lips drew back from her teeth in a smile. "Ah," she murmured, "nothing will happen to me. But it is nice to have your concern."

The group from the hill rushed full into the heart of the town. He heard Bob crying out, now lost somewhere in the rush of horses. A great figure of a man, blackly whiskered, led this bunch and his voice was a hammer blow against iron. "Knock them down— knock them down!" The quick, lean report of a rifle followed on his words and one rider gave a great cry and rolled like a drunk on the leather. Lifting his eyes, Goodnight saw a man in the window of the hotel's corner second-story room, both elbows on the window sill, his face hidden as he snuggled against the rifle stock and took aim.

The big bearded one shouted and pointed, and fired at the window. The horses milled, swung wildly around and came onto the walks. A horse backed full into Goodnight and lashed out with its feet and broke a board beside him, and swung again, pinning the girl against the wall. Goodnight reached up, caught the rider at the elbow and hauled him from the saddle.

The firing burst up with a sultry violence. The unhorsed rider struggled around and struck out with a fist, catching Goodnight in the throat. Goodnight hooked a punch straight up from his belt into the man's chin and drove him away in a spinning turn. He drew his gun then, expecting more of a fight, but the man never turned back; he ran and ducked through the confusion, trying to reach his horse. Goodnight heard Niles Brand's voice somewhere near. He turned and discovered his partner working a zigzag way across from the Texican. Niles reached him, softly growling, "There he is—with this new bunch!"

"Get away from me," said Goodnight. "You damned fool—get away!" The confusion grew greater and the horses were again breaking under the sudden fire of other rifles thus far hidden. He had his back to the girl, sheltering her body with his own as the horses reared around upon the walk and moved at him. He saw a thin, straight face move through the crush, a young face stretched thin by the heat and the lust of the fight. A rim of gray hair showed below his hat and he was grinning, and in a moment disappeared in the shadows. The big man with the rough black whiskers was calling them all out and the bunch ran back toward the head of the street and at last faded back into the canyon.

Dust was a silver screen through which he saw the turned shape of a man on the ground. Men, many men, came out of the town's black spots, walking toward the Texican. Bob was gone, and the pockmarked Slab, and all those who had stationed themselves by the Trail. He saw Harry Ide step from the hotel and he guessed it had been Ide who fired from the second-story room of the hotel. The hill crowd had set a trap, but the desert bunch had known of it and had set one of their own. He thought: "A hell of a lot of shootin' for no results," and remembered he had the girl behind him. He turned on her.

She watched him with the same expression he had

noted in the dining room—direct and speculative, barely showing interest, barely giving him hope. He watched her lips change and form a new shape; he saw her smile spread warm over her face.

He said: "Who was the big fellow with the whiskers?"

"Hugh Overman."

"That his crew?"

"They all came out of the hills," she said.

Harry Ide had gone into the Texican, the crowd drifting with him. Niles Brand stood over in the stable's archway, smoking a cigarette.

"I'll walk back with you," said Goodnight.

She gave him a studying glance and for a moment some answer was balanced in her mind; then she shrugged her shoulders and turned with him, walking over the dust toward her house beyond the hotel. Goodnight threw a glance at Niles; he made a small motion with his hand.

She saw that. She said: "You'll have to be more careful—you and your friend. This town has nothing but ears and eyes. You are being watched now. You'll always be watched."

"Kind of an uneasy town."

"This town," she murmured, and shook her head. She kept in step with him, across the dust and down the street. The old man, he noticed, still sat in the alleyway. The girl gave him a swift look and a sharp word. "Go somewhere else, Gabe."

Gabe murmured, "Yes'm," and faded back. When she reached the small porch of her house she stopped and faced him. He was full in the beam of her doorway's light, and by impulse she touched his chest and pushed him back until he was in the shadows. "You must be more careful," she said.

He came near her, looking down at her lips. They lay closed but without pressure, full at the centers. She had to lift her head to meet his eyes, and suddenly her eyes were heavy and the veiled expression broke and he saw want come to her. He put his hands at her hips and swayed her against him and kissed her full and heavy on the lips, and stepped back.

Her eyes turned blacker and the self-confidence grew oddly bitter. "You did it very easily, didn't you?" she murmured. There was the power of hatred in her and he felt it burn against him now, shocking him and shaming him. He came to her again, not touching her but so near to her that he caught the fragrance of her hair.

"I guess I've been alone too long. When I saw you in the dining room you were the strongest thing in this town."

"Any woman can do that to a hungry man."

"You're not any woman."

"What am I?" she said, letting her voice drop to a whisper.

"Not like anything I've ever seen before."

He turned to go and was stopped by the quick soft murmur of her voice. "What is your name?"

"Frank Goodnight."

"Do you know mine? Have you asked about me?"

"No."

She came near him, whispering in his ear. "Rosalia Lind. Will I see you again?"

"Yes."

She stepped back and he saw her self-assurance return. She had gone beyond her pride and she was annoyed at herself. "Be more careful than you have been," she told him. "The men in the Trail are all hill people. The Texican is only for men from the desert. You went to both places."

"You saw me?"

She watched him, her face shadowed and soft. "I have watched you," she murmured and turned into her house.

He looked both ways on the street and saw nothing

30

to warn him; and moved down the street idly to the shed. He paused here, making up a smoke. He heard Niles grumbling at him from the blackness behind the shed. "You're doin' mighty well for yourself as a pure stranger. You know who she is?"

Goodnight said, "Who you talkin' about?"

"The girl. That girl walkin' through this town like a dyin' man's vision of Paradise. She's Rosalia Lind."

"So she said."

"You see that hotel just the other side of the saloon? That's hers. You see the store next to it? That's hers. She had a father who started this town. I guess he owned the town. He's dead, and it is all hers. Her dad came from Kentucky. There were some other Kentucky men that came with him—and these people hang together awful tight. If she lifted her finger six men would show up from nowhere and cut your throat. The boys from the desert know that and so do the riders from the hills. They step around her pretty soft and easy."

"All right," said Goodnight. "You almost tipped over the cart, comin' to talk to me on the street."

"There he was. One bullet would have ended all this wandering around."

"I'll find him. The one with the sharp face—smiling?"

"That's the man. But try to get him out of those hills. He's smart. He got himself in with Overman. Try to get him away from Overman. It's the same as a bodyguard."

Goodnight drew his cigarette down to a bright butt and flicked it to the dust. "Stick around here, Niles. I'm going up in those hills."

"Doin' what?"

"Don't know yet. I'll catch him off first base. Sooner or later. You stay here until I shout."

He turned back. He walked to the corner of the Texican and rounded the corner, and came upon

Harry Ide standing there.

Ide grinned at him. "Well," he said, "you see what the town's like."

"That's right," answered Goodnight.

"Stayin' around," said Harry Ide, "or coming back to my place?"

"I'll be ridin' around," said Goodnight.

"Go ahead and ride," said Harry Ide. "But you see how it goes. A man can't stay in the middle."

"This Overman dug a hole for you," commented Goodnight.

"So he did," said Ide. "And we saw him dig it."

He kept his smile as he talked. It was a hard smile; it had weight and threat. He looked about him, keening the night for its treachery, and gave Goodnight a short nod and crossed the street, going into the darkness beyond the hotel.

Goodnight moved into the stable; he paid his bill and saddled the horse. He rode out and gave the horse a drink and afterwards started toward the hills, but within a dozen feet he turned squarely about and rode back, turning the saloon's corner. He stopped in front of Rosalia's house and got down, and saw her on the porch. He went to the porch steps and halted. There was no particular reason why he had returned, or if there was a reason he could not drag it out of his head. He stood puzzled before her, watching the door light make its streaming shine along the smoothed blackness of her hair. She watched him and she waited for him to speak; she was round-shaped in the light, she was still, with her lips lying together in gentle fullness. Her eyes were shadowed to him and he could not see the expression in them. Her breasts lifted softly and softly fell to her breathing. He came up the steps to her and he had the impulse to seize her, and fought it back with difficulty. The pull of her presence was that urgent, straining him forward against his sense of propriety. A woman had not done this to him before.

32

She said in a small, murmuring tone: "Why are you here?"

"You can pull a man against his wishes," he said. "You know that?"

"Is it against your wishes?" she asked him. He saw her draw together and harden her spirit against him.

He said: "Turn around."

She held herself still. She whispered, "What interests you?" But he didn't answer and in a moment she swung until her face was in the light. He looked at her eyes, at the glow which seemed to lie below the dark coloring. It came out of her from deep places. It wasn't just the lamplight shining; it was part of her spirit. He said: "A man can ride a long way on the memory of that."

Her answer came at him swiftly: "How far are you riding?"

"I don't know."

He returned to his horse and stepped to the saddle. He heard her say: "You can't escape anything by riding. It rides with you."

"I will see you again," he said and went on. At the corner of the Texican he had a view of the main road running back through town. Harry Ide had vanished in the darkness, but at this moment Boston Bill Royal stepped from the dark side of the store opposite and looked up at him, now not amused or indifferent.

"You scatter yourself in too many places, my friend," he said.

Goodnight said curtly: "You had better judge your own actions," and rode straight for the canyon's mouth, leading into the Owlhorns. A mile from town he felt the weariness of his horse grow greater and he pulled into the timber, made cold camp and fell asleep.

Boston Bill listened to the sound of Goodnight's

horse rattle against the stony underfooting of the road and entirely die in the timber above town. Afterwards he circled the Trail and walked quickly along the back end of a row of houses and came again to the street at the north end. He stopped here, watching the shadows for sight of Harry Ide. He saw nothing and in a little while he grew tired of the wait and moved back toward the saloon. When he passed the edge of the adjoining building Harry Ide's voice struck him from the rear.

"Just a minute, Bill."

Bill stopped, one foot in advance of the other. He waited, not turning and not drawing his feet together until Ide spoke again.

"Step back here. I want to talk to you."

Bill turned about and faded into the space between the two buildings. He reappeared ten minutes later and paused to look around him. He had not been seen, he thought, and he pulled his shoulders together and crossed over and moved down the inside wall of the hotel, thereby coming into the rear of Rosalia's house. He knocked on her back door and let himself in. She was in the front room; her face changed when she saw him.

He had sharp eyes and a quick mind. He saw the change and thought he knew its meaning. He said irritably: "Better be careful of strangers. You know nothing about that man."

"Next time," she said, "wait until I open the door before you come in."

"What did he want?" he demanded. "What brought him to you? How did he come to know you?"

She lifted her shoulders, facing him with a cold sureness. "Did you hear what I said?"

He came to her, smiling; he lifted his arms to her. She stood fast, commanding him by the stern expression on her face. She brought him all the way down from his careless confidence; she made him sober and restless and unsure. He turned irritable again. "I can't

34

keep up with your changes. You're warm, you're cold. One time you're charming. Now you freeze me with dislike."

"I never change," she said.

"You're something all covered over. I never am able to tear the covering aside."

"What do you think is inside?"

"Heaven or hell. In a woman there's little distinction between the two."

"You always want to explain things," she said. "Nothing's ever that mixed up. Everything's much more simple."

"When I first met you," he recalled, "you were charming. You liked me."

"Perhaps I saw something in you."

"Why have you changed?"

"Perhaps I see something else."

He flushed. His pride was injured. "Now you see something in a new man. But you will see something else in him. Let him alone."

"Who are you to say that?"

"Rosalia," he said, "I want you."

"Wanting's not enough."

"What is enough?"

She shook her head. "That is for you to find out."

"There's never been a soul in this world I cared enough about to change for. There's never been one for whom I'd give up all that I am, or have, and do what was asked of me. Not until I came here. You have that power."

"I don't want it," she said.

"There's cruelty in you," he said.

"Honest people are always cruel."

He studied her, his mouth small, his eyes half-shut. The color of his face was stronger than usual and pride caused him to keep his injured feelings hidden. He brought on a smile. "You are accustomed to a high hand. You've always had your way. You've used the

35

whip when you wanted. But remember this — you're a woman and a whip won't do if you want a man."

"Perhaps," she said.

Irony came quickly to him. He bowed to her, still smiling. "This seems to be a one-sided conversation."

"You use so many words to say so little."

That touched him and he grew openly angry. "I've heard that said before, today. By your friend — by the man who just visited you."

She said spare and dry: "Pull out, Bill. If you don't know it, Harry Ide's in town. Better watch him."

"I have known that for an hour."

"Have you?" she commented, and looked closely at him. He met her glance until he was warned by the things she might be seeing, and turned sharp on his heels and left by the rear door.

She was thinking: "He gave himself away. He has seen Harry Ide — talked to him. I did not know he would betray his people." She thought of it, but not for long. A sweet, sharp feeling ran through her. She stood still, letting all of it warm her and trouble her — and remembered the power of Goodnight's arms. He had come back to look again upon her, and she knew why he had come back. He had been uncertain of her. He still was. She thought: "I should not have let him kiss me." Her expression darkened and momentarily she disliked herself. "Why did I do it?" She tried to answer the question and could not, and turned impatient. "I did it," she decided, "and that's enough. If it isn't enough for him, let him never come back." She moved to the porch and she stood in the shadows, feeling the first coolness of night come. "How else could I have acted? If a thing happens, it happens. I hope he comes back."

THREE

SUN RANCH

At daylight Goodnight saddled and returned to the road, traveling steadily higher until he reached a creek boiling violently down the breast of the mountain. He crossed a gravel ford and now left the road, not intending again to use it this day. Deep in the pines he made up a short fire, cooked bacon and coffee and shaved; and resumed his journey.

The first sun was high beyond the stiff tops of the pines; this western slope was still gray and cold. There was almost no underbrush. The red-bodied pines lay heavy around him, the almost solid mat of their branches trapping the shadowy pearl light of dawn long after full day had lightened the sky. A thousand years of needle-fall made a spongy surface upon which the horse's feet dropped with scarce a sound; and except for the slight jingle of the bridle metal and the occasional chukkering of the horse's lips, and the now-and-then sharp beat of a woodpecker's bill, a churchly stillness lay all along the aromatic timbered reaches.

Occasionally he passed over a small cattle trail; twice he came upon a wagon's course. Traffic between desert and mountain summit moved in errant zigzags through the pines. He traveled without haste, and frequently stopped to let the horse take a blow. Far back in Oregon he had felt haste, but with all the weeks behind him he had developed a patience so that now time didn't matter very much. In the beginning he had felt a great wild anger; but that kind of anger could not sustain itself and had hardened into a fixed and patient purpose. The immediate desire to destroy Theo McSween in one swift stroke seemed now, after these weeks of chase, less than enough. All the days of thinking about it and all the nights of remembering his sister—whom McSween had betrayed and destroyed—made it necessary that McSween should face his crime, should suffer from the image of it, should have it as a weight on him that grew greater and greater until it carried him down in one long slow fall, he knowing his ruin as it came to him—forseeing it and suffering with it to the bitterest end.

He had never seen McSween until, on the previous night, Niles Brand had pointed him out in the group of horsemen. Born and raised in the Oregon high desert, Goodnight had frequently drifted from home. While he was returning from his last wandering, the story had started and had ended. This McSween, also a drifter, had come into the country, had made his gallant display, and had ridden away with Goodnight's sister. Goodnight's parents had objected to the man and so, the oldest tale in the book, his sister had run away to make a marriage. There never had been a marriage insofar as Goodnight could discover; following the trail to Nevada he had found his sister listed in the cemetery under her own name. He had located the doctor in the case. The doctor had said: "Looked to me like both of them had just kicked around without money, sleepin' any place and eatin' any place. Your sister was rundown and pneumonia did the rest. The man pulled

38

out." Then the doctor looked thoughtfully at Good-night as he added: "In fact he left her before she died. You could tell she had been a fine and pretty girl."

It was that last phrase which even now turned its knife point in Goodnight's bowels. Niles, being a home-town boy, had seen the man. Now Niles had identified him and Niles's part was over. The rest of it was his own burden, and that burden had changed him, it had burned away his carelessness and most of his easy faith; it had made him tough and disbelieving and sometimes sad. A simple world had turned into one with a thousand sides, with shades and colors he had never before seen, with questions that rang like footsteps in vast empty cor-ridors.

He threw off before another creek beyond noon, rested and resumed his way. After the first quick rise, the Owlhorns began to break into benches where short-grass meadows and finger-shaped valleys lay between the green tree masses. He crossed these openly, reached timber and climbed again to the next higher bench. The road which he had been paralleling at a distance all day suddenly swung around toward him. Thus far the timber had fur-nished good traveling, but at this point the land be-gan to break into canyons and sharp-backed ridges, through which the road made the only comfortable passage; therefore he took it. Sunset found him be-side a creek and here he stopped, put his horse on picket in a small flat of grass, and made his meal. He built the fire larger than his needs, drew his blankets beyond the reach of the light and watched the world plunge into darkness. Against the utter black heavens the stars swirled in the universe's yeasty ferment and a small wind, chilled by this ele-vation, moved against him and a moon hung tilted low to the southwest, so thin that it had only a faded glow.

He was not far from the road, and he was now near the summit plateau of the Owlhorns. Somewhere there would be ranch quarters and at some time or another travelers would pass and see his fire, which was as he wished. He smoked his cigarette in content, the ease of a long day's end coming upon him like softness. When he heard the run of a horse far down the grade he turned in his blankets and threw a handful of pine stems on the fire, lifting the blaze.

He listened to the horse come on as he had listened to the like sound on many another night in many another place, interest and caution rising together. He lay flat on his back, his head against the saddle and his feet to the fire. Sound and rider came quickly around a bend of the road, reached abreast, and stopped. He saw the rider's shape bend in the saddle and straighten back. He heard the leather squeal. A woman's voice came easy at him. "Hello," she said, and followed her call into the firelight.

She sat still on the side saddle, her arms folded on the horn. She wore a tan shirt and a long dark riding skirt and a man's hat sat back on hair the color of dark honey. When she looked directly at him he saw the lovely turning of her throat. She was on guard; not so much afraid of him as alert to his presence and skeptical of him. She said so at once. "Your story doesn't make sense. You ride away from the road all day, as though you were on the run. Then you camp where everybody can see you. Then you build a fire big as a house, and sleep back in the shadows."

He sat up. "How do you know I kept off the road?"

"Bob Carruth followed you for a while."

40

"Nothing better to do with his time?"

"You didn't think you could ride this far into the Owlhorns without notice, did you?"

"Why not?"

She said: "You must be green." Then as he got slowly to his feet her attention came close upon him. His smile was a white streak against the shadows and the fire threw its bronze highlights on his face, making it bony and rugged. Her eyes narrowed on him in appraisal, and opened wider. She looked quickly around, as though wondering if he were alone. "This is no place to camp. You'd get a bullet in that fire before another hour. You're running I suppose."

"No," he said, "just riding."

She listened to his voice, she weighed it. She had started out cool and suspicious of him, and she wanted to remain that way. Still, he saw the change of her lips and he saw a small gust of expression go over her face. "You're not green," she murmured. "And you're probably lying." She turned the horse, intending to move on. She reached the road and swung and stopped; she was beyond the firelight, deep in thought, and at last she spoke from the shadows. "Saddle up and come to the ranch. You'll have no luck here."

"What ranch?"

"Sun Ranch. Were you the man in town last night that hit Bob Carruth with a bottle?"

"He was a little suspicious."

"He had a right to be. You visited the other saloon."

He chuckled. "He had his rights. I had mine. So we're even."

Downgrade was the heavy murmur of horses moving fast. The girl said impatiently: "Saddle up and kick out the fire."

41

He made up his blanket roll in quick turns, threw on the saddle and lashed his roll. He gave the fire a sidewise kick with his boot, sending the sticks into the nearby water. He said: "Still, they'll smell smoke and stop," and rode beside her.

"You're not green," she repeated and set the pace up the grade. "You would have been picked up and brought in anyway and you might as well sleep in a bunk." At the top of the grade she turned into timber, leaving the road behind. Presently she halted. "If we go ahead of them they'll catch our dust and know we're around."

"That's all right, isn't it?"

"If you stay in the hills," she said, "you'll learn nothing's all right." There was, he recognized, a swing of regret and dislike in her voice but he thought little of it at the moment, being more interested in the sound of the horsemen coming along. They had not stopped at his camp, which made him murmur: "A careless lot. If they can't smell smoke . . ."

She reached out through the darkness and touched him; her hand squeezed down, commanding his silence. A group of riders ran by on the road and a little gust of talk fell behind from them, and then they faded on. The girl waited a moment before riding forward to the road. Goodnight came beside her; both horses traveled at a walk. "That was Boston Bill," she said. "He'll be at the house when we get there. When they question you, just say that you saw me on the road and asked for a night's shelter."

"This Boston Bill is full of questions," he said.

"It will be my father who asks the questions," she said. "My father — Hugh Overman." Then she remembered Goodnight's remark and commented on it. "How would you know about Boston Bill?"

"I met him out on the desert."

42

"He was out there in daylight?" Her voice came at him with a lift of interest. "Where was he?"

"At a ranch."

"Near Sherman City?"

"That's right."

"Ide's ranch," she murmured, and said nothing more for a long interval, apparently turning over the information in her mind. The road reached through another shallow canyon still rising. The canyon reached a level area surrounded by the shadow of ragged hills; a creek made its smooth run directly before them. Lights sparkled ahead and he saw shapes cut over those lights, moving around a yard. A plank bridge boomed a warning of their approach and in another minute they were at the front of a log house built low and long across the yard.

He saw first the huge square shape of a man in the doorway, the same black-bearded one who had led the hill crowd into Sherman City on the previous night. With him was Boston Bill, seeming small beside the older one's great shape. There were other men, Boston Bill's men, apparently, waiting by their horses along the yard. Goodnight passed among them as he walked forward with the girl to the huge one at the door.

The girl said: "I picked this man up on the road, Dad. He wanted a sleep and a meal."

Hugh Overman was a cold and distant spirit lost in thought. Goodnight watched the man pull himself into the present and look upon him, neither interested nor disinterested. He lifted his hand and made a strange, stiff upward jerk with it. "Strangers are welcome," he said. "Show him the bunkhouse, daughter. Show him the cookshack. See he gets a cup of coffee."

Boston Bill observed Goodnight with a small thin smile, and he sent a quick side glance to the girl.

He must have noticed something on her face, for his smile broke off and he spoke to Overman in a lightly provoking tone. "Charity is blessed, Hugh, but it might be well to consider this stranger."

"You know him?" said Overman.

"I've met him and there's some things about him I don't understand."

Overman placed his severe and powerful eyes on Goodnight. "You come here with honest intentions?"

Boston Bill broke in. "He was at Harry Ide's place when I saw him."

Overman's eyes grew agate-still and in their depths a great wrath slowly moved. "You're on my place and I have offered you puttin' up. But we'll see. Daughter, give him his coffee and bring him to the dining room."

The girl touched Goodnight's arm and turned him. He followed her to an ell of the main house, through the door into a kitchen. A light burned on a table and a pot of coffee sat on the back edge of the still-warm range. Virginia Overman lifted a cup from a hook, poured his coffee and pointed to the condensed milk and sugar box. She continued to watch him; she was puzzled and she was uncertain and this expression softened her face and gave it a sweetness.

"I wish," she said, "I knew what you were doing at Ide's place."

"I stopped for a drink of water."

"And I wish I knew what Bill was doing there."

She watched him as she asked it and when he only shook his head and smiled her expression grew lighter until she was smiling back. "You're like all the crowd. Never say anything."

"What crowd?"

"The drifters and the fly-by-nights and the line jumpers who hide in every canyon and behind every

44

tree of these hills. I like to go on quick judgment—and I wanted to think you were not one of those."

"Stay with your judgment," he said and finished his coffee.

She pointed toward an inner door. "Now you can go in and stand your trial." She followed him to the door and her voice called him around before he opened it. "There are two things to remember. These men all have past records. They'll be afraid you're after them, or they'll think you might be one of the desert men laying a trap."

She waited again for some sort of answer and he saw that she was anxious for him to speak and clear himself. She had some kind of hope in him, the reason for which he could not understand. And when he shook his head and turned to open the door he noticed the let-down of that hope. She followed him through the door into a room with a long table, flanked by a backless bench on each side. Hugh Overman sat at the head of the table, stiff and massive, his burning glance coming to Goodnight and staying there. Boston Bill was near him, and his nearness made a tremendous contrast. Overman was a solid one whose convictions were as thick as the polar ice, whose temper was a deep, constant flame; against him Boston Bill became a thin character with his small disbelieving smile and his sharp, agnostic eyes. A dozen or more other riders stood around the room.

Overman said: "I'll tell you at once that if I thought you were a spy I'd shoot you down. Now, man, what are you doing here?"

"Riding through," said Goodnight. "Or maybe staying if I like it."

"Your answer turns around upon itself and means nothing," said Overman. "There is a reason which drives every man. What drove you here?"

Goodnight pointed his finger at Boston Bill. He turned it, indicating all the group. "You know what drove these men here?"

Boston Bill said: "Maybe you better answer questions instead of asking them."

"Still," pointed out Overman, "it is a fair answer. I have taken all of you at your word. I can do no less with this man."

"What was he doing at Harry Ide's place?" asked Boston Bill.

"I stopped for a drink of water," said Goodnight. "What were you doing there, Bill?"

Overman answered that for Boston Bill. "It may have been to warn Harry Ide or it may have been to destroy him. Either thing would have been welcome to me."

"Except for his interfering," said Boston Bill, "Harry Ide would have been destroyed."

"I like to see a man get an even chance," said Goodnight.

Overman gave Goodnight a bright-black glance. "Fairness is a good thing and pity is blessed. But there are ways here you do not understand. The desert is an evil land inhabited by evil people. Evil is to be done by as it does. Keep your pity for better things. You interfered from good motives, but you were mistaken."

"He was in town last night," added Boston Bill, "steppin' around like a stray dog with its tail up. What was he doing there?"

"He dragged me off my horse," said a voice, and then a man came out of the crowd and walked on until he faced Goodnight. He was a solid shape burned black by weather, he was a hard one, scarred by trouble and still wanting trouble. Along the trail Goodnight had seen many like him, restless and narrow of mind and governed by passion.

46

"Brother," said Goodnight, "you ran your horse into me and missed a woman by six inches with its kickin'."

The man was hungering for a fight; it was a shine in his eyes and a shape around his mouth. He looked aside to Boston Bill and a thought passed between them. He squared himself at Goodnight. He said: "I didn't have time last night to take care of you. No man can drag me off a horse . . ." He never finished the sentence. It was a feint to cover what he meant to do, for he swung his hand all the way from his belt and missed Goodnight's face and fell against him. He caught Goodnight around the waist to protect himself. He lowered his head and shoulders and struck sharp up, his head cracking Goodnight's chin.

The blow roared through Goodnight's brain; he heard Boston Bill say in a casual way: "Bust him up, Ad."

Ad's weight carried him back toward the wall, other men swiftly sidestepping to avoid the fight. But one bystanding man — Goodnight never knew which one — reached out and hit him on the jaw and backed away. Ad had him tackled around the waist and Ad's shoulders slammed him full force into the wall. He shifted his body, knowing what Ad would next do, and thereby avoided the jolt of Ad's knee as it aimed for his crotch. The maneuver threw Ad off balance, so that his grip around Goodnight's body relaxed, and at that moment Goodnight whirled free of the man and swung and caught him on the back of the neck with all the driven-down weight of his forearm. A thinner neck would have cracked; as it was, Ad emitted a small wince and fell in a curling drop to the floor, knocked out by the blow.

Goodnight stood away from Ad, feeling blood in his mouth from the butting of Ad's head. The fight broke his restraint and a wildness grasped him and he made a quick circle on the balls of his feet, watching the others; he had lost his hat and his long hair dropped over his eyes. "Anybody else," he said. "Anybody at all?"

He heard the girl speak behind him. "You should not have permitted that, Dad."

Old Hugh sat stone-still in his chair and Goodnight then noticed something new in the room. All the crowd had stood in a scattered way around the table before the fight, but in the half minute of action they had shifted and now he saw four men placed shoulder to shoulder against one side of the room, facing Boston Bill and Boston Bill's group across the table. The fight had shaken them apart, or distrust had shaken them apart — the ranch crew to one side and Boston Bill's riders to the other. One of the men in the smaller group was Bob Carruth. Then the door opened and another rider came in and put himself with the ranch four. It was Theo McSween.

Overman still had his daughter's reproach in his mind and now spoke: "Right makes right. If a man is just and honest he will have more strength than the man who is not. This young man whipped Ad. Therefore he is honest."

Boston Bill gave Overman a cynical grin. "Suppose two dishonest men got in a fight. You'd say the one that won was honest?"

"Less dishonest than the other," stated Overman.

Boston Bill ceased to smile. The arrogance that lived around his mouth and in his eyes suddenly jumped to his voice. "I don't want this fellow around."

Overman looked at Boston Bill and then Goodnight saw a flaw in the old man's complete self-assurance as Overman said: "I will not turn a man off Sun Ranch without reason."

48

"My say-so is reason enough," stated Boston Bill. "You do it or I'll do it."

Overman lifted his great head and his temper flared; yet he held his feelings down and his answer was less than Goodnight expected. "Never mind, Bill," he said, and he flung his arm stiffly up and stiffly down.

Goodnight nodded at Boston Bill. "You have talked too much again. Now it is put up or shut up."

Boston Bill's pride was yeasty in him. His color burned in the light and his big beak nose tipped hawklike at Goodnight. The crowd waited for him to move, to answer; the compulsion of their judgment was on him as he stood brooding in his tracks, trying to beat Goodnight down with his glance. Then he shook his head. "You're on Sun Ranch. I won't touch you here. This is the second time you have called me, friend. You're a clever man in pickin' a safe spot to call."

He nodded at his partners and went quickly out. In a moment Overman rose and followed him through the door, and the other crew members one by one disappeared until only Goodnight and the girl and Theo McSween were here. McSween showed a puzzled interest in Goodnight.

"I've seen you before, ain't I?"

"No," said Goodnight. "Maybe it was somebody that looked like me."

Theo McSween said, "Maybe," and started for the door. He turned in it, looking back with a rapid flip of his head, as though prompted by suspicion or a fresh thought. He stared steadily at Goodnight and he murmured, "Somewhere," and left the dining room.

Goodnight thought: "Why not have it over with now—I've caught up with him?" But he knew it had to be another way, for the memory of the doctor's words in Nevada was a fresh scar in his mind. He watched the door, nothing on his face; he listened to Boston Bill's men run out of the yard. The girl stepped around him and faced him.

"You're not green," she said. "You've got a lot of experience — the same dirty kind all the rest of them have."

He said: "Do you know that your father's afraid of Boston Bill?"

"Yes," she said. She looked long at him, something half formed on her lips. He saw caution hold her back. Then she said: "So am I."

FOUR

TURN OF THE SCREW

He said: "What's to be afraid of?"

Virginia looked over her shoulder to the door;
and turned to it. She stepped into the yard, and
stepped back, coming toward him again. The big
lamp on the table threw its lush beam against her,
staining the skin at her throat to a smooth butter
yellow. Her lips lay softly together and light points
danced in her eyes as they met his glance. She had
smiled only once at him, and then faintly; distrust
and reserve remained always with her. But below
that he saw fullness waiting, and the fullness was a
promise and a temptation to him, bringing on his
smile, and when he smiled recklessness came
quickly to his face.

She watched it and understood it and her expression grew smooth and tight and a disturbed breathing lifted her breasts; her glance held him and for a
moment warmth ran between them, and the knowledge of a swift and common thought was between
them. She dropped her glance. She murmured:
"Who was the woman you were talking about?"

He had to remember her name. He bent his
head to think of it; her kiss was a better memory
than her name. Then he remembered. "Rosalia

51

Lind."

Her glance was cool and distant. "Gallant of you. She's a friend of yours?"

"Just ran into her."

"As you ran into me," she murmured, and was displeased with him.

"What's the difference of all this?" he said. "The day comes and the day goes and you'll forget you ever saw me in another week."

The roughness of his talk brought a break of surprise to her face; it arrested her interest, and she watched him again with a close, wondering attention. "Are there no honest men left in this world?" she asked.

"Honesty is common enough. Is that what you're lookin' for?"

"More than that, perhaps. A man should be . . ." She shrugged the rest of it away.

He said: "You ride alone too much."

Surprise showed on her face again. "How do you know that?"

"The thinkin' that comes from ridin' alone takes you into a lot of queer places."

"Not queer," she murmured.

"Better not to think," he said. "Nothing's as good as we think."

"I'm disappointed in you," she said, and then corrected herself. "No, not disappointed; I hadn't expected much. All stray riders are the same."

He said: "What are you afraid of?"

"I think," she told him, "you know enough about Boston Bill to take care of yourself. He warned you. You probably know enough about any of these riding bums to watch them wherever you are. You've probably spent your life with them."

He said: "You can ease off with the spurs."

She had her own temper. He saw it come to her face and lips; he saw her eyes narrow and lose warmth. She said: "That is the only way to handle your kind. These hills are dangerous. I know that. I've had to carry a gun whenever I ride. Why should I take you for anything better? But it isn't what I wanted to tell you. You're on Sun Ranch. My father is hospitable in his own way, but I wouldn't want his hospitality to fool you. If he should ever become convinced that you came here to betray him or to betray any of the crew, he'd never give you a chance to explain. You would be shot without any warning. That has happened here."

He said: "I'll be gone from Sun Ranch after breakfast."

She said nothing at the moment. Turning, she went to the door again and stood there, facing the shadows. He watched her profile, he noticed the curve of her shoulders and the rich yellow gleaming of her hair. She had been angry with him, she was cool and suspicious now; even so, the shape of her lips and the lovely turnings of her body and the melody of her voice made a cover for the heat and the dreaming and the rich longings of a woman. She faced into the night, and spoke to him from that position.

"No," she said, "I want you to stay."

"Why? What's one saddle bum more or less?"

"Stay and find out," she said and turned back to him. "Unless the threat Boston Bill made is enough to send you away."

He smiled, and then he laughed and she watched him with her eyes half-closed. She was still prying into him for his worth and his real character. He said: "I wouldn't run because he wanted me to, and I wouldn't stay because you used him to get at my pride. But I'll stay for my own reasons."

She showed relief; and then relief faded and she grew brisk with him. "Never let your reasons out. The bunkhouse is just across the yard. Throw your horse into the small pasture behind the bunkhouse. What's your name?"

"Frank," he said. "That last man who left here—what's his name?"

"Mac," she told him. "Probably borrowed, like yours." She came over the room to him, looking up. She came near enough to be touched, and he wanted to touch her—for her nearness sharpened all his longfelt hungers and the sight of her struck through him—the fair things he saw and the warm things he felt in her. He held himself still, meeting her eyes. They were cool and speculative; they knew him and they were puzzled with him. She said, very softly: "Are Rosalia's lips as soft as other women's?"

He felt the quick heat in his face. She had thrown him off balance, as she had been trying to do since the meeting on the road. It turned him angry, but he held himself in. "I've wondered about yours," he said.

"You'll never find out," she said and suddenly swung from him. At the door she paused to say: "But it was nice of you not to speak of Rosalia. Some men do not even have that much decency." Then she left the dining room in a way that made him feel her spirits had lifted.

He turned down the lamp and went into the yard, seeing Overman and his daughter on the porch. Dust still lay in the air, stirred up by the departure of Boston Bill and his partners; starlight was a cloudy glow all down the heavens' slopes to the horizons. He took his horse to the small pasture, unsaddled and carried his gear back to the bunkhouse; when he stepped inside he saw Theo McSween sitting at the table, his hands idle on a deck of cards. McSween faced the door watchfully. Three other men lay on the bunks, awake and interested. One of them was Carruth, one was Slab, the fellow with the pock-marked face who had been bait in the Sherman City fight, and one was new to him. There had been still another in the dining room, lined up with these. He had gone.

Goodnight pegged his gear and found a bunk. He sat on the bunk, crouched over while he rolled a smoke, feeling the eyes of the others lying steadily against him. They were all the same kind of fugitive men, and they feared him or distrusted him. When he lighted the cigarette he saw McSween's steady, light-colored stare. McSween's arms were idle on the table and he had pulled himself back in the chair, slightly away from the table. He had dark hair turned white at the edges and he had the kind of face that would catch a woman's interest and perhaps the kind of tongue that could softly play on a woman's weaknesses.

McSween said—and his voice was slow and weighted with curiosity: "You ever around Tempe, Arizona?"

"No."

"Maybe," said McSween, "it was up in the Horse Heaven country."

"No."

McSween caught at his tobacco pouch in his pockets and began to build a smoke. His fingers were small for a riding man; his clothes were clean and he kept his hair cut and his face well-shaved; he was a fancy Dan. He put a match to his smoke and drew in a long breath of smoke. But he was still disturbed and now said: "Maybe over in Harney County, Oregon."

"You never saw me there," said Goodnight.

"Well, by God, I've seen you somewhere."

"You're a damned fool for talk," said Goodnight.

McSween blew out a gust of smoke behind which his light-blue eyes showed a sparkling resentment. He had small-cut lips, he wore his sideburns long and his dark hair had a heavy wave. Goodnight stared at him steadily, remembering his sister, his sister's voice and his sister's impulsive love of things that were light and gay and human. She had been a clean girl, and this man had dragged her through mud. This man had charmed her as he had no doubt charmed many another girl; he had done it as coolly as he would have set about breaking a horse.

He never took his eyes from McSween as he thought of it. His sister must have known the truth about this man before the end. Somewhere along the dismal trail, sleeping in sheep camps, drifting through rain, the dream in her must have died by the time they reached the Nevada town. When it died, her pride and her hope and her desire to live had likewise died. The doctor had been kind enough to call it pneumonia. Goodnight rubbed his big hands together, made hollow by the torture of his thinking; and the fury and the need of vengeance which had burned away so much of his youth during these last weeks of pursuit now came up to his face. The destruction of McSween was the only object he now had, the only thing he wanted out of life. Here the man stood, yet as much as he wanted to destroy McSween he knew so swift an ending would leave him unsatisfied. This man had to suffer and squirm and sweat and cry before he

56

died. He faced Goodnight as a man whose evils had never left a mark on him, careless and arrogant and without remorse. That had to be beaten out of him until he was a cringing shape filled with fear, until he flinched at the sound of a voice and begged like a dog for food and water and the very right to live. This thinking took a hungry, cruel shape on Goodnight's mouth. McSween saw it and rose and kicked back his chair. He gave Goodnight a strange stare.

"What you lookin' at me like that for?"

"Ask me any more fool questions and I'll slap out your teeth," said Goodnight.

He stood up from the bunk; he took a step nearer the table, watching McSween's face grow firmer and show a decision. McSween even grinned. "Boy," he said, "you're talkin' to the wrong man. If you want trouble with me you can get it."

He was ready to fight, but he was puzzled and so stood still. Goodnight took another step, suddenly seized the edge of the table and tipped it against McSween. McSween dropped his hands to knock the table aside. Goodnight circled swiftly, hit McSween a great blow on the side of the jaw and knocked him to the floor. He saw McSween roll and turn and grab at his gun; he had expected it and now he stepped on McSween's wrist and bore his full weight down, the sharp boot heel grinding into McSween's skin. McSween gave out a yell and rolled against Goodnight's knee. Goodnight dropped his knees straight down on McSween's ribs, seized the gun and rose back, waiting.

He looked around him at the other three men solemnly watching all this from their bunks. They were wild ones and they wouldn't interfere; they were the kind who had long ago learned not to mix in another man's business. They were probably enjoying the fight. He watched McSween rise from the floor. McSween said, "You like rough stuff, boy? Here's some . . ."

He came at Goodnight from a low, bent-over crouch, springing suddenly at his hips with his reached-out arms. Goodnight let him close in, took one step nearer as McSween's arms seized him and then, before McSween came out of his crouch, brought his knee full up into McSween's lowered face. The crack of that knee on McSween's mouth was sharp in the room. McSween's arms fell away and he dropped on his hands and knees. He never fully collapsed. He held himself painfully off the floor and some memory of other fights made him hunch himself together to protect his vital spots while half-unconscious. He shook his head and lifted it and cautiously searched the room with his glance. When he located Goodnight near the door he caught hold of the nearest bunk and pulled himself upright.

Goodnight's knee had smashed his lips into his teeth, drawing blood, and Goodnight's boot heel had badly sprung his wrist. He stood uncertainly erect, drawing heavily for wind, shaking his head free of dizziness. He rubbed the back of a hand over his mouth and stared at the blood drawn away. He spoke without much feeling, tired but still not beaten.

"I'd like to know where I've seen you before. Then I'd know what all this was."

"Stick around and you'll find out, maybe."

McSween gave him a tough glance. "You don't think I'm goin' to run from you?"

"You'll try to run," said Goodnight.

"The hell I will," grunted McSween. "I'll stay long enough to crack your skull." He sat down on the

58

edge of his bunk and started to pull off his boots.

Goodnight pointed a finger at him. "Find yourself another bunk. I'm sleepin' in that one."

McSween dropped his feet to the floor. Half humped over, he threw a malign stare at Goodnight; he hadn't been humbled, he hadn't been made afraid. He still wanted to get at Goodnight, but knew he couldn't. He drew back his broken lips, like a dog growling. He pulled himself together and got up and moved to the other end of the room. He stopped at a wall mirror and saw his face. It shocked him. He touched his lips with a point of a finger; he turned on Goodnight. "Damn you, you've scarred me."

"Tough," said Goodnight. "Be harder for you to attract the ladies."

McSween stood silent, thinking of that. The words stirred something and he straightened and looked at Goodnight with a sharper attention, still seeking to identify him. Recognition didn't come and, turning around, he crawled into another bunk and lay face upward, gently groaning. The three other men, Goodnight observed, were watching the door; swinging around, Goodnight observed Virginia Overman looking in from the yard.

"A bunkhouse," said Goodnight, "is no place for a woman. You know that."

She had been watching part of the fight; the expression of dislike was in her eyes as she looked at him. Then she turned into the night.

Goodnight wheeled to Bob Carruth. "No hard feelings about that crack over the head?"

"We'll wait and see," said Carruth.

"Where's the other man—the other one that stood by you in the dinin' room?"

"He left," said Carruth.

"Your boss," said Goodnight, "came to town with a big outfit. Where's the rest of the crew now?"

"You're lookin' at all the crew he's got," said Carruth. "The little party in Sherman City was too warm for the others. They just faded over the hill this mornin'."

"Ide outguessed you. Or maybe your intentions leaked out."

"So we discovered," said Bob Carruth. "Sure strange how news gets around."

Goodnight removed his boots and his pants. He hung his gun at the corner of the bunk and he rested back. He said: "Mac, go blow out the light." He waited and heard nothing. He let the silence pile up, and spoke softly, "Better mind."

McSween dragged himself off his bunk and stood in the room's center, looking down at Goodnight. For the present, his vitality was gone and he had nothing particular on his face. It was blank, as though he had wakened from a hard sleep. He said nothing, but turned and extinguished the lamp by sweeping his cupped hand across the chimney. Goodnight heard him roll back into his bunk, and in the darkness, never trusting McSween, he reached to his holster and lifted his gun and put it under the straw.

Virginia Overman crossed the yard to the main house and found her father sitting in a corner chair, plunged in his odd thoughts. He had his hands on his lap, palms upward; his chin lay dropped on his breast and she stood silent and watched him for a full minute and realized he was unaware of her presence.

"Dad," she said, calling him back from the distance. "That man may stay."

He lifted his head. "He would be useful."

"Any man would be useful," she said. "Bob and Tap and Slab and Mac are not enough. We might have kept the other five a long while if you hadn't tried to raid Sherman City."

"I will always fight evil," said Overman.

"Nothing good came of it. One of our boys was killed and four more ran away, fearing what Ide might do to us."

"They ran out of weakness. Let them run."

"It leaves us stripped."

"We have friends."

"Don't trust Bill too far."

"Why do you think this new man will stay?"

She walked a slow circle around the room, tall and calm and confident. She had gray eyes, after her father. She stopped near the doorway of her bedroom. She said: "I think I know how to make him stay."

FIVE

FIRST WARNING

Goodnight ate breakfast in the dining room with the crew and with Overman and Virginia. When he finished, he moved at once into the mountain's bright light, into its thin and winey air. The rest of the crew crossed the yard and were soon in saddle, moving into the trees, downgrade. McSween went with the group and for a short moment Goodnight's thoughts ran fast and uncertain. If McSween kept on going it would be another weary search to catch him again, but presently he made up his mind and turned away. McSween's pride would not let him run. McSween would return.

Virginia came out of the dining room and saw him. She said, "Saddle up and ride with me," and went on. Goodnight returned to the bunkhouse for his gear and continued to the small meadow. His horse ranged down-pasture with half a dozen others but when he drummed up a signal on the gate post with the flat of his hand, the horse came out of the bunch to him. He saddled and stepped aboard; and he sat through his morning exercise, the horse bucking in short stiff-legged hops, because of the goodness of the day. When Goodnight got back to the main yard the girl was waiting for him, and set

62

out with him across the short mountain meadow. A road split the meadow and presently reached timber. They passed into the cool morning twilight, going steadily upgrade.

"Where's this road go?" he asked.

"Over the mountains. The way you'll be going, I suppose. On east."

"Maybe," he said.

She sat square on her saddle, not looking at him. "I have had a hard time getting men to stay on this ranch. Keep your hands off Mac. I need him. Don't drive him away." Then she turned her head and he saw the dislike she had for him. "You're like the rest of them, lawless and on the jump. You are also brutal."

"This a way of giving me my walkin' papers?"

"No," she said, "I want you to stay. I have no choice."

The two horses walked sedately side by side as the road looped between green walls of timber. Now and then Goodnight sighted the dark shoulders of granite peaks south of the road; and now and then they came upon gravel fords over which clear and sparkling creek waters shallowly rushed. It occurred to him that this was the second time Virginia Overman had let drop the hint of her worry and her insecurity; and so he asked the same question he had asked the night before.

"Why?"

"You can see for yourself can't you?" She looked at him, her dislike thawing. He had the idea that she wanted to trust him and could not. She placed him as she placed the other men in these hills, just one more rider with a dishonorable past. In addition she thought him cruel; that latter judgment bothered him, for sometimes on the long march to

63

this point he had wondered at his own newly acquired bitterness, his terrible judgments of all things and all men. Life had ceased to be the same. He woke no more with the keen, fine eagerness of morning upon him, he rode no more with the old free spirit, and at night the heart of his campfire burned dull, its mystery gone.

She had waited for his answer. Not receiving it, she murmured: "You're a gloomy cold man." Then she bent a little in the saddle, her glance nearer to him, and she was a moment silent. "Why," she said, "what troubles you?"

"Maybe you'd better not ask," he said.

"Running away," she said in a smaller voice, "is a miserable thing. You'll find out you can never run far enough." She shrugged her shoulders. "Never mind. It is your business. You can see what's happening on Sun Ranch, can't you?"

"Your father seems to know what he's doing."

"My father never came here with the intention of setting up headquarters for the wild bunch. He ran his cattle and minded his business until about ten years ago. Then the desert outfits began to resent his being here, because he used the grass they'd been summer-ranging. They tried to run him out. You have seen my father. You know how he would answer. It has been a fight ever since my childhood. The hill people against Harry Ide and the other desert ranchers. My father hates all desert people and would willingly wipe them out. He is unforgiving. Perhaps he has reason to be. I have no love for the desert ranchers. They're greedy."

"All people are greedy, one way or another," said Goodnight.

She gave him a keen glance, arrested by the remark. "I wonder how deep your resentment is. You don't have the face of a lawless man. It isn't lined with evil or dissipation. Are you sure you are as disillusioned as you think?"

"Shouldn't matter to you."

"It does, very much," she told him in a completely matter-of-fact voice. "I do not admire your actions — such as I've seen of them — but I need a man like you. This country has become a jungle in which all sorts of stray and vicious beasts have sought shelter. It used to be a lovely country. All through my childhood it was a land of delight. The shadows were clean shadows, made by the mountains and the timber. It is not so now. I used to travel this road, never thinking of danger. I never ride on it any more without a gun, always expecting the worst from each bend. It is a terrible thing to do that to so clean a spot of earth."

"You were young and never saw the evil which is always around us. Now you're older and you see it."

She looked at him. "Do you like to think of it that way? Don't you want to fight it?"

He said: "I'll take care of my chores but no other man's."

She showed him the disappointment and the faint contempt she had earlier revealed; and again he felt it keenly. She said: "I should have expected nothing more from you. Yet I need you. My father is in trouble."

"You want another gun to throw against the desert," he guessed. "Therefore you are mixed up in the evil you've been talkin' against."

"As long as my father fought to protect himself against the desert people he was doing what had to be done. They have tried to drive him away, but he has outfought them. I'm glad of that, for they've been wrong and lawless about it. Now it is worse.

65

The feeling is so bad between hill and desert that nobody regards any kind of an act to be wrong. My father has taken his help where he found it. Much of that help has come from the wild bunch, which has grown powerful enough to control the hills. The hill ranchers fought to keep back the desert crowd. Now they've got a worse danger in the wild bunch. Some of them know it. My father is troubled, though he doesn't tell me. He used to be very honest and very strict. The wild bunch has taught him to think anything is fair against the desert crowd."

"Boston Bill?"

She turned in the saddle toward him. When she spoke again he noticed she did not directly answer his question. "The wild bunch has corrupted some of us; the rest of us it has made afraid." She stopped her horse, turned it and started back. "I should not have trusted you with this. You're the same as the rest."

"Then why did you?" asked Goodnight.

"Maybe," she said, "it was something I thought I saw."

He rode downgrade in silence, her talk working through him. Her judgment of him was a slow acid burning his conscience and her hope in him waked those old easy and straightforward and simple things he had since put away. He was a different man, embittered by injustice, and he knew it and could do nothing about it; yet the recollection of what he had once been would not leave him.

"You should trust no man," he said. "You should not have trusted me."

She glanced at him. She said nothing but her attention thoughtfully remained upon him. Presently she straightened and when he looked at her he saw that she was quietly smiling. She put her hand on his arm and coquetry danced in her eyes; it was a charm suddenly turned on. She said: "Stay and help me," and spurred her horse into a reaching canter. He followed her down the road to the meadow and along the meadow to the yard, puzzled at the change of her manner but warmed by it. As he came into the yard with her he saw Overman, Boston Bill and a third man waiting by the porch. The third man was the old fellow who had been in the alley beside Rosalia Lind's house the previous night. Old Gabe.

He dismounted, turned cautious; he saw the jealous suspicion in Boston Bill's blue eyes, he felt the massive temper of old Hugh boil against him. Overman said: "Daughter, I have spoken to you of riding with strangers." Boston Bill's eyes went to her with curiosity, and came again to Goodnight, bold and discontented.

Old Gabe reached into his pocket and produced a slip of paper which he handed to Goodnight. Three neat feminine lines of writing said: —

Your friend has been hurt and is in my house. Come to the back door after dark — down the alley where the old man was.

The second sentence was to take the place of the signature, to remind him secretly of Rosalia Lind. He stood with his head bent, troubled as to Niles, doubting the message and the messenger. How had this man come so openly upon Sun Ranch and how was it he stood here now with so much certainty? The three men were watching him with their various attitudes. Virginia regarded him with a noticeable distrust.

He pointed to the messenger and spoke to Overman. "You know this man?"

"I know him," said Overman.

The old man grinned his red-gummed grin. "Everybody knows me," he said. "And," he added shyly, "nobody cares about me. If anybody cared I'd be dead before now. It's the little folks that ain't worth botherin' about and never amount to nothin' who outlast the folks that try to run everything. Us no-accounts own this world and get the fun of it. You got an answer fud that writin'?"

"I'll carry my own answer down."

The old man turned to his horse. He gave the group an insolent grin from the saddle, knowing his age sheltered him. "Never knowed a heavy gambler ever to win. You're all bound to lose. You're livin' like fools." He turned his horse about and went away confidently, lumped like a squaw in the saddle, his old legs banging the sides of the horse; and so disappeared in the timber.

This scene and the delivery of the note seemed neither to have increased nor decreased Overman's suspicion; it had not changed his judgment. But Boston Bill had been touched on some vulnerable nerve by the scene and held himself still with difficulty. Goodnight folded the note and slid it into his pocket, not entirely sure of the next few moments. He said: "I've got to go to town," and turned to his horse. The silence of the three people was oppressive behind him and when he swung to the leather and again faced them he realized that all three were debating his departure. A clear, cold antagonism had returned to the girl's face.

"Are you coming back?" she asked.

"Yes."

Boston Bill gave Virginia a blank look. "Why

68

should he come back?"

"We can use another pair of hands."

"You've got plenty to call on," he reminded her.

"Sun Ranch hires its own crew, Bill."

"So far we've gotten along," he said. "I'm here when you want me."

She lifted her head, she straightened and laid her voice on him, even and definite. "Don't interfere."

Boston Bill flushed. He still had his anger and wanted to use it. But he was somehow held back, as though he desired no quarrel with her; and at last he managed a graceful gesture. "Only trying to help. After all, what do you know of this man?" He swung on Overman as he asked the question. Overman, Goodnight observed, was solemn and aloof and would not come into the argument. Goodnight knew then he would have no protest on his departure and swung around toward the meadow. Boston Bill's voice followed him: "I'll ride with you, friend," and in a moment Bill trotted abreast. Looking behind, Goodnight saw the girl poised watchfully in the middle of the yard.

The two men passed shortly into trees, dropping downgrade. Goodnight looked at Boston Bill. "Get it off your chest."

"What takes you to town?"

"That's my business."

"Sure—sure," said Boston Bill resentment singing in his voice. "My friend, I misjudged you yesterday. I figured you for one more bum. I see now you're able to take care of yourself. That's perfectly agreeable to me, but I just want to make sure you stay out of my business. You do that much and I'll keep clear of you."

"Say the rest of it," said Goodnight.

Boston Bill gave Goodnight the benefit of his

hard blue eyes. "The rest of it is that you've been bumping into me and I have not called you. Thereby you may be figuring me wrong. I don't believe you know my style. I'm not one to go harum-scarum into a fight. I never fight except for a purpose. So far you have not really provided me with a purpose. If you ever do I shall certainly fight you."

"You could have said it in less time," observed Goodnight.

Boston Bill showed him a thin smile. "You have never run into a man like me and therefore you constantly make mistakes. These drifters around here are dogs without brains. They fight out of pride, nothing more. Any man with a brain can handle them. You're the first one I feel is anywhere near me in intelligence. Therefore you may be dangerous to me and I may be dangerous to you. These are big hills. There's room enough for both of us. But keep out of my pasture."

"Where's that?" asked Goodnight.

Boston Bill rode on the best part of a quarter mile before he gave Goodnight a hard, fresh grin and a knowing glance. "You're not bad at pumping out what you want to know. I don't believe I shall give you the ground plan of my venture, old boy. I simply say, don't interfere with me. And, look here, there are other hill ranches to work on, if you must stay and work. I suggest you leave the Sun outfit."

"I'll be going back there," said Goodnight.

"I hold your future in the palm of my hand," pointed out Boston Bill reasonably. "If I ever swung the old man against you, you'd never live to leave the place."

"You've tried," said Goodnight, "and no luck."

Boston Bill halted his horse and swung it, directly

facing Goodnight. He was alert and was angry, but he continued his cool way of handling Goodnight; his mind controlled his temper. This man, Goodnight understood, was not the kind of fighter and not the kind of simple bad one with which he was familiar. Looking into the man's eyes Goodnight had an odd feeling that he saw there in the coolness and the brightness the dull shadow of something ruined and dying. This man had an education and came from a good place; but he was here now, far below his station, somehow corrupted. That shadow of dullness was a real thing, the reflection of inward shame. There was never anything as wicked as a good horse turned bad, or a good man turned bad.

He said to Boston Bill, gravely, with deliberation: "Only one thing I'm not sure of about you. Whether you'd give a man warning or crack him from behind."

Boston Bill's ruddy cheeks showed a sharper color at once and the anger in him slipped its control and shaped his face with arrogance. He searched for an answer to that charge but apparently the streak of fatalism in him knocked the answer aside. Turning, he rode back toward the ranch.

When he reached the yard he went directly to the house. Virginia was in the room but old Hugh had gone back to his bedroom for his customary nap. Boston Bill watched Virginia closely, his smile coming short and pressed around his mouth. A little flash of excitement showed on his face and he ducked his head toward the old man's room, murmuring: "In there?"

She nodded. She stood by the table, her hands on it. She looked down at her hands and he was sharp-eyed enough to notice that her heart struck sharp against her waist. She lifted her head and

71

gave him a rapid side glance and turned, moving toward the end of the room. The main door stood open. Boston Bill swung and closed it and he waited a moment, staring across the width of the room at her; and then he thought he saw his invitation and went to her. He looked down at her a moment; he waited for her glance to come up to him, with its shadowing, its disturbance. He touched her with one hand, lightly, and let it rest tentatively a moment, and then held her with both hands and pulled her forward. He let his mouth drop gently to her lips, but that was the end of his gentleness, for the effect of her closeness completely threw him off balance and he tightened his grasp around her waist and bore down insistently with his mouth.

She was willing to have it that way. He felt her fingers dig into his back and he felt her own desires rush at him. He thought: "She's hungry for this—I could have done it sooner," and the next moment her hands slid against his chest and pushed him away. Her eyes were darker and wider and her mouth had become heavy. She breathed rapidly, she held her palms up, protecting herself, still pushing at him, and a violent dislike jumped into her face and pulled it tight. She shook her head. She motioned at her father's door and shook her head again. When he reached for her, still unsatisfied, she knocked his arms aside. "All right—all right," he grumbled, and swung on his heels, leaving the room.

She listened to him ride away. She rubbed a hand across her mouth; she tucked in the edges of her hair and felt pleased with herself, knowing she had broken through his guard. She had meant to let him have his kiss, realizing he had long wanted it; she had not meant to let him have enough to be too confident. He was an overbearing man, a difficult one to keep in hand. She distrusted him and sometimes hated him because he felt himself stronger than she. She wanted to break him and make him manageable, and yet could not do so. Still, this had not gone badly. That single kiss had put a rope around him and he would be tantalized by it and would come back, and would try to please her.

She stood this way, analyzing him, and presently she began to compare him with Goodnight. They were both difficult men to handle but she thought of Goodnight: "I can make him want me, too."

Six

Death at Night

Goodnight left Sun Ranch around ten o'clock. Running downgrade, now on the road and now in the shelter of the timber, he reached the break of the hills—with the housetops of Sherman City below him—near four. It was still three hours until sundown and although the message from Rosalia Lind was urgent enough to make him restless, he could not shake away his suspicion; therefore he made a wide detour to avoid entering town from the upper side and presently cut the road which led out upon the prairie. Dropping back to the trees he sat against a pine until the sun fell and the shadows began their inward night-tide. He rose and crossed the road, coming upon Sherman City from the lower end. Reaching the old shanty where he had met Niles the night before, he left his horse and walked behind the line of buildings.

He came to the rear of Rosalia Lind's house and he stood well covered by the darkness of the house adjoining. A light came through her window and painted its dim yellow cone on the muddy night. Beyond the reach of that cone lay the back ends of other buildings, undressed and unlovely; and bleak alleyways and between-building spaces promising trouble.

74

He did not trust the old man's message and he did not trust Rosalia Lind. This town and this country lived in its own evil. He stood still, watching the lighted windows, and then he noticed that the back door of the house stood open and as he watched this, the light went out; and he heard a voice grumble: "What's the matter?"

It sounded like Niles Brand's voice. He moved through the yard toward the door; he came soft-footed across the small back porch and found a shape in the doorway. He took one step aside, still keyed to danger, and then he saw Rosalia's face move forward. She whispered something under her breath and her hand reached to him and drew him in. There was a complete darkness in the house, and the sound of a man's heavy breathing, and then he heard Niles speak again. "Where'd you go to?"

She still held Goodnight's arm, the pressure of her fingers speaking for her and her presence sending its warmth against him. She waited there, saying nothing, arresting him with the unseen sweetness that came so powerfully out of her. He put his arms around her and felt her lips come up quick and eager. It was like falling into softness, through layer upon layer of softness, all of it closing about him warm and painfully good. The feeling of it was a sustained wave through him, this same goodness without shame; and when he stepped back he heard her let out a small sigh and he thought she was smiling although he saw nothing of her face. Her finger tips brushed across his lips and she swayed until she was against him again, whispering into his ear. "I've been waiting for you." She pulled away and in a moment found a match and lighted a lamp.

He closed the rear door, standing against it, watching her go about the room to pull down the window

75

shades. She faced him over the room's length; he saw happiness shape her lips, he saw the glow of her eyes as she watched him and remembered the kiss. Light and shadows lay against her, darkening her eyes, rounding her shape. Her lips moved slightly, speaking to him without sound, and she turned lovely and alive before him. She moved her head at the open door of another room. "In there."

It was a bedroom, with Niles Brand lying on the bed, bare from his waist upward. A harness of cloth, looped around his neck and around his chest, anchored a bandage against his left side. He had one arm thrown back over his head, grasping the bed post. He said to Goodnight, "Nice weather, pilgrim," and tried to grin away the hurt of his injury. Sweat lay beaded along his head and upper lip and the day's heat, trapped within the house, flushed his face to a cherry color.

"Bullet?" asked Goodnight. "Where'd it land? Who did it?"

"Shaved a rib, or broke a rib — or somethin' like that. I was crossin' the street from the stable. The thing plowed downward across my flank. So it was fired from above me. I was facin' the hotel. So it came from the hotel, second floor. That's all I know about it. I told you this was a damned queer town. This girl and an old guy with whiskers pulled me off the street." He looked at her. "What did you bother for?"

She stood by the bed, her manner of dark assurance returning. "You're this man's friend, aren't you?"

"That's the reason?" he asked, in a puzzled tone; and he looked at her close and careful. She was a mystery to him, not smiling at him and making no attempt to please him. She had helped him, but the help was not for him. He saw that and shrugged his

76

shoulders, and the shrug brought on a fresh stab of agony in his side. He bared his teeth and gripped the bed post more tightly. "Give me two or three days, Frank. But meanwhile, where do I hang out?"

"Here," said the girl. "You're safe here. Nobody would dare touch you in my house."

"You big enough to hold 'em away?"

She showed both men a lift of her chin and an imperious gesture with her hand. "You're safe here."

Goodnight said: "No reason for you to be potted, Niles, unless somebody knows you are tied up with me."

"That was known half an hour after you came," said the girl.

Niles gave her a bright-sharp stare. "You got your fingers on a lot of things."

"Two men riding into Sherman City, a day apart, would be suspected. This place is full of men who know all the tricks. You couldn't fool them. I know who shot you. I know why. I know more than that. You stay here until you can take care of yourself. It will be a week, and not two or three days."

Goodnight said: "If you're safe here, I'll have to duck back into the hills."

"You find out anything?"

"Yes," said Goodnight. "It's only a question of time."

Niles said in a gritty voice: "Do it and be done with it."

The girl stepped from the room, both men listening to her footsteps recede toward the rear of the house. Goodnight bent down, murmuring: "He's on Sun Ranch. He won't run. I'm going back there. When you're ready to ride, ride back home."

"You damned fool," said Niles, "you think you can get out of here alone? We're both in trouble. I don't

77

think we could ride out if we wanted. It's—" he scowled at the ceiling, seeking words, and added, "just too many things workin' too many funny ways."

The girl came back with a drink of water. She stood over him, supporting the glass while he drank. Water spilled down his bare chest and he squirmed on the bed and tried to smile again. "Remember how a cow tries to get out of quicksand, Frank? Same thing. We're in quicksand. Maybe you could turn down that light. Believe I might be able to sleep. Sorry I got your bed, lady."

She took up the lamp and moved from the room with it, Goodnight behind her. She put the lamp on a table, turned down the wick, and swung to face him; all her austere self-possession went away in that one moment, leaving her a beggar waiting his nod, his word, his summons. Heat lay heavy in the house, swelling through him; he dropped his head, thinking of the suddenness of their meeting and the rashness of his first impulse toward her. And he wondered now at the strange things she did to him, making the moments sharp and all his appetites keen. She brought him back to his older days of carefree thinking, when all the world had been good. She brought that back.

She came across the room, touching his arm, moving with him back through the house and out to the rear porch. She sat down in the deep shadows, pulling him beside her. Her voice dropped low. "You're safe on this porch, Frank. There are three men in those shadows. Nobody could get into this back yard."

"I got in."

"You were permitted in," she told him softly.

"Odd thing."

"Not odd. My father started this town and left many friends when he died. You're walking on my ground, anywhere you walk in Sherman City. I have men who'd never let you leave here, if I said so. Perhaps" — and her voice held its secret amusement — "I'll have them keep you here. What are you going to do now?"

"Back into the hills."

She remained silent over a long period, bent forward, her arms across her knees. She looked into the darkness, indrawn and sober. When she spoke again there was a drag of sadness in her voice. "I do not know what brings you here and I don't know what you want. Men do things for so many reasons and some of those reasons are foolish. But they are men's reasons. I never question them. If I like a man I'll help him, whatever he wants, and no matter what kind of a man he's been."

"Don't trust me," he told her.

"That is a silly thing to say. If I didn't like you I'd let you die and not care at all. But if I like you I'll trust you. How else can people live? This is a lonely town for a woman. I've seen men come and go. Now and then I see one I like. Sometimes I've attracted their attention, and then found nothing I've wanted."

"Better be careful of the kind of men floating through here."

"Listen to me. I'm not afraid of fugitives or wild ones. All I ask of a man is that, bad as he is, he has something in his heart, and be simply a man. I would overlook everything else. Even a life of sleeping in the rain from pillar to post. I don't like cautious men, or smart ones, or careful ones. Just plain ones who are what men are supposed to be, nothing more. Don't go back into the hills."

"Why not?"

"You don't want to be in this quarrel."

"I'm not in it."

"Go back to the hills and you'll be in it. You can't stay out."

He said nothing and she touched him with her arm, bringing his face around. He saw her smiling for him. "You won't mind me, which is the way a man has. All right. But don't go back tonight. This is the one night you should stay under cover."

"Why?"

"Take my word for it."

He was thinking of Theo McSween. He had banked on McSween's pride, but he was now not sure that McSween wouldn't run. It made him uneasy and restless to think he might lose his man. "I'll be back on Sun Ranch by daylight," he said. "But thanks for the warning."

"Sun Ranch," she said thoughtfully. "That's where Gabe found you?"

"Yes."

She rose, drawing away from him; and her voice drew away from him. "Go there and you'll never get out of trouble."

"Why?" he asked again.

Her voice stiffened. She had a great deal of pride. "Do as I tell you. Isn't that enough for you to know?"

He rose and stood close beside her, smiling through the shadows at her. He denied her authority over him with a smooth murmur: "So-long until I see you again."

She hit him with her suppressed irritation: "I got you out of the hills once. How many more times must I send in a man to pull you clear of trouble?"

"Is that what you did?" he asked.

"Do you suppose they would have let you leave Sun if it hadn't been Rosalia Lind's man delivering the message? They knew where Gabe came from and they knew better than to hold you back. Go up there now and I'll not lift my hand again."

He was still smiling. He laid his hand under her chin, lifting it. He bent and kissed her and felt the anger dissolve out of her. She pulled back from him, staring at his face. "Ah," she sighed, "how funny. The men I like are all headstrong. Why is that? Do you hate a woman giving you orders?"

"No," he said. "I've got to go back. That's all there's to it."

"Not tonight," she whispered. "Not tonight."

"Be good to Niles."

She said: "I could lift my voice now, and you'd never leave town."

He ceased to smile. He said: "Don't interfere."

She stared at him a long while, troubled for him and angry with him and yet drawn to him; and at last she shrugged her shoulders. "So-long," she said. She watched him swing from the porch and cross the yard; she watched him disappear in the shadows and she listened to his footfalls die sudden-out. She drew a long breath and put a hand on a breast and pressed it tight, and turned into the house. She heard Niles turning restlessly on the bed and took the lamp into his room. His eyes turned on her, full of pain and yet shrewd.

"I heard the argument," he said. "Don't try to change that fellow. It will do you no good."

"Is he stubborn, Niles?"

Niles rolled on the bed, easing his weight from side to side; he gripped the bed post and silently struggled through the hard pulse of his broken flank. "I grew up with him. Everything was fine and everything was swell. I stayed home and he hit the trail, just for the hell of it. You know — a lot of life in him that had to spill out somewhere. Just shout because you can't keep still when you feel good. That was Frank, until a

81

few months ago. Now you've got a tough man on your hands. He's got to go into those hills and nothin' you say will stop him."

"And nothing," she said, "will keep him from being killed. He doesn't know those hills as I do."

"Dammit," he groaned, "I wish I could go with him."

"Niles," she said, "I'll help him."

He was sweating and he was flushed and he was restless. She put down the lamp and went for a glass of water. She sat on the edge of the bed and supported his head while he drank. Her hand accidently brushed his bare chest and he showed his instant embarrassment. "Better if I had my shirt on."

"Never mind."

He looked at her with a moment's penetrating attention. "I don't quite know about you."

"For you," she said, calmly dismissing the statement, "that doesn't matter."

"Not thinking about me," he said. "Thinkin' about Frank."

"That's his business, and mine."

"The hell it is. If I don't think it's a good idea, Rosalia, you'll have to break through me to get at him. I'm tellin' you that."

She wasn't listening. She rose and took up the lamp, looking down at him with her thoughts elsewhere. "It will be the girl," she murmured. "I know the way she'll handle him."

"What girl?"

"If you want anything, I'll be in the next room," she said, and left him.

Goodnight reached his horse and made the wide circle of town again. When he got into the timber he

82

traced his way to the main road, drew slightly aside from it and looked down upon the town's housetops. The two roads were solid streaks of dust formed into a cross, glowing silver in the shadows, turned to amber-gold where the storelights shone upon them. One horse stood swaybacked and sleepy before the hotel and one man sat in front of the stable; otherwise the town showed no life. The fact struck him and he watched the front of both saloons for a matter of five minutes. In that length of time no man entered or left either place. The hill people were absent this night, and the desert crowd did not appear.

He turned back to the road and moved up, now in more of a hurry than he had been. The thought of Theo McSween left unguarded disturbed him anew. Moreover, he was aware of Rosalia Lind's repeated warning: "Don't go into the hills tonight." It was a signal of things to come which the town, by its emptiness and by its suppressed quiet, seemed to heed. He thought of Rosalia Lind as he moved steadily forward at the bottom of this deep black trench cut out of the timber. The thought of her evoked warmth and satisfaction and a feeling of something new discovered, making him eager even as he possessed his doubt. One moment she had been cold and strange to him and then she had answered his kiss with a swift rush of willingness, with a desire as great as his own; and he had felt the receiving softness of her body and the need of her lips. A woman like that, he thought, so quick to give, so easily surrendering—Yet he was ashamed of the thought and would not listen to its suggestions. What was time? A woman might look coldly on a man and hold him away even as she desired him, out of a sense of propriety, and make him come back time and time again until she had proved her value and her will to him. Another woman might stake everything on the impulses of her heart. Which was the better woman—the cool one who waited her time, the warm one who suddenly answered? In which one ran the fire, in which lay the depth?

He was five miles into the hills when he heard the first rumor of another rider in the night, coming behind. He turned off the road and waited until the man went by at a punishing pace. He stood still, realizing that his own dust wake must have been a warning to that rider; but the rider's echo was a steady abrasion in the night, presently dying. Goodnight swung back to the road. Starlight made a trembling glow above the narrow-slashed pathway of the trees and wind flowed downhill with its faint pressure against him. Near ten or eleven o'clock he felt the slackness in his horse and thought of stopping, and would have stopped had not he picked up a sound to his right, like the gentle, slow scrubbing of knuckles on a washboard. This was on some other road or trail in the timber which appeared to slant toward him, for the sound grew greater, reached a peak not more than three hundred yards from him, and began to fall off. It was a group of riders pushing hard against the hills.

A little later he crossed that road as it swept around from the southwest and intersected the one on which he traveled. He was by now half the way around Sun Ranch and gave up the idea of camping. The horse frequently slowed, knowing its own mind; he urged it on, watching the gray-black foreground of the road with greater attention. Dust stayed with him to indicate other travel; and the silence of the hills had in it the tag-end of sounds not quite faded out and he got the impression of men crisscrossing the dark mountain slopes with their urgent hastes. Midnight brought him to the mouth of a canyon somehow familiar and shortly he recognized his previous night's camp spot, whereby Virginia Overman had met him; and he was here when he caught the first distant break of guns.

This was from higher away, from the Sun Ranch meadow; and these shots grew and came down to him with the small wind, making faint flutters in the air. He was in the notch of the canyon, the high round walls holding him strictly to the road. He had half a mile of this, as he remembered, and urged the flagging horse to a quicker pace. The firing stayed brisk, not heavy volleys, but as spotted shots following one another at intervals.

Halfway up the canyon, with a quarter mile still to go before reaching the shelter of the timber, he heard the firing die into a silence made hollow by the racket which had gone before; and after that he caught the on-traveling murmur of horses. He was still trapped in the canyon and now brought down his spurs, sorry for his horse as he did so. The horse jumped into a dispirited run, its shoes striking sharp against the rocky underfooting of the road; the canyon wall began to drop down. Ahead of him a ragged burst of shots broke the lull, the last rear-guard action of the fight, and then that ceased and a heavy party ran at him.

He looked anxiously at the shadow bank to either side and knew he could not yet climb from the road; nor had he time now to turn and run, for the head of the oncoming column was a vague motion before him. Someone in that party shouted, "Harry, hold it," but the column came on at an easy run. Goodnight shoved his horse flat against the left-hand bank, thus to be absorbed in the black shadows of it. He heard the man cry again: "I can't make it, Harry."

The column was dead on him, slacking speed. It

ran abreast of him, the nearest rider within arm's reach. Someone said: "Hold up," and the column broke and turned back upon itself; one rider swung about, his stirrup touching Goodnight's stirrup. "Who's hit?" said that one.

"Me," said a voice in a steady fall of tone. "I can't make it back. I—"

"Grab him before he falls," said the voice.

"Come up—come up," said the hurt one, and after that Goodnight watched a shadow waver and sink away. He heard the man strike ground and grunt. The column turned into a close bunch and men got down, working their way through the horses.

"Dead?" said the voice.

"No," said somebody.

"Yes," another voice added.

"Who is it?"

"Charley Tevis."

Goodnight found himself boxed against the wall of the canyon, a rider crosswise before him, a rider behind him. When this group moved on again he would be in the current, moving with it and unable to break clear of it without being observed. The collection of men and horses choked this narrow way, swaying in confused motion, men riding back and forth restlessly. Goodnight grumbled in half a tone: "I want to see Charley," and wedged his horse into the jam. Men gave way to either side, but one of them said: "Keep your shirt on—he's dead." A match burst near the ground near by and he saw the sharp silhouette of a face—Harry Ide's face—bent toward the dead man; the match went out, making the blackness greater than before. Goodnight's horse had stopped, its progress barred by another horse in front of it. Harry Ide said: "Give me a hand. We'll sling him across his saddle."

86

Somebody else got down and all the horses stirred again.

A thin gap showed ahead of Goodnight, into which he worked his way, his knee scraping another knee. He got into a more open spot and half turned his horse, wanting to make no show of hurry in all this.

"Harry," said somebody, "he'll slow us down."

"We're not runnin' from anything, are we?"

"I don't want to be in this timber by daylight. These hill people will be behind every tree."

"You got a better idea? Lift him up, boys."

A rider drifted forward from the rear; he came coasting up beside Goodnight. He bent nearer Goodnight. "Match?"

"No," said Goodnight.

Harry Ide was speaking again to the group around him. They had the dead man in the saddle. They were holding him while Ide made a quick hitch with his rope, ducking up and down in the blackness. The dissenter still disliked the idea. "You'll have a hell of a time making any hitch hold him on the leather. He'll slide and scare the horse into a run. You'll have him draggin'. At the foot of the hills you'll just have bones left. Dump him in the timber. We can come back and bury him tomorrow night."

Harry Ide said: "That'll stay tied," and pushed back through the crowd to his own horse. "Everybody else here?"

The man beside Goodnight had found his match. Goodnight saw his arm lift and he heard the match scrape against a thumbnail, and at that moment he swung his head and bent down, as though to check his stirrup, thus turning his head from the man's sight. The match flared and its light hung on, and went out. Straightening, Goodnight saw the man's face pointed to him. At the head of the column Harry

Ide called: "Let's go." and the mass began to shift and sort itself into column again. Suddenly the near man swayed forward to bring Goodnight's face into view. He said nothing but he seemed ticked by suspicion. "Who's this?" he suddenly asked and reached out to grasp Goodnight's arm.

The head of the column moved on. Goodnight had jockeyed himself near the foot of it, with three or four men behind him. The near-by man said, "Ride beside me," in a changing, toughening voice, and let go his grip, and moved ahead. Goodnight murmured: "I'll ride back with Bill," and swung his horse toward the rear at once. The use of the name was a fair risk—in this group there had to be at least one Bill. Meanwhile another man came up from behind and passed him and the man who had grown doubtful now was too far ahead to work his way back. But his voice lifted: "Don't let that fellow drop out!"

Goodnight was at the end of the column, only one man now near him. He said to this one: "Who the hell's he talkin' about?"

The rear man grumbled: "Who's talkin' about what?"

Harry Ide's voice sailed down the column. "What's up?" The column, not yet wholly straightened into a marching line, lost speed. The man adjoining Goodnight drifted ahead to catch up and as he did so Goodnight turned his horse, walked it upgrade fifty feet and wheeled against the bank of the gulch again, blending himself with the shadows. The column had wholly stopped, its tail a hundred feet below him. A voice said:—

"There's a sleeper in this outfit. What I saw of him don't look familiar to me."

Ide said impatiently: "We're wasting time and we're in a bad spot."

"Still, there's somethin' funny."

Ide said: "Soon settled. Light up and take a look at the man next to you. Hurry it up and don't keep the matches burnin'."

Goodnight turned half in his saddle, watching the uneasy shift of the column's shadow; he saw the matches flare and make prickling flitters of light and he saw faces vaguely. Then the matches died, to be followed by somebody else's voice: "Where's that man who was ridin' behind me?"

"Behind who?"

"I was on the tail end. Then somebody dropped back behind me. Who dropped back behind me?"

There was a delay, after which Ide spoke: "We started with fifteen horses. We still got fifteen. What the hell's the matter with you fellows?"

"Yeah, but where's the one that dropped back?" insisted the voice. "I'm goin' to take a look."

A single shadow broke from the column's massed shadow and moved up the road. He was fifty yards from Goodnight when Harry Ide called after him. "That's enough. Let's ride." The column moved again, leaving this single man with his lonely scouting. He came on steadily and stubbornly until he was twenty feet below Goodnight and there he stopped, trying to penetrate the blackness with his glance. He bent forward in the saddle and seemed to stare straight at him; he stayed that way, completely motionless, listening and staring until Goodnight feared his own horse would break the silence.

The column had gone on and the single rider at last grew weary of the waiting and turned about and went away. Perhaps a dozen yards onward he stopped and made one more quiet stand, and then went on again, finally fading from sight. Goodnight delayed until the sound of the man had dropped to a scuffling murmur. Thereafter he turned upgrade again and came presently to the head of the canyon.

The road at this point reached level ground, passed through a short belt of timber, and came upon the meadow of Sun Ranch; and in the belt of timber, he well knew, some of the Sun Ranch crew would be stationed, waiting for trouble. He left the road and cut a considerable circle, reaching the meadow at a distance from the house. There was a light inside the house and as he watched he saw a door come open and men move awkwardly through it, carrying another man inside. He crossed the meadow, still circling, reached timber, and came cautiously upon the house from the eastern side. The length of the dining room and kitchen was before him, all dark; he skirted this, turned a corner and stopped at the edge of the yard. The door of the main house was still open — a careless thing he thought — and he saw the girl sitting silent on the porch steps.

He said: "Virginia," and looked sharply around the yard to see what effect the sound of his voice might make. A shadow broke from the corner of the bunkhouse, stepping into the yard; and a man came at once from the main house. The girl, still seated, spoke indifferently: "Who's there?"

"Goodnight," he said and rode over the yard. He stepped down and faced her. She looked up at him and he saw that she had been crying. She gave him a stone-still glance and her voice was hard and turned against him.

"Why bother to come back?"

"What's wrong?"

"My father's dead."

Theo McSween was on the porch, his light face turned sallow and sharp and cool. He held his hands on his hips, waiting out Goodnight; two other men moved in from the yard, behind Goodnight. He heard their feet slip along the ground. He sat down on the porch beside the girl and he watched the way her mouth struggled to hold its tight shape and gradually grew loose. She wanted to cry again and she wanted to hate the world. He put his arms around her and drew her against his shoulder, and listened to her fresh crying begin. Her body trembled and her tears ran down her cheeks and fell warm against his hand.

One of the men in the yard said to McSween: "Shut that door, you fool. You want to make targets for Harry Ide to shoot at?"

SEVEN

THE WILLFUL WAY

Holding her, he felt the misery that made its havoc in her, and for the first time in many months he had pity for another human being, and this surprised him, since he had thought himself toughened beyond any such feeling. McSween, who now stood on the porch behind him, had turned him against the race of man. Nevertheless, the girl's broken crying hurt him and caused him to think of Harry Ide with anger.

He could not turn his head and he disliked McSween's presence behind him. He said so: "Get away from my back." The three other Sun riders, Bob Carruth and Tap and Slab, had moved out of various corners of the yard and collected before him; they looked dead-beat.

He said again to McSween: "Step around where I can see you."

The girl pulled herself out of his arms and checked her crying. He watched her put away her tragedy and bring her will like iron hoops around her feelings. Her mouth pressed together and at the moment she showed them all a bitter face. McSween had not moved. Goodnight rose and turned, facing the man and watching his expression grow balky. He stepped up to the porch, coming near McSween. "Mind me," he said. McSween

92

spoke through the quick short lifts of his breath: "You ridin' me again? Nothing you can do will budge me if I don't want to budge. I'm one horse you don't break."

"Move down," said Goodnight.

"No," said McSween, "not until I'm ready."

He expected trouble and he had himself braced for it and cocked for it; still, he was slow and Goodnight's fist cracked him in the belly before he got his arms lifted. It drove the wind out of him; his hands dropped, fingers fanwise over his stomach, and his mouth sprang wide open and he stood there in an agony, without breath and unable to get it. Goodnight struck him lightly on the shoulders, swung him and caught him with both hands and flung him off the porch. McSween's boots caught on the steps and he fell on his knees and hands into the yard, and remained like that, his head lopped down. The three other Sun men said nothing.

The girl looked on McSween with a kind of impersonal interest. She turned to the doorway, speaking to Goodnight. "Come in here a moment."

McSween got to his feet slowly and faced Goodnight. The color had entirely gone from his sharp countenance, the insolence and the pride in his own power was vanished. Even so, there was something left — a brand of fanatic stubbornness that made him meet Goodnight's glance with a dead stare.

"Give me my gun back and we'll get the whole thing done with. That's what you want, ain't it?"

"Go on back to the bunkhouse," said Goodnight.

McSween spread his legs. He closed his fists and let them hang beside his legs; he had the air of a man talking to himself in silence, commanding himself to stand fast. He never said anything and he seemed half drugged. Goodnight came down the steps at him, waiting for McSween to break ground, to show fear. He didn't get the chance to see it, for one of the other Sun men pulled McSween around and shoved him toward the bunkhouse.

Goodnight said: "Don't lend the lady-killer a gun, boys," and turned into the house. He closed the door and waited for Virginia to say what was on her mind.

She was in a corner of the room, waiting for him, stony-patient. "You've met Mac somewhere before?"

"No."

"Why ride him then?"

"I can't tell you that," he said.

"I can. Just to be top dog. You hate anything that won't buckle under. I thought you were cruel but then I thought you might have something better in you. I guess I was right in the beginning. Well, that seems to be all that counts here. Do you want to stay on?"

"Yes."

"You know what's happened?"

"I got mixed up with Harry Ide's bunch when I came up the road."

"So it was Ide?" she said. "I knew they'd be from the desert but I wasn't sure he led the party. You see what it's like. Where are your sympathies — or does it matter?"

He could have told her that her hurts mattered, but he did not. All he said was: "It doesn't matter. They've probably got me tagged as against them anyhow, since I'm here."

"I've got to keep this ranch. I don't want to be driven away."

"We can try," he said. "There ought to be men enough in the hills to lend a hand."

She said: "That's what I fear."

He studied the answer. He pointed to the lamp on the table near her. "Turn that down," and he gave a glance round about to the windows of the room. She lowered the wick, throwing the room into half-darkness as he said: "I'm not certain of Mac."

"Do you doubt he'll try to kill you now?"

"He'll try," said Goodnight. "I was just wondering

which way he'd try."

"Tell him to ride on if you want."

"I want him here. If he leaves I'd have to go after him."

She made nothing of that and shrugged her shoulders. "How far do you have to follow a man if he won't bend to your liking?"

He said: "You're worried about Boston Bill."

She showed him an expression that meant nothing to him. The man's name affected her or had power to disturb her, and when he realized it he looked at her more carefully, not so sure as he had previously been of her attitude. He said frankly: "Or maybe it isn't worry."

She avoided answering the implied question by changing the subject. "My father tried to play the kind of a game he wasn't meant to play. Other men influenced him too much. I don't want it to be that way with me. All I want is to keep this ranch."

"Boston Bill is willing to help you do it," he reminded her.

Her voice revealed some strain and some emphasis. She kept stubbornly to her point. "I want to keep this ranch and I want to run it. You're brutal enough to make men mind you. How would you like to be foreman?"

"If I'm supposed to keep off the thing you're afraid of," he said, "maybe you better tell me what that is."

"You'll see."

He turned to the door, but he changed his mind and crossed the room and went through the kitchen and left the house by the back way. Reaching the edge of the house, he caught an incomplete glimpse of the yard and saw nothing; but the feeling was on him—that feeling which had so many times come out of the primitive recesses of his body to warn him—and therefore he moved back into deeper darkness, cut a wide circle and came up in the rear of the bunkhouse. Stepping beside its end wall he reached the edge of the yard and found McSween in the middle of the yard, facing the porch with a rifle in his arm.

The girl had turned up the house lamp and she had opened the door to let out the day's heat condensed inside; and therefore McSween was a revealed shape in the yellow glow. Had not Goodnight hated the man so thoroughly, he would have admired him, for McSween waited there openly, with a kind of dumb patience and a stolid desperation, as though his own pride could not be satisfied with any other way.

Goodnight stepped into the yard, lifting his gun on McSween. "Stand fast," he said. "Drop the rifle."

The sound of his voice made McSween flinch. Goodnight noticed a short, stiff shudder go through the man. McSween stood rooted, not turning his head as he grated back his answer: "Why didn't you do this square and meet me head-first? I was right here where you could see me."

"Drop the gun," said Goodnight.

McSween let the gun fall, and then turned. His face was old and showed something close to despair. "When do I get the chance?" he said. "I got it coming to me."

"When you can find it," said Goodnight. "Get into the bunkhouse." He walked past McSween and picked up the rifle. McSween stood indecisively in his tracks, watching Goodnight with his balked glance. Goodnight rammed the muzzle of the rifle into the man's back. "Move on," he said. The pressure stirred McSween. He marched to the bunkhouse with his fist doubled; and swinging he went into the bunkhouse and moved like a man half-asleep to his bunk in the corner; he sat down on its edge, still staring at Goodnight. The other three had turned in for the night, but they were awake, watching this scene.

"Who lent this greenhorn a gun?" asked Goodnight.

Bob Carruth said: "It's my gun."

"Man should be more careful with his weapons," said Goodnight.

"He said he only wanted to fire one shot. Didn't think it would hurt the gun."

"He was braggin'," observed Goodnight.

"So it appears," agreed Carruth gravely.

"It was a nice play," added Goodnight. "He stood in the light, knowin' I'd see him. Knowin' I'd surround him and take his gun away."

"Still," said Carruth, "he could of shot through the window, or stayed in the shadows and hipped you."

"Maybe he thought of that," said Goodnight. "Then he got to thinkin' that maybe he might miss his first shot and wouldn't get in the second. So he did it the way it would look the best and hurt the least."

"That might be a fact," said Carruth. "Man never knows. Still, why wouldn't he make the try, with him so far on the worst end of it?"

"Lady-killers," said Goodnight, "have no guts."

McSween sat bowed over on the bunk, head between his hands. His eyes were yellow-gray in the light, winkless as they watched Goodnight. He said nothing at all; he only let his dead-set face show its expression. The three other men looked on, neutral and interested. Carruth, thought Goodnight, was willing for McSween to use the gun because he was curious as to how it would come out. Carruth—and the other two as well— had no conscience in the matter. They were spectators interested in the show, watching one dog bristle at another dog, and coolly laying bets on the outcome. He knew that. He knew, too, they would forever watch him for whatever danger he might be to them, to discover if he came out of their own past lives to catch up with their crimes; and he knew that if they feared him they would try to do away with him, but meanwhile would respect whatever power he showed. That was their kind.

"Bob," he said, "who's been foreman around here?"

"I been."

"Hope you liked it while it lasted."

Bob Carruth took the news with his usual grave and indifferent manner. One eyebrow lifted, opening one eye fuller; the other was a streak of light between closing lids. Finally he turned over on his bunk, putting his back to Goodnight. "That's fine. Now you can do the talkin' when Boston Bill shows up tomorrow."

One wave of sunlight broke over the hills, shattering the morning twilight, the suddenness of it like sound whirling down the meadows, through the glens and pockets and narrow rock canyons. The pines standing in massed shadows above Sun Ranch heaved suddenly out of obscurity, their green needles shining. At this hour the air was thin and clear and cold and the strike of Goodnight's foot on the water trough ran its echo straight out along the earth and split into double echoes at the timber's edge. Breakfast was done and he had gone for his horse when he heard the on-reaching running of horses coming from the ridge trail. Coming back to the yard he found Boston Bill at the porch, talking to Virginia Overman. Half a dozen of Boston Bill's men sat asaddle, waiting.

Carruth stood in the bunkhouse doorway, watching this with his usual cool reserve. Carruth murmured to him, "Now you can figure this one out," and seemed amused.

Goodnight thought of something. "Where's Bill's headquarters?"

"Back on the ranch that used to be Clark Morphy's. Two miles up."

"He could have heard the shooting last night."

"He could have," agreed Carruth.

The idea stuck with Goodnight as he went over the

98

yard. Boston Bill, at the moment, reached out and touched Virginia's shoulder and spoke to her. "All you need to do is tell me what you want."

Goodnight observed the half-reluctant interest on the girl's face. Bill's presence and his personal attraction reached her, even against her judgment. It was something like this, he thought, as he arrived at the porch. Boston Bill swung around to meet him, the charm fading. "You're back?" he said, and then thought of something else. "You in this fight last night?"

"No."

"That's right," said Boston Bill. "You were in town." He turned to the girl. "Don't trust men you don't know."

His charm returned as he looked at her. He was a tall one, bold and arrogant when he chose to be; he was capable of swift changes and he had unexplained qualities—and therefore he fascinated her. Goodnight was aware of this as he watched her eyes drop. She said hurriedly: "Frank is foreman here, Bill."

Bill gave Goodnight a steady stare. "That trip to town saved you a lot of trouble."

"Where were you last night?"

Boston Bill said: "That's none of your damned business." Then he remembered the girl, and gave a better answer, grudgingly: "We just got back to our place after a night ride. Otherwise we'd been here."

Goodnight looked back at the riders still sitting asaddle and saw no night weariness on them. What was the man trying to avoid? Meanwhile Boston Bill put his hand on the girl's arm and said, "I want to see you alone a moment." He led her inside and closed the door.

Goodnight got out his tobacco sack and poured a cigarette. He drew a long breath of smoke and he watched Boston Bill's men and was aware of their covert amusement. McSween appeared and stood beside the stirrups of one of the riders and watched him with a hungry anticipation, as though he saw the chance for which he waited. Over by the bunkhouse the three other Sun men held their places, also watching and judging him. This whole scene made him or broke him as the moments ran on.

The door opened and Boston Bill called out: "Virginia wants her dad buried next to her mother — over there beyond the trees. Get busy on it, and send somebody to Roselle for the minister."

It was Boston Bill's signal that he proposed to take control. Goodnight knew it and the crowd knew it and something went over the yard, making him smaller before all of them. He nursed the cigarette, saying nothing and doing nothing. The mounted men got down and started toward their chore.

Eight

At Roselle

A minister came out of the hills sometime before noon on an old gray horse, conducted the funeral and took his dinner and went away. Goodnight said to Bob Carruth: "Where'd he come from?"

"Roselle."

"Where's Roselle?"

"Summit of the Pass Road. Was a mining town."

Goodnight went back to the corral and took seat on the top bar. He had a view of the main house whose door was again closed. Boston Bill's men sat around the yard, in the shade and in the sun; the day inched along, meaning nothing to anybody. This was one of those times when, as in a poker game, luck ran low and the players sat disinterestedly by, waiting for a break to come, for a fat pot to build up. He realized he had taken a bad beating during the morning. In the space of two minutes before the critical audience Boston Bill had cut him down so that he was a lesser man in the eyes of all of them, so that whatever pressure or weight he used against any of them would need to be greater than before. Boston Bill was clever and fought with many weapons.

He had stood back in the small crowd at the funeral and he had watched the girl; she had shed no tears and it seemed to him she had changed greatly. Her way of standing, her gray eyes looking down at the earth, her fixed composure — these things reminded him somehow of her father. He thought of her very steadily as he balanced on the corral bar and watched the house.

Meanwhile Boston Bill sat on the corner of the living-room table, inside the house, and considered Virginia Overman. She sat in a corner of the room, perfectly composed. Not once during the funeral, and not since, had she given way. She had excellent control of herself, a thing which impressed him. Yet he doubted the sincerity of any woman and believed all of them to be actors who suited themselves to any part and any emotion, playing whatever role they thought would show them to advantage. He spoke softly even as his critical eyes searched her.

"It is very tough. You know very well I'll do whatever chore you want done. I've told you that before."

"Yes," she said, "I remember."

"Virginia," he said, "how are you going to run things?"

"As they have been run in the past."

"You must be aware of the difficulties. The kind of men we have to use around here do not take to a woman's instructions."

She looked at him intently. "A woman can do things a man cannot. Has that occurred to you?"

He smiled with some indulgence. "A woman's knuckles were never meant for a fight."

"A woman has a smile," she said. "I could smile your whole crowd away from you."

"Why," he said, "what goes on in your head?" He was sober now, and he thought carefully of what she had told him. He looked at her in a different way; he permitted more of his natural cynicism to show. "You're talking in a very realistic manner."

"Bill," she said, "I can read your mind. You're sorrowing with me today and doing it well. You do many things so well. But tomorrow or the next day, or next week, you'll suggest how lonely it is for me and you'll propose. That's about right, isn't it?"

He stared at her, considerably surprised at her cold and rational analysis of him. It irritated him to know that she had played with him precisely as he had played with her. He said pointedly: "The truth is, Virginia, you're not particularly forlorn because of your father's death."

"I will do what my father did not do," she said.

"What's that?"

"Don't be curious."

"You will do it with my help," he said, "or you will not do it. Don't let your fancies get the best of you."

She studied him over a thoughtful interval. "You're pretty blunt when you don't feel you have to be charming. Sun Ranch is mine. You had a better grip on my father than you have on me. You knew him better. You knew how to work his prejudices and how to appeal to his streaks of hate and justice. He had more justice in him than I have. He could hate, but I can hate harder. He was a simple man, and you studied him and knew him, and used him. Had he lived you would have made yourself so necessary to him that he could have done nothing without you. I'm different. You don't know me as well and you'll never be certain I'm standing where you think I am."

"My God," he said, "is this what has been going on behind your smile all these months? You sound as though you despised me."

Her glance ran over his face and a flicker of expression came to her lips and eyes. Then she looked down. "No, Bill," she murmured, "I don't hate you."

He was trying to judge her and having a poor time of it. She had changed on him, throwing his reasoning out of line; now he tried to re-establish her in his scheme of things. "It would be foolish of you to send me away, Virginia. Where will you get other help?"

"I'm not sending you away. I only want it clear about Sun Ranch. You can change your plans."

"What plans?"

"You're not the usual kind of a brush jumper. You ran away from something much better than the average man.

103

I think you sometimes hate yourself for running. You are very proud of your brains and you have a contempt for most men around you. Well, here you are. You think you could make a little world of your own and run it as a perfect king."

"Sun Ranch," he pointed out, "is just a mountain meadow surrounded by trees. You could make it bigger if you wished. You could have cattle over half the mountains, if you wished."

"Cattle rustled from the desert?"

"How does it matter where we get our beef? These men will take what they can from us. We can take what they have with equal right. Sun Ranch could stretch from summit to the desert. It could go out upon the desert twenty miles. If you want it."

"All that is nice to dream about, Bill. You're a great one to dream and talk."

"I can draw twenty or thirty men to me," he said. "What's to stand against us? It won't be hard to knock out the ranchers who have been trying to ruin Sun. Once they're gone, who cares? If it were back East we'd have some kind of law on our trail. But this is just empty country and it is a matter of indifference what happens. How do you suppose big outfits ever got started in the first place, if not that way? Ten years from now, when settlers catch up with us, it will be too late. It isn't too late now."

"You've been here long enough to have tried it. Why haven't you?"

"I came here green," he said. "I had to learn. I had to build up my crowd. I've built it."

"You always talk well. You started out to catch Harry Ide. You didn't do it."

"This stranger rode up and spoiled my play."

She said: "What really made you go to see Ide?"

He gave her a strange look. "I have told you."

She watched him so steadily that he grew impatient, and afraid. He held her glance, knowing he could not show weakness now, but the effort was hard and he broke it up by bringing a smile to his face. "You're touchy."

"Go back and do what you intended to do. Then I'll listen to you."

He said slowly: "You're asking me to go kill Harry Ide?"

"Yes," she said.

"I realize how you feel. This thing has hit you hard and Ide deserves to die. He probably will in due time. But I hate to hear you speak so coldly."

"Now you're just talking again. If you're afraid, don't bother. All the hill outfits are friends of Sun. They will do what you haven't done."

"I do not like to hear that from you."

"For that matter," she said, "Goodnight will take care of Ide for me. You can ride along on your own business, whatever it is."

He said angrily: "I don't want him around."

She swung about, her will as strong as his. She flung her question at him. "Why didn't you settle that also when he stopped you at Ide's?"

He said, very slowly: "Are you asking me to go out there and draw on Goodnight?"

"No," she said. "Let him alone. But don't talk of things you never mean to do."

He said: "I'll see you again in a day or two," and left the house. She followed to the doorway, watching him swing to his horse; and wait for his men to gather. All those men were wild ones, fugitives and without much conscience; yet Boston Bill had done one thing to them, had bound them together and had made them loyal to a certain extent. Presently he wheeled and led his outfit away.

"Bob," she called, "saddle up for me." She let out a long sigh. The stiffness on her face, the cold containment, slipped. She was tired and showed it and she was thinking: "I shall have to handle him better than that or he will slip through my fingers, or destroy me. He is a clever man. He is more subtle than a man. His brain is like a woman's—like mine.

105

He reads me almost as well as I read him."

Bob brought her horse forward. Going to it, she spoke to Goodnight who still roosted on the top corral bar. "I wish you to ride along, Frank." She waited until he had joined her and afterwards turned to the meadow road.

He said nothing to her. Depression obviously chilled her spirit; she struggled with her thoughts, with her eyes fixed ahead and seeing little of anything, with her lips compressed. The meeting with Boston Bill had left her displeased and he had also noted that Boston Bill's expression, on leaving the house, had been stormy. These two had clashed.

They reached the timber and came upon a trail running upgrade into the high country. She sat like a man in the saddle, her stirrups low, her legs straight and her body swinging in easy motion. Once she looked around at him, as if some sudden thought had compelled her. Her lips were clear and ample against her face and her eyes had dark depth. The lightness of her skin and the color of her hair made her seem a laughing girl, easy and teasing and buoyant and quick to love. The suggestion of it went deep into him and produced its effect.

They came to a summit of the trail. Here she stopped and pointed her hand down a ravine, at the lower end of which a small meadow opened. Following her gesture, Goodnight noticed a log house and a weather-gray barn sitting in the meadow. "That's where Boston Bill stays," she said. "I wanted you to know where it was. This is not the closest road to it. The best road goes straight from Sun. Remember that."

She went on, crossed a short bare bench and reached timber, again climbing. She appeared pressed for time and she drew back again into her thoughts and made no further attempt to talk to him. Half an hour onward they came upon a narrow footbridge slung over a canyon thirty feet wide and sixty feet deep, at the bottom of whose dark slice a creek ran swift and white. Somewhere nearby, out of sight, a falls made a steady racket and the

106

mist of its spraying lay damply in the air. Now the road reached a clearing scarcely more than a foothold at the base of a cliff, and ended in front of a cabin and a corral and a log lean-to. Behind the cabin rose a cliff, gray and weathered and cracked. In all other directions the pines marched away in ragged up-and-down formation, covering the sharp breaks and ridges roundabout.

A mustard-colored dog, long and lank, scuffled around the cabin with its red mouth showing, and a man as lank as the dog stepped from the lean-to, holding a rifle loose in one hand. A short beard covered a face that might have been old or young; he had a hatchet chin and agate-black eyes and a faint streak of a mouth. He was about six feet tall, nothing but bone and hide, with the round shoulders of one who bent to watch the trail as he walked or rode. His voice, when he spoke, was an old man's voice: "Git down, Virginia."

"Just came to introduce you to a man, Ned. This man. His name is Frank. He's working for me."

"For you or your old man?"

"My father is dead. Harry Ide's crowd shot us up last night."

The old man stolidly accepted the information. He shrugged his shoulders and his lids crept nearer together, accenting the beady brightness of his eyes. "We can remember that," he said. "One day Harry Ide's goin' to have a hell of a time." He looked at Goodnight and said: "Whut about this feller?"

"If he comes up here for anything, remember he's from me." She turned to Goodnight. "This is my father's oldest friend — Ned Tower."

Ned Tower laid his glance on Goodnight like the edge of a knife, motionless but ready to cut. He was one of the lone sort, Goodnight judged, answering to no man and responsible only to his own conscience; and his conscience was tough enough for anything that had to be done. He nodded his head: "I'll know him if he comes, Virginia. That all?"

107

"All now," she answered.

"No," he said, "it ain't all. Whut you goin' to do with Boston Bill?"

"I'll use him," she said.

"Will you now?"

"I'm not as easy as Dad," she said.

"We'll see," he said.

She turned away and led Goodnight downgrade, saying nothing again until they were near the main meadow road. The sun was low and the shadows streamed far out from the trees and the heated, spicy air began to tremble with oncoming coolness. She looked at him, her troubled mind now seeming to relax. "Ned Tower is a man I can always turn to. He knows all the other hill ranchers. Up here we're very clannish. A word to one is a word to all."

"Doesn't seem to trust Boston Bill."

"Nobody does. But if a dozen men ride into a hill rancher's yard, what can he do? Best to feed the crowd and hope for no trouble."

"I'd guess," said Goodnight, "it has been profitable all around. He's brought you a lot of desert beef in return for his meals."

She hardened against the suggestion and had an instant answer. "I've no regrets for the desert people. I'd like to see them destroyed."

He said nothing and when they reached the bottom of the trail and came into the Pass Road, she turned to him. "Why should you care?"

"It is entirely your business," he said.

"But you disapprove."

"Hate to hear hardness in you. In a woman."

"There's hardness in you."

"Yes," he said. "Maybe a man, made out of plain clay, wants a woman to be better than that."

She stopped, she put out a hand to stop him. She turned and looked fully at him. "That's the most revealing thing you have said. How can you pack two different things around in your heart? How can you be two men?"

108

He moved into the Pass Road. "Dust still here. Some-body's passed by." He looked at the tracks in the ground and presently motioned upgrade. "That way."

"Just another fugitive going over the hill." Then she added, "Same kind of a man as you are," and watched him with sharp eyes. He said nothing as they moved down-grade side by side. The suggestion of other travelers turned him alert, she noticed. He sat straighter in the saddle and he watched the trees with a restless attention. He had a great assurance about him, he had no doubt of himself. Behind the temper that drove him was great per-sonal warmth, and his infrequent smiles had made a strong effect in her. She thought of the women he had known and felt angry at him for knowing them. They trotted into the yard at sundown.

She stepped from the horse and said, "Please come into the house for a moment," and led him inside. She closed the door and turned to him with a changing expression on her lips. They lost the day-long hardness and her eyes widened and met his attention and glowed. Her breath-ing ran faster and suddenly she was a woman, fair and wishing to be noticed. "Frank," she said, "you'll stay on won't you?"

"If I'm not pulled away."

"What could pull you away?"

"I can't tell you that."

She said: "I don't know what you're running from, or what you're after. I've seen you do some terrible things. Yet I trust you. Even when I saw you at your campfire I trusted you." She let her voice sink and soften; it blew on him like pleasant wind. "If you were truly bad you wouldn't look at a woman as you do. If you were really cold you wouldn't speak of a woman as you do. Don't you suppose I want to be the kind of a woman you think about? Don't you think I am? But how can I be anything but hard? The men in these hills will take whatever they can. These are the men I've seen all my life. If I think all men are like that, you must not blame me. How many

109

times I have ridden these hills wondering if there was another kind of a man."

He watched her closely and she saw his imagination come up and catch fire in his eyes. It was like a voice singing to him, like color showing through dead black. Then she said, still in her soft way: "You'll stay?"

He came nearer and noticed the pulse in her throat beat quick and hard; he watched the flurry of strange, unguessed things come to her eyes and he saw her lips loosen. She dropped her glance, but brought it quickly back, neither offering nor asking. But she waited and he wondered about the waiting. Then he said, "Supper time," and left the room.

She stood still, listening to his steps scrape across the porch. The supper triangle broke the stillness of the yard, flinging metal echoes outward to the hills, that sound breaking far up and far away. She dropped her head, staring at the floor. For a moment she hated him for refusing what she had silently suggested to him. He had recognized the suggestion; she had observed its effect on him. It had swayed him and he had used his will to pull away. Why had he done that? Her pride was hurt by it, yet presently she said to herself: "He'll stay," and went to her room. She made herself neat for supper and looked carefully at herself in the mirror. She combed her hair and stood back, coolly thinking of herself as she would be to him, and moved on to the dining room.

Goodnight stood at the foot of the table; the three other hands were already seated. Goodnight said: "Where's Mac?"

Bob Carruth looked up, gray and disinterested and reserved. "Left."

"Left for where?"

"Didn't say."

She watched Goodnight grow cold, grow keen. "Which way did he go?"

"That way," said Bob Carruth and waved his knife. "Towards Roselle. Over the mountain. That's the way they

110

all go. He stayed a week. That's a long time for his kind."

Goodnight started for the door. Virginia came around the table to halt him. "Where are you going?"

"After him."

"Then that's what brought you here. Why didn't you say so? And if you wanted him, why didn't you take him when you had him?"

Goodnight went by her without answering. Carruth called out: "Hope you find him. He took my forty-four."

Goodnight reached his horse. Turning in the yard, he looked at Virginia. She said at once. "Will you come back?"

"Maybe," he said and ran on.

She watched him until he was far down the meadow. Afterwards she went into the dining room. She stood a moment, undecided, and then returned to the living room, her appetite gone. She felt strange, she felt lonely. She walked slowly around the room with her complex thoughts. "I should have warned him that Mac is treacherous," she told herself. "I hope he knows it." She folded her arms across her breasts. She said: "I had depended on him. What will I do now with Boston Bill?" She went into the bedroom and stopped before the mirror. She was a cold woman, she thought, and cared nothing for Goodnight as a man. She had permitted Goodnight to see warmth in her, knowing that it would draw him and hold him on the ranch. It had been only for that reason. She scanned her face, she drew a thumb beneath her eyes. She thought: "Is that all of it?"

Twilight came on, lingered briefly, gave way to dark. Goodnight reached the end of the meadow and ran on between black hedges of pine. Now and then he pulled to a walk and gave his horse a breathing spell, but he hated the delay and scarcely could abide it; for the fear of losing Theo McSween dominated him and he cursed himself for ever permitting the man out of his sight. There was really nothing else left in him except this one desire. It had changed his life, it had changed his mind and his heart and now that he felt Theo McSween slipping away it made an emptiness in his belly.

He had not figured the man would run. McSween had stood up to him, had defied him, had come back for more punishment, had begged for a gun and an even chance. What had changed him? Maybe, Goodnight decided, the thought of more punishment had finally worn the man's courage thin. It was what he had wanted — to destroy the pride in McSween, to make him cringe and beg, to break him down and gut him of every thread of self-respect until he stood stripped and wrecked of manhood and knew it and hated himself for what he was. There never had been a waking hour in the last three months when Goodnight had not thought of how it was to be done; he thought of it now and had his greedy eagerness. It looked like he had broken McSween; and that was near to the end of it.

He reached a flat stretch and set his horse into a steady canter. Mountain cold blew against him and the stars spread their milky ferment through the black sky. He was high up and he had the feeling that the whole weight of the hills suddenly tipped from west to east. Out east was another sea of desert; if McSween intended to run, he would run straight — the same way he had been running ever since leaving Nevada. Across that eastern desert he would go, more weary days on end.

Goodnight was two hours from Sun Ranch when he felt the peaks on either side shove their shoulders toward the road, cramping it. Creeks ran down those high slopes to make a little river that flowed with the eastward-falling grade, and around a bend of the road he caught the dull shine of house lights, thus coming upon Roselle, in the jaws of the pass.

He drifted forward with caution, observing that this town was nothing but a huddle of old shacks split by the road which went straightaway through. Against the nearby hillside he made out the yellow scars of mine dumps and the scaffolding of buildings stripped of their covering lumber. When he reached the side of the nearest house he stopped in the shadows to have a look before him; a two-story building stood ahead of him with an outside stairway leading from street to second floor. There seemed to be a saloon on the ground floor, with a few horses standing before it; across the road from it was another large building whose windows and doors had been removed.

He studied the horses and did not identify McSween's mount; he remained in his saddle for a few minutes, carefully waiting. A man passed out of the saloon, and one man passed into it; that was all the town showed him for his waiting, and afterwards the sense of time wasted pushed him forward. Dismounting before the saloon, he stepped inside the place. Four men sat at a table, playing poker; and all four ceased playing and looked at him with a dead steadiness. One of the four rose and moved behind the small bar; he lifted a bottle and glass and set it on the counter.

"Where would a man eat?" said Goodnight.

The saloonkeeper pushed his thumb behind him. "Go sit down in the back room. I'll fix it."

"Where would a man sleep?"

"Take your blanket up the outside stairs and pick a bunk."

"I'll eat first," said Goodnight and poured himself a short drink. He held the glass between his hands a moment. The bartender now did a queer thing; reaching down, he got an empty bottle and turned and banged the bottle's bottom against the wall at his back.

"What's that for?"

"Tellin' my old woman to fix another supper," said the bartender.

The three other men hadn't stirred since his entry. This country roundabout was the same as that near Sun Ranch, full of dodgers; and probably the best trade this saloon had was from these fugitives. Goodnight held the drink in his hand and moved quickly on the door to the

113

rear room. He threw it open before him and saw a table with a red oil-cloth top. There was a plate on the table with a steak half cut through and a cup of coffee half emptied. A chair stood away from the table, as though a man had hurriedly kicked it aside, had hurriedly departed. An open door at the rear of the room showed the direction of his departure. Goodnight turned back and laid his whisky glass on the bar. The barkeep said: "You want that meal now?"

"Fry it up," said Goodnight. He went rapidly over the saloon to the front door, and cast a sudden backward glance at the three men at the poker table as he left the place. They were sitting by; they were not in this deal. The bartender had given the signal to the man eating in the rear room, but that was probably only the kind of protection he would have given any stranger on the run — just a rule of the house. Coming to the road, he looked to both directions, made a quick decision and swung to his left, running the front width of the house and turning the corner of it sharply. It brought him to an alley lying between the saloon building and a small adjoining house. He saw a shape weave at the far end and he heard the ragged run of steps; he followed the alley and came out at the back edge of the town. He heard the faint crush of a foot to his right, and looked that way and saw nothing. The man had disappeared in the darkness but a horse stood to Goodnight's left, behind the hotel and saloon. He hugged the hotel wall and stepped toward the horse. When he came upon it and looked closely at its markings he knew he had caught up with Theo McSween. He was on the near side of the horse, and reached out and untied the latigo and hauled off the saddle and carried it on until he came against a pile of boxes and rubbish behind the saloon's rear door. He dumped the saddle in the pile. If McSween ran away now it would be bareback; he wouldn't get far before being overhauled.

Goodnight paused a moment, trying to guess the man's actions. McSween was behind him, moving to-

114

ward the other end of the building line, circling and re-treating and trying for a fair shot. Therefore Goodnight continued on until he reached the corner of the saloon building and crept along the side of its wall until he reached the road and the front edge of the building. He looked down the street and saw nothing; and observed that the few lights which had been in this town when he had entered it were now dimmed down; Roselle, living on the trade of fugitives, gave its customers an even break — no more and no less. One dull lance of light filtered through a crack of the saloon's closed door; directly across the street a yellow stain of light showed on the drawn shade of a window. That was all. He and Theo McSween were alone on the street, maneuvering and creeping while the rest of this town watched the game go on.

He still stood at the side of the saloon, thereby exposed if McSween backtracked and came upon him from the rear. He slid around the edge of the saloon to the front side and stood there, watching the lower end of the road. He was debating: If McSween crossed over the road he'd be somewhere in the shadows of the opposite buildings. If he hadn't crossed, he'd be waiting at the lower end of town, or crawling back for a surprise play. There was no way of knowing. He could wait and break the other man's nerve — he could make McSween move and betray himself; or he could start hunting.

It was not in him to wait. He had traveled too far and he had hunted too long. Turning, he rounded the corner of the saloon and quietly retraced his way down the side of the building to the rear; and hugged the back wall as he moved toward the lower end of town. He passed McSween's horse and he reached the narrow alley between the saloon and the next building. He stopped here to listen, and crossed the mouth of the gap in three long, soft steps. The next houses sat close together; at each between-space he paused and looked along it to the front — to the road whose deep yellow dust threw up a faint glow. It was like looking down the black barrel of a

115

gun at a white piece of paper in front of it.

The end house was two hundred feet below the saloon and when he got to its edge he faced the irregular floor of the short meadow upon which Roselle lay. The road's yellow streak of dust ran on back toward Sun Ranch, and the nearby hills lay above him, ragged against the sky. Close at hand something stirred and someone murmured. He put his ear against the house wall and heard the low speaking of one voice and then another; townsmen were inside, waiting out the fight.

He rounded the corner and advanced to the road and stood at the house's edge, considering the short row of buildings across the way. Three small houses squatted low in the night before him; the windowless and doorless two-story building faced the saloon with its black blind eyes. Watching it, he saw a faint glow in the second-floor window, like the low burning of a cigarette tip, and he stared at it steadily until it occurred to him that this was the night's light catching on a splinter of glass still hanging to the window frame. The window, he now observed, commanded the road and the house-tops of the town. From that position a man might see many angles he could not see from the street level.

He backed away from the edge of the house and retreated to the deeper shadows. He crossed the road and circled behind the buildings on the north side and came against their ends, now again looking down the between-spaces as he passed them. When he reached the rear of the two-story building he spotted a doorway and moved to it and listened inside.

The smell of an abandoned place came out to him, musty and dry, with the remnant odors of a thousand things once held within the place still clinging there. He looked at a farther partition which seemed to divide the lower floor and he saw another doorway in that partition, its blackness less than the blackness of the partition. A rat ran across the upper floor, producing a scurried, gritty wake of sound. That was the only sound. Nothing came

116

from the town and nothing else came from this abandoned building which once held its treasures.

He set one foot forward and down, testing the floor. He let his weight fall easy and slow, and tested with another foot; and found there was no floor but only a hard-packed earth. He slid on until his foot struck a sill, and small as the echo was it seemed to swell and grow large; he stopped dead and he listened and heard nothing, but coolness of some kind ruffled the back of his neck. He reached the doorway through the partition and stepped over another sill and found himself in the forward half of the lower floor. Onward he saw the dull-gray square of the door and the windows to either side of it — these opening on the road.

He had begun to smell dust dragged up by his own feet, a dust dried by the years and turned to powder. He looked to left and right and discovered nothing, but he knew there had to be a stairway or the remnant of a stairway somewhere close by. He made a guess and turned to his right, still treading hard earth, and put out his hand. Another two paces onward his forward-stretched finger tips brushed a board slanting upward before him. He came near it and sightlessly explored with his hands and felt the steps; and when he slid his hand across one of the steps he touched a damp, cold object that made him jerk his arm away. His wrist struck the edge of the stairs, producing a definite noise. A voice came straight down on him.

"That you, Goodnight?"

Goodnight sucked in a long, heavy gust of wind; he let it come out in slow pinches. He stood rigid. It was McSween's voice, and it came again. "That's you, ain't it?"

"Come down out of there."

"Your last name's Goodnight, ain't it?" said McSween, doggedly curious. "You're Mary Goodnight's brother, ain't you?"

"Come down," said Goodnight.

"There was somethin' about your face that bothered

117

me — ever since you hit Sun Ranch. Three hours ago it just came to me."

"I'm coming after you," said Goodnight.

"Everything's been bad enough without this," said McSween. "I wish I had never met your sister. My luck changed the day I saw her. It just ran out and nothing went right afterwards."

The emptiness of the building diffused McSween's voice so that it was hard to know where the man stood. Goodnight got to the front side of the stairs and laid his weight on the treads. They gave and groaned, but they held him. He went up slowly, flattened as he climbed. He heard McSween's body move; he heard the boards of the second floor whine. McSween's voice came louder at him. McSween's words fell out, hurried and breathless.

"She came of her own accord. I didn't drag her away. She was old enough to know what she wanted to do. Why blame a man for that?"

Goodnight's hands touched the second floor's level. He paused, still uncertain of McSween's whereabouts. He heard the man breathing and he heard the boards whine. McSween was doing a strange thing — backing away into the blackness without a shot. Goodnight lifted himself out of the stairway in one sudden spring, whirling away from the stair wall. He stopped, he stood fast, listening into the fathomless black. McSween's breathing was swift and short, somewhere ahead.

"I wish," groaned McSween, "I knew what happened. When I touched her I lost everything. I knew then something would happen. It just came over me. So I hit the trail, but there never was a minute I didn't know somethin' was comin' behind. If you was any other man I wouldn't run."

Goodnight pulled up his gun. He pointed at the sound and he fired. He heard the bullet smash through wood and brick. He heard McSween shift direction.

"Listen," sighed McSween, "I'll never touch another woman."

Goodnight fired again. The burned powder bloomed blue-crimson in the black; and then muzzle light leaped back at him and this second floor roared with the quick explosions. He fired four times and somewhere in the heart of the racket he heard McSween shout up a great cry, and then sound and cry faded and the stink of powder swirled around him and he heard the shallow, slow gathering of McSween's breath. He stood still, coldly and patiently waiting to put in a last shot.

McSween groaned and his body twisted against the rickety floor, sending vibrations through the building. "A man and a woman," he sighed. "A man and a woman—" He ceased to speak and Goodnight thought he had died. But McSween caught his breath and went on. "A man ought to be free. But he can't do without a woman and the woman takes his freedom. Your sister smiled back at me, Goodnight. Now I'm dyin' because of it. Is that fair?"

Goodnight said: "You'll be in hell a long time, remembering that you took her away, used her, and left her to die."

"Ever kill a man before?"

"No," said Goodnight, "but I've got no regrets over this. I'm happy it's done."

"You'll be in hell, then, a long time before you die," said McSween.

He had been slowly stirring on the floor, and now ceased to move. Goodnight listened and heard no breathing, and went forward cautiously. His foot touched McSween's body and he bent over the man, shaking him with a hand and feeling the lumped looseness give and fall back. He thought of Carruth on Sun Ranch and reached down and got the gun from McSween's hand; and climbed down the stairs.

He made his way to his horse in front of the saloon. The door was open and the saloonkeeper stood in the light. Looking around, Goodnight noticed other men now showing in doorways. Lights came on again from house to house and a woman's pale face appeared at

119

a window. He got to his saddle.

"You want that supper?" asked the saloonkeeper.

"Hold it for the next brush jumper comin' through. It won't be a long wait." He turned west and rode away, Roselle behind him, and two hours later reined in at Sun Ranch's yard. The echo of his horse on the meadow road had run ahead of him. Carruth came to the bunkhouse doorway and Virginia stood at the break of the main-house porch, watching him as he rode over to Carruth. He handed down the gun McSween had borrowed. Carruth took it and had a look at the cylinder. He gave Goodnight his gravely disinterested stare. "It was loaded when he took it. Empty now."

"He had his chance," said Goodnight.

"I guess," remarked Carruth, "he wasn't the shot he thought he was."

"As men go," said Goodnight, "he was at the bottom of the pile."

Virginia called: "Come inside."

"I'm going to town."

"What's there for you?"

"A bottle of whisky," he said.

"There's a bottle here."

"I never get drunk on the ranch I work for."

She drew herself straight, hating him for his stubbornness. She said: "If you find comfort in her, go on. You're of no use to me."

He turned away, easing his horse into a slow canter. He heard her call after him in another voice. "Will you be back?"

He didn't know and therefore he didn't answer.

NINE

TIME FOR WONDER

He reached Sherman City before midnight, left his horse in the stable and strolled as far as the hotel corner. He wanted to go directly to Niles Brand but he knew it would be best to be seen by Rosalia's men before attempting to enter her house. Therefore he loitered a few minutes, crossed to the Trail for a drink, and came out again to find Rosalia's chore man, Gabe, standing on the corner staring at the sky. As he went past, the old one murmured: "Go into the back door of the hotel and turn right." Then the old fellow resumed his absent-minded study of the stars.

Goodnight moved toward the screening blackness at the street's end. He reached the shed whereby he had earlier met Niles, turned by it and came back along the rear side of the row of houses. He crossed Rosalia's yard and let himself into the back door of the hotel. A spot of light came through the keyhole of another door directly to his right. He hit it once with his knuckles and stepped inside. Niles Brand sat up on a bed, propped against pillows. Rosalia stood at the corner of the room.

The sight of her struck him. He met her glance, its dark depth and its growing glow; her lips changed faintly and then he remembered the shape of them and the heaviness of them against him, and all that had its

121

way in him as he looked back upon her. Niles Brand said in a softly ironic voice: —

"Well, Frank, how's the big world?"

Niles was cheerful and grinning, but it appeared he had been through his torment. His face was pale enough to show the freckles ordinarily hidden by heavy tan and his lips were cracked from fever and his cheeks were lanker than usual. There had been a doctor working on him; he was properly bandaged and he wore his shirt.

"You eatin' well enough now?" asked Goodnight.

"Appetite came back today, like a rain on a dry land."

"What you doing in this room?"

Niles showed a bit of embarrassment. "I wouldn't take a lady's bed from her."

Goodnight looked at the window, at the door. He said: "Not protected much."

Rosalia moved over the room and opened its door, Goodnight looked across the hall to another room whose door also stood open. A man sat in a chair, facing them with a rifle over his knee. She closed the door, making no comment at all.

"You see?" grinned Niles. "There's another fellow outside by my window. This lady owns the town." He had been studying Goodnight all this while with the critical and experienced eyes of a friend, and what he saw took the cheerful grin from his face. "Somethin' happened in the hills?"

"Yes."

A glinting expression showed on Niles's face. "Catch him?"

"Yes," said Goodnight. "That's done."

"Then," said Niles, "we can turn around and go home."

He had no answer from Goodnight. Goodnight showed him nothing; he was dry and tired, and beyond that lay some kind of unpleasant feeling. Niles said:

"Better get a room and go to bed. Then we can play rummy a couple days until I'm ready to ride."

"I'll see you tomorrow," said Goodnight, and turned out. His steps struck the hallway floor, going forward to the front of the hotel. The girl listened to them thoughtfully.

"Not like him," said Niles.

"What has he done?"

"Killed a man," said Niles. "A man that ran away with his sister and left her dyin' somewhere out in Nevada. Been a hell of a long trail and I'm glad it is over. But he don't take it right. He ought to be pleased."

She turned back to Niles. "Then he never was running away from anything?"

"He's an honest man," said Niles. "But there's something wrong."

"What was he like? Before all this happened to his sister?"

"Everything," said Niles, "was fun. Always smilin'."

"I've never seen him smile," she said. She stood soberly by the bed, looking at Niles. But it was now as so often before—she looked at him without seeing him. She was far from him.

"I don't know what's workin' on him," said Niles.

"I do," she said. She turned out his light and left the room. She stood in the darkness of her own yard and she called, easy-voiced: "Syd," and waited until a shape drifted up from some yonder patch of blackness. "Go to the Trail," she said. "There's a man in there—you know the man—and he'll be getting drunk. Don't let anything happen. When he's good and drunk, bring him to me."

Goodnight walked through the small lobby of the hotel, waking a man who sat sprawled asleep in a chair; the man opened his red eyes briefly and closed them

123

again. Goodnight reached the street, looking both ways. There was an occasional light burning out of a window but nothing showed on the street except for a fellow sitting on the edge of the walk in front of the Trail, drunk and fighting to keep erect. Goodnight turned toward the Trail. The drunk saw him and the drunk murmured: "It's my legs, that's all. They went to sleep on me. Ain't that the damnedest thing?" The Trail had a swinging door with a window in it made of colored glass, green and red and blue; the lights of the saloon came through it and turned the drunks face rainbow colors.

There was a card game going on inside the saloon — four men deep in smoke, with the bartender standing by. When Goodnight arrived the bartender turned behind the bar; the other four kept on with their playing. They hadn't looked directly at him but he knew they were conscious of his presence.

The bartender knew him from his prior visit, and distrusted him. He watched Goodnight with his Irish brows dropped down like sagged awnings. The barkeep wanted to bounce him out of the place, but didn't dare to and so he nursed his jealous resentment in silence. He put up a bottle and a glass. He let them drop harder against the bar than was usual. Goodnight stared at him steadily, he held the barkeep's glance and he put his elbows on the bar and bent across it, murmuring in a little voice: —

"Get the hell out of my sight."

It was plain that the barkeep fancied himself a tough one, ready to answer any challenge. No doubt his imagination had supplied him with many a fight into which, in fancy, he had hurled himself with a snarl and a terrible wrath, and out of which he had emerged victorious, his opponent senseless on the ground, himself without a scar. Now he stood before an actual challenge and the reality of it stiffened him. He had belief in himself and an immense pride fed by his dreaming, yet all this began to crumble. Goodnight saw him struggle with his courage; he witnessed the barkeep's pride waver forward and back, unequal to the issue. Coldness came to the barkeep's belly and the coldness weakened his legs and fear was a water dissolving his manhood. Suddenly he lowered his eyes and stepped away.

He stopped at the end of the bar, half turned aside, but Goodnight had a casual glimpse of his face, the sharp lines of distaste, the strange putty look around the mouth. This man faced his own private ruin; his admiration for himself died and he knew self-hate, born of his weakness, so that from that moment forward he would never again feel fully equal to other men. One single yell and one impulsive swing of his fist would have saved him; no matter what defeat or pain he may have suffered in a fight, he would have arisen with his manhood still intact. But he had failed himself and his face revealed the sickness of it. A thousand times in the future he would review the scene and know at which point he had failed, and would wish with all his heart he had acted differently — and yet would know he could not have done so. This night the barkeep became a different man.

Goodnight forgot him almost immediately and, save for the occasional reminder of chips clacking behind him, he forgot the four men playing poker. He was nursing a very odd feeling and the drink he swallowed did not materially help. This mood, this irritable and unsatisfied and formless feeling, would not dissolve; it had come upon him at the moment of McSween's death, had ridden all the way to Sherman City with him. Once in the past, he had come down with typhoid fever, and remembered the sensations of unease that preceded it; this was somehow similar.

He stood loose in his joints, his weight largely on his elbows. He took a second drink, and a third, aware of a new man quietly come to the saloon. He looked at the man and thereafter ignored him. He ran a hand softly over the bar and was relieved and satisfied to feel its cold, smooth solidness. The solidness helped him; it was the only solidness anywhere. That was a queer thing to think about. In the old days he traveled and had no cares and everything was fun and the days ran on, hot or cold, but all of them strong to his senses and all of them good. The past meant nothing and the future never came; only the immediate day and its fun had mattered.

Then for three months one thing alone had claimed his mind and his heart. He had thought of nothing but his sister's tragedy, and of McSween's downfall. His last remembrance before sleep was of McSween, and his first waking feeling was of an impatience to be on the trail after McSween. It had hurried him, it had crowded every hour, leaving room for nothing else. Now it was all done and he could be himself again.

He reached out with his thought to the old carefree times. He said silently to himself, "I can go back to everything that used to be." He let his weight settle heavier on his elbows. He lifted his head and stared at the back-bar, looking beyond it, and far away from it, with a solid net of lines across his forehead. His long face showed a flush and it showed the intensity of his thinking; he was a bent, angular shape against the bar, gone out of this world. He reached forward with his senses to catch the smell of the cold wind coming down from the high peaks against his campfire, to recall the shade of the dry desert at sunset time — all a melted yellow surface; he reached farther and farther, but each time he grasped nothing. Nothing came back. None of the sounds and smells and tastes and none of the feelings came back.

He didn't feel free again; he couldn't capture the feeling of freedom for all his trying. He felt burnt out and

126

useless. Somewhere after his fourth drink he understood he could never return to his old days. A man — and the weight of the knowing came down like the hammer of a pile-driver on his skull — a man never went back. Each day changed his bones, his flesh, his blood. Today's sunsets were never the color of yesterday's. The time never would come again when, riding the trail with the whole day before him, he could sing and dream and never care where night brought him. He wasn't the same man. He was another man standing at the bar, eyes half closed to catch the smoky tan light streaming through the pony of whisky.

He looked at the bottle which had been half full and found it almost empty. His weight was on his elbows but he felt only a slight pressure there. He thought: "I have got to have something to do." He thought of his sister and that memory hurt him until he could no longer bear to think of her, and his old great rage against McSween was as bitter as it ever had been. Even with McSween dead, there was no peace and no sweetness; everything was just the same. McSween had said: "You'll be in hell a long time before you die." Now what had McSween meant?

A man said to him, from a long distance: "Your treat, ain't it?"

He turned and saw the man — the same one who had so quietly entered the saloon a long time before. "Sure," he said, "there's the bottle. Barkeep, bring another glass."

The barkeep came up with the glass. He looked at Goodnight, darkly hating him, and he looked at the other man with some kind of appeal in his eyes. He said: "I got to lock up sometime, Syd."

But Syd said: "What's your hurry as long as you got customers?"

Goodnight turned, remembering the poker players. They had gone and it surprised him to know he hadn't heard them leave. He stared at the barkeep. "What's the time?"

"Two o'clock," said the barkeep sullenly, and moved away.

"Plenty of time," said the man and drank his drink. He was heavy at the shoulders; he had white heavy teeth and his grin was white against the mahogany burn of his skin. His eyes were a smart gray, and his neck was solid.

"What's on your mind?" said Goodnight.

The heavy one looked at him with some care. He was sly and he moved easy, studying Goodnight as he moved. "When you're through here," he murmured, "she'd like to see you."

Goodnight reached into his pocket, glanced at the bottle, and threw out a pair of silver dollars; they rang dull on the counter and that warned him of himself. The sound was too far away. He dropped his knuckles sharply on the bar, feeling little. He stepped away from the bar and stood a moment. "Let's go see her," he said.

The heavy man went before him. At the doorway Goodnight looked back at the barkeep who stood with his hands below the counter. He stopped dead. Suddenly the barkeep lifted both hands into sight and placed them on the bar. He sent his hate over the room like a hot gust of wind but he didn't stir.

The street was dark except for the lone lights of the saloon. The drunk lay in the dust, curled and shivering as he slept; starlight turned his face pale. Goodnight looked at him and shook his head. "There's a man turned into a dog. Whimperin' in his dreams like a dog. When he was a baby his mother probably said: 'He'll be somebody great when he's big.' What makes men great and what makes them little?"

The heavy-set Syd said: "He's asleep, which is happiness. What more could a man want?"

"Not enough," said Goodnight.

128

Syd stopped, his feet close by the drunk. "What more does a man want? Or if he wants it, how much chance does he have of ever gettin' it? If I kicked him he wouldn't feel it. But when he's awake he's full of misery and everything hurts him. Better to be asleep."

"Ought to throw a horseblanket over him," said Goodnight.

"No good. He'd sleep warm this once — and every other night he'd sleep colder and be whinin' for the one warm night he had."

"What makes him lie in the dust while I stand straight?" murmured Goodnight. "What's the difference?"

"Somethin' the Lord gave you, friend."

Goodnight shook his head. "There was good in him. He had some kind of dreams in his head. He rode his horse as a young man and saw the shadow grow tall on the ground. Some woman smiled at him. Some man was his best friend. He knew evil and was ashamed. He could be made to cry over small things that were good. He came from the same place as the stars. Then he fell and a star went out. Why is that?"

The heavy man said: "I thought you were drunk, friend."

"The world is a brutal thing. Full of scoundrels and made up of torment. There is a curse upon it, made by men. The race of man is small. We're nothing better than ticks scattered in the sage. Maybe we started clean but now we're livin' in filth made by ourselves and we breed upon our own ignorance and vice, the smell of which rises to heaven. One day a big wild wind will blow out all this, all men and all the foolish little lamps of men, and it will sweep away all the dirty houses and sand will fill up all men's small scratches upon the earth. And then the world will be clean again and maybe someday there'll be another breed better than we are."

Syd said nothing. He rolled a cigarette. He lighted it and he drew in a breath of smoke. Then he pointed at the drink. "None of all this bothers him," he said practically, and turned over the street. Goodnight followed him down the dust. Syd paused at the alley behind the hotel and gave a sharp look around him. He made a signaling duck of the head to some unseen man in the pre-dawn blackness and entered the alley. When he came to Rosalia's rear yard he stopped and touched Goodnight's shoulder. "Go on in," he said, and faded away.

She was on the porch waiting for him. She rose out of a chair as he came up. He stumbled on the top step and she caught his arm and drew him on into the house, her voice murmuring at him. He stood still in the house's darkness, hearing her move away, and then a lamp's light came on and he caught the outline of her face as through a film. He knew then he had taken too much whisky, but even with the dimness of her face he noticed the long line of her lips, and the dark, deep color of her eyes as she watched him.

"You wanted to see me?" he asked.

She came forward and took his arm again, guiding him into her bedroom. "You shouldn't be alone in town tonight."

"I'll crawl into the hotel."

She said: "Lie down there," and put her hand against his chest. He dropped back on the bed. He pulled up his feet and lay on his back, his eyes closed. "Late for you to be up," he said.

"It took you a long time to get your drinking done, Frank."

"You been waitin' for that?"

She didn't say anything for a while. Presently he opened his eyes to find her looking soberly down, darkly in thought. Light from the lamp glowed through her hair; light drew a full encircling pair of shadows

130

across her breasts. She was thinking of him and those thoughts showed, even though the film remained in front of his eyes.

Her voice took a faintly rough edge. "I had to wait, didn't I?"

"No."

He had closed his eyes again; he was falling asleep. Tenderness showed on her lips and then vanished, and a dark wave of harshness caught her face—and then that too vanished. She spoke in a whisper, as if afraid he might hear, yet wanting him to know. "You could make me lie down in the mud and wait for you."

She knew he hadn't heard, and the tenderness came again. She moved to the foot of the bed and pulled off his boots and laid a quilt over him. She stood at the bed's side, her absorbed glance upon him—upon the width of his chest and the relaxed smoothness of his face. Lying this way, with the black trouble out of him, he was at peace, and on the edge of smiling. He had a face for smiling; there was recklessness at the corners of his mouth and eyes. She saw him as a handsome man.

When she spoke her voice was rough again. "Does it help you to get drunk?"

He opened his eyes and looked at her. "You know, Rosalia, it's very funny. A man can't go back."

"Where do you want to go back to?"

"I don't know." He was silent and the shadow of trouble appeared again in his eyes. "Nor can a man ever wipe the slate clean."

"Are you sorry for killing McSween?"

He shook his head. He turned on the bed, placing his big hand over his face. He spoke in an uneven way. "It still hurts like hell to think of my sister. Nothing repairs that. It's a senseless world. I hate the whole damned race and I'll never lift my hand to help a living soul. From now on—" He lifted a fist and closed it and made a motion.

131

She stood by and watched him fall asleep, she watched the trouble die out of him. She brooded over him, knowing the depth of his hurt, and knowing too on what dangerous ground he stood. For it was out of such injustice and personal loss that outlaws were made. He balanced now on the very edge. He was strong and his feelings were great, so that he would never be a halfway man. If his bitterness grew still more it would destroy all his kindness and all his faith, and he would lift his hand against other men and so would destroy himself. In the beginning she had thought him already this kind of man, since almost no other kind came to these hills. Attracted to him, she had accepted him for what he was and had made up her mind to fight for him. Now that she knew he was not a fugitive and not an outlaw she was relieved — yet worried at what he might become. All her protective instincts rallied; she wanted to keep him as he was.

She remained over him, resisting the powerful impulse to bend down and kiss his heavy mouth. Tenderness and wanting swayed her. She held herself away, grown strong by his need of her, hardened by his hurts and the things that threatened him. Presently she left the room and made a bed on the couch in the living room. She blew out the light, hearing afterwards a slight tapping at the back door, which stood open. "Ma'm," said a voice, "what you want me to do?"

"He stays here tonight, Syd. Where's Harry Ide?"

"In the hotel asleep. Room's dark. Those other two fellows that came with him are bunkin' in the livery stable."

"Get Gabe to watch the street. You go to bed, Syd."

Syd said doubtfully, "Ide ain't here for fun. He's been lookin' around. You know what I think? I think he figures Goodnight's in the hotel. He thinks it's Goodnight instead of Niles Brand in that room. He's lookin' for Goodnight, shore enough. You know why, don't you?"

132

"I know why, Syd. Ide thinks Goodnight is going to run things at Sun now that the old fellow is dead. Get Gabe to watch. You sleep until breakfast."

Syd delayed to say one more thing: "You know, that's not a bad fellow. Him—Goodnight. We had quite a talk when I was bringin' him here. Yes sir, quite a talk."

"What did he say, Syd?"

Syd grunted. "Can't say I really know. But he sure swamped the subject, whatever it was. I gather he don't like some things."

Harry Ide kept a rented room in the hotel the year around. Sometimes it served him as a place to stage a roaring poker game with the owners of other desert ranches, sometimes he used it as a shelter when, full of liquor, he could not make the long ride back to his own place; and sometimes, fearing ambush on his ranch, he came here to hide away temporarily, to watch his enemies.

He had been in the room that afternoon, seated before the window; and thus saw Boston Bill arrive; and he spent the next two hours watching Bill drift into sight, disappear, and show up again. At supper time Ide went down the back stairs and ate in the kitchen; and climbed back to his room. When he stepped inside he found Boston Bill waiting for him.

It gave him a start, although he was far too cool a hand to let Bill see this reaction. Bill lay stretched out on the bed, smoking a cigarette; and Bill grinned at him, enjoying the scene.

"This makes me one ahead of you."

"My turn next time," said Ide, making himself agreeable.

"It should demonstrate something," said Bill. "Anybody can get the drop on anybody else at any time. So why should we fight at all? You've got your

133

business and I've got mine."

"That's right," said Ide.

"A proposition then?"

"Depends on what you want."

"I've got what I want," said Bill. "Just stay away from Sun. I don't care where else you go."

"That," said Ide, "is a bargain."

Bill got off the bed. "You'll have no more trouble from Sun. You may have trouble from some of the other hill outfits."

"I'll take that in hand."

"It would be a good idea."

"For both of us," agreed Ide. "Whatever I do up there will also help you. That's why you suggested it, isn't it?"

"Sure," said Bill and moved to the door.

Ide said casually, "You're a damned cool customer, Bill."

"It may be," assented Bill. "I like to do things the easy way. A shooting is a foolish thing between us."

Ide nodded and watched Bill go. Ide listened to the tall man's steps drop down the stairs. He went to the window and saw Goodnight go into the Trail, and afterwards, half an hour or more, he saw Goodnight on the street. Ide thought: "Very cool—too cool. I cannot depend on him. It will be only a matter of time before he wants me out of the road. Same as he wanted Overman out of the road. He may try it himself, or he may talk this Goodnight into trying it."

He thought the whole thing over very carefully as he sat before the window with his cigar.

Somewhere during the night a flurry of sound struck down through the woolly layers of sleep to reach Goodnight, like the fall of a board and its after echo. He heard it as he would have heard the sounds of a dream, and then it faded out and when he awoke he remembered nothing.

He looked around him and was puzzled; he saw his bootless feet showing beyond the bottom of the bed-cover. His mouth was dry and his surroundings strange and he lay a moment, backtracking his memory. He was in a room whose door was closed, with the sharp morning chill in it and the smell of coffee and bacon strong in it. Someone moved around outside the door.

He got up and put on his boots and sat on the edge of the bed and rolled a cigarette. He remembered the saloon and he remembered something about a man talking to him; he remembered the night air and the alley — and then he knew where he was. He got up and looked at himself in the bureau mirror and found himself ragged and needing a shave; but his head was clear and he felt fine, he felt fresh and sound and ready for anything. He opened the door and walked across Rosalia's living room to the kitchen. She stood over the stove, making up breakfast. She heard him and came about, as grave as he had ever seen her, and she looked at him in her searching way — reading what his face might hold.

He smiled at her, the first real smile she had seen from him; he was embarrassed but still he was cheerful. "I remember passing a drunk sleeping in the dust last night. When I woke this morning I thought for a moment maybe that drunk was me, and that maybe I just imagined I was on a bed. Your bed, isn't it? Nice of you, but I didn't help you by bein' here."

"This town," she said, "knows better than to question what I do."

"That's right," he recalled. "It's your town."

"I had one of the boys bring over a razor and shaving soap. Here's the hot water."

He got the shaving gear and he took the teakettle from the stove and went to the back porch, shaving by a small mirror tacked to the porch wall. He washed his face with a blubbering racket and dried himself. He

135

stood on the porch a moment, watching first sunlight break the glassy morning air, and for a moment the good feeling came back with its edge, its promise, its never-ending surprises and pleasant moments. For a moment it came back; after that the old recollections took it away and left him with his nagging emptiness. He returned to the kitchen and took his chair at the table. She had his coffee for him, his bacon and eggs and fried potatoes, and baking-powder biscuits out of the oven.

She sat down with him, sipping at a cup of coffee but not otherwise eating. She was watching him in the same manner he had noticed earlier, out of extremely grave eyes. "Frank," she said, "how old are you?"

"Twenty-nine."

"Last night," she said, "you were bitter. So you tried to drink it away. But you were bitter still when you fell asleep. The thing that hurt you most was that you couldn't forget your sister. Nothing wiped it away."

He said: "Who told you about all that?"

"Niles," she said.

"It's a fine breakfast," he said and rose and stood in the doorway, looking out upon the yard. "Time to go, I guess."

"Where?"

He held his silence for a matter of minutes or better, and at last said: "I don't know. I haven't thought of anything else for three months. Just this one chore. Now it's done and I can go back to riding. Yet there's nothing in that any more. There's a time for drifting, when a man feels that way. But when the feeling runs out, drifting's no good."

"Why," she said, "should you hate the world so much?"

He studied the question and he tried to answer it, and could not. He lifted his palm and held it open, and closed his fingers hard down. And opened his palm

136

again. "Nothing there. When I think of the misery dealt out to a girl who was straight, who never—" He stopped, unsettled by his feeling, brought back again to his terrible memories. "Why should I feel kind?"

She said: "Don't be like the rest of the men in these hills. Don't nurse grudges and hate until you're rank inside. You'll be an outlaw and your own worst enemy. It doesn't matter about many of those men. They were born with kinks; they'll never be better, only worse. You weren't meant to snarl at the world, to ride against people, to destroy and to die alone without friends."

"There is nothing," he said, "for me to hang to."

"Find something. Otherwise if you do nothing but hate and disbelieve you'll be no better than George McGrant's dog—skulking in the darkness, waiting to jump out and bite somebody. Hate will ruin you."

He said: "I've got to thank you for the meal, and for bein' kind." He turned again, saying, "Going over to visit Niles. Maybe play a little rummy."

She said in a thin voice, "Wait—turn around," and watched him swing. She had something to tell him, but the telling of it was a hard thing to accomplish; it quickened her breath and laid a strictness around her mouth. "Niles," she said, "was killed last night. Somebody got to his window and shot through it. He was asleep."

TEN

WOMEN MEET

He stood wholly still as she told him; she saw his lips stretch thin and very tight. His eyes changed, opening fully on her with an expression she could not fathom and never afterwards understood; but at the moment it was as though he hated her and wished to kill her.

She dropped her eyes out of pity and heard him draw a long breath. Afterwards he turned from the room. She followed him to the porch and watched him walk across the yard toward the hotel, very slowly, with his head down and his shoulders sloped. He went into the hotel.

Syd came along the back side of the hotel, intending to follow Goodnight. She checked him with her hand. She murmured, "Stay out of there." Syd moved away into the alley. Rosalia waited, her shoulder touching the two-by-two post. She waited with her eyes fixed to the hotel doorway into which he had gone, patiently and darkly foreboding, inexpressibly sad. Her lips were long and heavy and she could easily have cried. What prevented her was her will, and her fear for him. When he came out of the hotel five minutes afterwards she was in this same position. He had closed up entirely; he was soft and painfully quiet with his words.

"You have any idea who did it, Rosalia?"

"Yes," she said. "I know."

He waited and his eyes begged her, but his rigid training in minding his own counsel told him well enough the question was foolish. He gave her time to speak, if she chose to speak, hopefully waiting.

"There were three men in town all night," she said. "Two from the desert and one from the hills. That's why Syd came to the saloon to meet you. I knew they were here. We had somebody watching Niles's window and somebody in the hotel, across from his room. But the man watching the window stepped away at three o'clock to get a cup of coffee."

He said: "What'd they want Niles for? He wasn't in any of this. He was out of it." He thought of it slowly, his mind reaching forward and around the whole thing. She saw the truth of the matter come to him in slow stages, forming around his mouth and darkening his expression. "They were after me. They thought they were shooting me when they killed Niles."

"Yes," she said, not wanting to say it.

He drew in his breath; he let it softly out. "You know who did it," he said, and again waited with his hope.

"I know," she admitted. "But I'll not tell you."

He spoke in a mild tone, as though it were something which interested him but did not stir him. "I'll find out."

"I suppose you will. Now you've got something to do, haven't you? You've got another chore. I'm sorry for you."

He bent his head, puzzled. "Why?"

"The end of the first chore left you empty. How do

you think this one will leave you, if you live through it?"

"Strange talk," he murmured. "Very strange. What would you have a man do?"

She shook her head and the softness and the sadness went out of her face; she had been a woman anxious to please him and she had been a woman whose spirit was warmth and color, whose voice carried out to him the resonance of her wanting, her depths, her dreams, her hungers. She had been soft and giving; she had watched him to find his mood so that she might fit herself to it. Now she stood straight before him and had her say. "Nothing but what you must do, Frank. No man can go back on himself. You'll hunt and you'll fight and you won't rest until you've balanced the ledger for Niles." She paused and when she spoke again her voice was sharper, "I'm not arguing against you, am I?"

He shook his head and turned off, walking around the corner of her house to the street. After he had gone she went into the kitchen and stopped there. She thought: "No use arguing now. But if he kills another man out of revenge he'll be an outlaw the rest of his days. If there was a way . . ."

Sunlight reached the town, filtering into the blistered surfaces of board walls, glowing upon the molded and edgeless patterns of the street dust, glittering upon clean windows and grayly burning against dirty ones. Sunlight was a tide moving inward, breaking the dullness of alleys and sending its straight fanwise lines farther and farther around corners; and each up-stepped degree of light made the town more homely, made it smaller, burning away the false mystery of night-time until at last Sherman City was only an ugly yellow break in the timbered

140

greenness flowing down the undulating pitches of the Owlhorns.

A dog lay in the dust, slightly panting, and rose on its front legs, too uncomfortable to stay in the sun; but it fell back again, too lazy to move out of the sun. One rider came into town, threw a package into the doorway of the hotel and moved back upon his trail. A storekeeper swept the litter of his shop onto the sidewalk, a woman opened her second-story window and threw a pail of water down upon the street, and the gray old man, Gabe, sat against the base of the Trail, half keeled over but not quite fallen. He had both eyes shut.

Goodnight thought: "He was on guard last night. He knows." He went into the Trail, into its stale stillness. The barkeep stood behind the counter, drearily polishing glasses; he looked at Goodnight and a fresh job of memory struck the raw spot made the night before. He stood a moment, staring at Goodnight, suffering and making a test of his courage again. Presently he dropped his eyes.

Goodnight said: "Did I pay you for the drinks last night?"

"You paid."

"When did those four poker players leave?"

"An hour before you."

Goodnight had said it casually and followed it with the same half-interested tone: —

"When did Ide pull out?"

"Ide? I never saw Ide. It was his foreman, Jack Drew." Then the barkeep looked alertly and suspiciously at Goodnight. "How'd you see him? He was out of sight."

"What was he afraid of?" asked Goodnight. "Boston Bill?"

But the barkeep now guessed he had been used.

He gave Goodnight a sour, half-worried look. "I never said anything about anybody bein' here. Don't say that I did."

"Never heard you say a thing," promised Goodnight and left the saloon. Gabe had disappeared from the side of the building; when Goodnight crossed to the Texican he found the old man stretched full length on the top of a pool table, face upward. He had his hat over his eyes. He removed the hat to catch a look at Goodnight.

"You lost a lot of sleep last night," observed Goodnight.

"I lose sleep every time you come to town," grumbled the old man.

"I'm obliged," said Goodnight.

"Not to me — to her. She's the one that tells me stay up."

Goodnight said: "When did you leave the street to get that cup of coffee, Gabe?"

"It was Syd. Around three o'clock. And he didn't leave for more than five minutes. He heard the shot. He came around the hotel corner and saw the fellow fading up beyond the corral. He took a shot and missed. Fellow was on a horse by then, going up the hill road."

"On a sorrel gelding?"

"Who could see a color on a black three-o'clock mornin'?"

"Stockin'-legged front feet?"

Gabe gave him a blue, disillusioned stare. "You're askin' too many questions," he said and fell back on the table. He pulled the hat over his face and his voice came muffled through it. "Never pays for a man to know too much, my friend." Then he said another thing in a lower voice that Goodnight didn't hear.

"What was that?" said Goodnight.

"I said," growled the old man testily, "you ought to get out of the country."

Goodnight drifted from the Texican and turned to the stable. He stepped into the runway's rank cool semi-darkness, the sound of his feet dying at once on the mushy underfooting of loose dirt and straw. He came to his horse and slid into the stall. He stood there, not sure of his next move, one hand on the big gray horse's back. Voices came from the rear of the stable, rolling up slow and idle—one tired voice answering another that fed in curious questions.

"You up then?"

"I was asleep, but it woke me. I got up . . ."

The horse stirred and looked at Goodnight. He ran his palm along its shoulders. He remembered Niles saying: "Better get some sleep. We can play rummy tomorrow." Niles was the last tie he had. These two—his sister and Niles—had come out of the past with him, out of his boyhood they had been together, the three of them particularly close. He remembered how much he had wished that his sister would marry Niles, as Niles had wished. It seemed it would work that way, until McSween came along. He remembered—and this was again a knife slice through him—that when he returned from Nevada with the news of her death he had found Niles playing solitary pool in Cochran's saloon. Niles said nothing, turned, racked his cue and walked out of the saloon.

A little later Goodnight had found him behind the City Corral, crying.

That was over. These two fine parts of his life were cut out of him.

". . . I got up and ran forward. He was just goin' past."

"Where was his horse?"

"Down there in front of McDarmid's house. Syd shot once but then this fellow was aboard and runnin' for timber."

"You saw him?"

Goodnight had heard this talk break against him, had heard single words of it as he struggled with his own thoughts. Now, suddenly he caught that last question and grew attentive. There was a delay and afterwards a sly, slow answer.

"Maybe I did. He was a tall man."

"With a big nose?"

"The nose," said the other, "might have been a big one."

That was all. One of the men came forward through the stable's gloom and saw Goodnight. He stopped and a queer expression jumped over his face. He watched Goodnight get his gear and slap it on; he watched Goodnight go into the saddle. He had a curiosity which at last made him speak. "You just come in here?"

"Just came in."

"Hear anything?"

"A big wind," said Goodnight. "A big wind comin' over the mountains." He rode out and paused to give his horse a drink and afterwards urged the horse around the corner of the Texican and stopped in front of Rosalia Lind's house. He was about to get down when she appeared at the front door. He straightened back in the saddle, removing his hat and holding it. "This may sound queer to you—but I don't want to stay here. Will you take care of Niles?"

"Yes," she said.

He rode to the porch and he reached into his pocket and handed down a letter to her. "Put that in

144

his pocket. I found it in my sister's coat in the hotel room in Nevada. She wrote it to Niles but she hadn't mailed it. So I took it."

"You never gave it to him?"

"Someday I meant to, but that day never came."

"But why not, Frank?"

"He was in love with her. Whatever she said— whether she had no regrets or whether she wished it had been different—it would have still cut him up. He was cut up enough. I figured to wait until he got used to the idea of Mary being gone."

"You haven't opened it?"

"It was from Mary to Niles," he said. "Maybe it's best the way it came out." He shrugged his shoulders, slowly adding, "From Mary dead, to Niles dead." He drew up his reins, turning the horse. He checked in and looked back at her. "A man would have to be wiser than I am to explain why all this happened. And if he found a reason that sounded fair, he'd be lying. The whole damned world is a lie." He urged the horse forward until he reached the hotel window through which the bullet had traveled. He stopped and studied it—and went on.

He moved up the trail, along the gulch, into the forest-shadowed road, the strong smell of pine coming down about him at once. Night's coolness still held and night's shadows lingered in the long vistas. Now and then one slanting shaft of sun slid through to burn a golden patch upon the yellow dust; and after he passed over this bright spot the rising dust moved upward along the column of light in cloudy brilliance. He felt better at once with the timber around him and the town behind him; but at the same time caution came back to him and therefore he heard the waking echoes of riders upgrade long before he saw them. He went steadily on and started

145

around a curve of the road and met them there, Virginia Overman and Bob Carruth.

They ran down upon him and came to a sharp stop. Bob Carruth said with some evidence of irritation. "Don't you know better than to ride down this road like a dreamy parson?"

It was a strange concern, coming from so hard a customer as Carruth. But it was stranger still when Virginia murmured in one long outflow of breath, "You're alive!" She crowded her horse near him and put out her hand, touching him. Her fingers closed upon his arm in a firm grasp and he saw her face break out of astonishment and grow gay.

"Am I supposed to be dead?" he asked.

Carruth eyed him closely. "Then who was killed last night in town?"

"How would that news get to Sun so fast?"

Carruth shrugged the question aside as being wholly immaterial. "Who was it?"

"A friend of mine."

"Must of been a twin for likeness," commented Carruth, "or they'd never made that mistake."

"Who are you talking about?"

Carruth closed his strong fleshy lips and said nothing more. Virginia Overman meanwhile dropped her arm. He watched her smile and her self-possession return; and afterwards, as a contradiction, he saw her reserve rise against him. "You're a trouble maker. Can't you ever stop hunting it? Coming back to the ranch?"

"Yes."

"Just for a meal, or to stay long enough to be useful?"

"I'll be around," said Goodnight.

"I'm going into town," she said. "Wait for me."

"I'll go with you," said Carruth.

"No, stay with Frank."

Carruth sighed. "Well, all right. But buy me a pint."

She swung and broke the horse into a canter, sitting in easy balance and swaying slightly, and so passed around the bend.. Goodnight watched her supple figure until it was beyond sight, and turned to discover Carruth's eyes fixed upon him. Carruth nodded. "Just to remind you, Friend Frank. She's as good a rider as you or me, and damned cooler in managin' things than you think. Well, we got to wait."

He dismounted and pulled his horse into the timber, Goodnight following. They rested back on the ground, a small lane between the trees giving them a view of the road. Somewhere a bird made a fluttering racket in the forest, to which Carruth gave a moment's attentive interest.

"How'd the news of the shooting get to Sun?" asked Goodnight. "It happened at three o'clock. It's eight now. Five hours. Somebody had to carry it through in a hurry."

Carruth had been lying back in full length. He sat up now and brought his hands sharply together, the sound of that impact going on and on through the timber. He grinned. He said, "News travels that way," and dropped back again.

"Any travelers come by the ranch in the last two-three hours?"

Carruth said in a wholly lazy voice: "I wouldn't remember about that."

He was, Goodnight realized, the same as the others; he would bear no tales and he would not involve himself in a quarrel before the proper time. He was forty or a little more, stained dark by weather, with a wrinkled face

147

and a heavy jaw and a short-bristled mustache.

"You been on Sun long?" asked Goodnight.

"Twelve years of seein' 'em come and go. Scoundrels and greenhorns and them that wanted adventure and riches, coming out of the East over the mountain. Pretty soon them that stay alive come back in a hell of a hurry. Some—" and he laid the weight of his judgment on the sentence—"stay in the Owlhorns. I sure hope she don't forget that pint."

He closed his eyes, completely relaxed—a man who knew how to take his quick moments of ease when they came. Goodnight rested his shoulders against a tree, smoking through a cigarette. He had his mind wholly on the night's tragedy and its aftermath of little hints dropped by one man or another. According to the barkeeper in the Trail, Jack Drew had been in town, he being Harry Ide's rider. It could have been the desert outfit which had hunted him and had gotten Niles. His presence on Sun Ranch probably had turned him into an enemy according to Ide's way of looking at it.

He searched that side of it carefully, giving it all the weight he could; for in his own mind he thought he knew who had shot Niles Brand. The stableman had made a break in saying: "He was tall. Maybe his nose was bigger than usual." That would be Boston Bill, and Boston Bill hated him for intruding.

One thing did not square. He had not believed Boston Bill would come from behind, or shoot through a window at a sleeping man. It was not as he had read Boston Bill; yet the wind blew that way.

Carruth said, "You got enough lives for a cat," and broke into Goodnight's thoughts. He turned to find the Sun man's gray-green glance on him, amused but penetrating. "Never figured you'd come back from Roselle. Never figured you'd come back from Sherman City this time. You're lucky as hell. No, it ain't luck." His eyes narrowed. "You're cut out for it."

"What for?"

"For the gun. That's it. I been wonderin' what made you smell different. You got somethin' kickin' you in the back, makin' a sore spot. The sore spot will grow. You're goin' to be a bad one, friend." Then he grinned amiably. "We'll see if you come out of the next one. There's another man around here who moves faster than you think." He closed his eyes again and laced his hands across his belly, and seemed asleep, still smiling.

Virginia put up her horse before the hotel and went inside. She had one errand but the accomplishment of it bothered her pride and she fought against her pride and brought her strong will forward until her mind was made up. She said to Barge Baxter, who ran the hotel, "Get me a pint for Bob Carruth, Barge," and waited until he had left the lobby. Then she turned down the hallway, let herself into the rear yard and arrived at Rosalia Lind's porch. She knocked at the open doorway. Her breath quickened and her lips moved together, but this excitement passed and when Rosalia came from the front of the house and faced her, Virginia was composed.

"I wished," she said in a inexpressive voice, "to say something to you."

Rosalia said, "Come in," and turned back. She walked into the living room, Virginia following. She swung, facing Virginia, and for a moment she watched the other girl. There was no question of her feelings; she showed her dislike and she revealed it

149

when she spoke.

"Glad you came. Sooner or later I would have had to come to you."

Virginia said: "Who was the man killed?"

"Niles Brand, Frank's friend."

Virginia frowned. "I didn't know about him. How did he get into it?"

"It wasn't Niles they were after."

"That's what I wanted to know," said Virginia Overman. "The bullet was meant for Frank, and hit this other man?"

"Yes," said Rosalia.

"Was Frank in the room at the time?"

"No. He slept here last night."

Virginia showed the effect of the answer by a flattening of her lips. She had been hurt, and the knowledge of that pleased Rosalia and made her smile. She was as cool as the woman who had come here to face her down—she was as rough a fighter as she had always known Virginia Overman to be. She had no illusions concerning Virginia Overman, no liking and little tolerance. Therefore it satisfied her to see the other woman betray her feeling.

"I wish you hadn't told me that," said Virginia. "It wasn't necessary."

"It is what you came to find out, wasn't it?"

"No," said Virginia.

"Then why did you come?" insisted Rosalia, harsher with her words.

"Was Boston Bill in town last night?"

"Yes," said Rosalia.

"When the shot was fired?"

"Yes."

She watched Virginia's expression change again. Her mouth lost its firmness, her lips came apart slightly and she seemed to be struggling with fear.

She lost color and her eyes grew round. She shook her head, speaking in a fainter voice. "You're to blame for it."

"I thought you might mention that," said Rosalia.

"You are," repeated Virginia. "Bill's been down here before. Visiting you. I always knew that, for when he came back he never was quite the same toward me."

"He's been down here," said Rosalia. "He's that kind of man, thinking himself very charming. I suppose he thought a woman couldn't resist him. That's his weakness, among other weaknesses. But he never came into my house at my invitation. He walked in of his own accord, and he soon walked out. I don't think he knows how close he came on one or two occasions to being shot by my people. He has never been in Sherman City without being watched every step of the way. If I had ever encouraged him he never would have come back to you. I wouldn't worry about that, Virginia. He got no help from me. I thought him a fool. If your tastes are different, you're welcome to him."

"You're to blame," repeated Virginia. "When he knew Frank Goodnight was seeing you it made him jealous. He came to town last night and shot the wrong man."

"He can thank God he didn't shoot Frank," said Rosalia. "Do you think he would be alive now—"

"Ah," said Virginia. "That's the way of it."

"Yes," said Rosalia.

Virginia's voice grew scornful. "So he sleeps in your house. Is that the way you hold a man?"

"It would be nice to know—if I held him."

"Why else did he come?"

"He was drunk," said Rosalia. "Not knowing there were four men in town waiting for him. I brought

151

him here."

"Drunk?" breathed Virginia.

"Do you know why? Because he was troubled. He had shot a man, out of revenge, and the satisfaction that should have come from it didn't come. Everything was the same as it was before. He couldn't understand why. So he got drunk, thinking maybe he'd find out why. But he didn't." She paused, and went on. "You came here to ask me to let him alone, didn't you?"

"I did," said Virginia, "but I suppose it was a foolish hope. You'd do anything to hurt me."

"Now I'll say something you won't understand. If you keep him on Sun he'll soon go bad, doing your dirty chores."

"I have got to defend myself against Harry Ide. Is that a dirty chore?"

"You've got Boston Bill and all the men you need."

Virginia shook her head. "I'm not sure about that."

"What you mean is that you are not sure of Boston Bill," pointed out Rosalia. "I can see all the way through you. You use Frank to whip Bill. Bill is cool to you and you think perhaps another man will waken him."

Virginia stared at her, revealing nothing. Virginia said: "Maybe."

"Or perhaps you wish two to choose from. That would please you a great deal. All you've had up there so far have been bad ones not worth a second notice. Yes, I think that is perhaps something in your mind. As I said, you're stone cold, afraid to give, or too selfish."

"I think," said Virginia, "I know a better way to handle this. I'll have Bob Carruth tell Frank about you."

A storm, a fury, an actual hatred came across Virginia Overman's smooth, confidently beautiful face. She pressed her mouth together, making it small, making it unlovely. She said: "What have you done to him?"

"I've kissed him," said Rosalia.

"I can do that," said Virginia. "Or any woman."

Rosalia showed a gleam of interest in her eyes. "Why don't you? It would tell him more about you in a minute—"

"Yes," said Virginia, "I think I'll have Bob Carruth speak to him."

"And what could Bob say?"

Virginia turned, walking to the door. She swung there, a suppressed triumph on her face. "I think anything he said of you would be true. But true or not, a word from a man to another man, a change of his tone, can damn any woman."

"Good-by," said Rosalia and watched Virginia Overman go away. She stood still, weary to the bone from the meeting. She had matched the iron in Virginia Overman, she had struck as she had been struck, and now the letdown was something in her flesh and nerves. Virginia would do as she said she would do. She would send Carruth to Goodnight with some story or other and that would be enough. A woman's reputation never stood up under that kind of attack.

Then she thought: "If he believes the story it will mean that I was never anything to him but a woman who kissed him. But if he has any tender thoughts about me—"

Syd came to the doorway, knocking. He said: "She don't know it but there's eight of Ide's men in town, watchin' her."

"They'll leave her alone," said Rosalia.

"But whut they in town for?" suggested Syd. "Somethin's boilin' up."

"Something's always boiling up," she said.

"Sure a funny country."

"Funny," she said, and made him throw his head back by the sudden energy of her cry. "Funny? Go on away, Syd!"

Virginia met Goodnight and Carruth on the road and the three went along at a climbing walk, saying almost nothing. At noon they came into Sun yard, both men stopping at the bunkhouse. Virginia continued to the porch of the main house, but before she went inside she turned and looked back. Goodnight had a fair picture of her at the moment, sunlight strong against her, lightening her hair. She glanced directly at him, asking for his attention and holding it; her lips were strong against her skin, and half smiling. She knew how she looked to him, for she saw the reaction on his face and she thought: "I can make him forget."

Bob Carruth swung away, but he turned back and stared at her, impressed by what he saw. He cast a quick side glance at Goodnight, and then looked keenly again at Virginia. He was a smart, practical man and all this he had seen before; and knew now what it meant. He cut behind Goodnight, bent for the mess room; realizing that had he gone in front of Goodnight, spoiling the effect she was creating for him, he later would have caught hell from her. She was a woman who wanted her own way. He grinned to himself.

The effect of it rolled powerfully through Goodnight. He didn't know why and he didn't ask himself why. Simply she stood in the sunlight, rounded and tall, a woman untouched and warming before his glance and opening to him — graceful and lovely and attracted to him. It was all there in that single sunlit picture.

He heard her voice call to Carruth. "Step in a moment, Bob."

ELEVEN

WRONG TURN

Carruth dragged his spurs over the yard, raking up little snakeheads of dust. He followed Virginia into the big room of the house; he took off his hat and watched her with his wary eyes. She faced him but she looked beyond him for a moment, through the door, and her eyes traveled slowly left to right. He heard somebody moving across the yard and then he knew she was watching Goodnight. The information mildly surprised him and his eyelids crept nearer as he thought about it and he studied the expression on Virginia's face with a greater interest. At this moment her attention was completely taken by what she saw. She didn't realize she was giving herself away to Carruth. He thought: "Why, she's interested in the man. It ain't entirely business."

She brought her glance back to Carruth and looked at him a thoughtful moment. "You've been here a long while, Bob. You're the only one I can really trust."

"I knowed you when you could just hang on a horse," he said. But to himself he reflected: "She wants somethin' of me." He knew all the signals. When she wanted something of a man she was always

156

nice; she always made the man feel she was interested in him. He had seen her do it many times.

"I need a little help," she said. "You're the only one who can do what I wish."

That was familiar too. She made a man important. And still, as clearly as he realized all this, he felt himself warm to her. After all, he had known her for many years. "Do what I can," he said.

She watched him steadily, holding him to her with her eyes. "This Lind woman has seen him. He stayed in her house last night. You know her kind."

Carruth dropped his glance and felt embarrassment; it was unseemly to be discussing it and therefore he said nothing. He was a rough-and-tumble sort of man with many sinful episodes behind him, yet he had his own notions of propriety.

"She hates me and she's trying to pull Goodnight off Sun, knowing we're fighting for our lives. She wants to cripple us." She waited until he lifted his glance again. She was unhurriedly persuasive, she appealed to his loyalty, to his partisanship, saying the one thing which she was sure would arouse him. "I think she's on Harry Ide's side of the fence. I've suspected it for a long while. We can't afford to have Goodnight go, Bob. He's the sort we need."

"What sort?"

"He's not afraid to use a gun."

"No," admitted Carruth, "he ain't afraid of that. But you got a lot more help, if you need it. I'd guess Boston Bill would take the job any time you said so."

"You know Boston Bill," she said.

He scratched the back of his head, wondering how she meant that. She observed his uncertainty and added: "If we ask a favor of him he'll move in for good. We'll never get rid of him."

He put a pointblank question at her. "Always

157

looked to me like you encouraged the man. Don't you want him?"

She had a self-confidence that never failed to draw his reluctant admiration. She never was shaken off her feet, she never seemed to forget her own interests. She looked at him with a poker expression, with no trace of womanly confusion. "I'd never permit Bill to think that I needed anything from him. He's too sure of himself as it is. That would make him worse. If he comes to me, he comes on his hands and knees."

"Why, my Godfrey," murmured Carruth, completely astonished at her frankness. Then he had his practical doubts. "You'll never find him on his hands and knees, Virginia. Not him."

"Wait and see," she said.

"Well, now, about Goodnight—"

"Sometime today when you are together, just drop the hint that many men have slept in Rosalia's bed."

Carruth blushed. The skin of his face was too darkly sunburned to show it, but the back of his neck flamed red. He could not meet her glance. He lowered his eyes and he was so confused that he began to reach into the wrong pockets for his tobacco. She waited for his answer. Not receiving it, she spoke more insistently. "It's true enough. Why look so odd about it?"

He said doggedly: "I don't know that it is true. Neither do you. In fact, it ain't true. She's a straight woman."

"Bob," she said, now severe, "who are you working for?"

Now he lifted his eyes, driven against the stubborn wall of his principles. "If a man spoke of any woman like that, in my presence, I'd bat his ears down to his boot tops. Any man speaking of any woman. I'll be damned if I do it. I will say furthermore, Virginia,

I'm ashamed to hear it from you. You ought to go wash your mouth with soap."

She was silently and enormously angry with him. Her eyes laid threat against him and she attempted, without speaking, to bend him to her will. It was for him a bad moment, but he kept his glance steadily upon her, until her whole manner changed and softened. She shrugged her shoulders and spoke as if none of it mattered. "Forget it, Bob."

He shook his head and turned out of the room. The two other Sun men — Tap and Slab — were in the mess hall with Goodnight. Bob Carruth joined them and ate his quick dinner. Nobody said a word. Tap and Slab ate, rose and departed and Goodnight soon followed. Carruth filled his coffee cup a second time from the big pot on the table and nursed it between his hands, drinking like a Chinaman. He was greatly disturbed; he had been left with a bad feeling. Virginia was a headstrong girl, a dominating type of young woman, always cold-blooded about getting her way. That was nothing new to him; he had always known it. But this was a different thing. It wasn't clean.

It shook him. His own life was filled with its gray things, its unpleasant memories, its moments of lust and evil; still, he had always been loyal. But that loyalty, being the one good thing in him, needed something equally good to fix itself upon. Old Man Overman, for all his narrowness and his moments of bad judgment, had been a righteous soul in whom Carruth had believed, now it was different.

He brooded over his second cup of coffee. The China cook came in, irritated at Carruth's dawdling, and displayed it by the way he cleared the table. Carruth gave him a bleak stare. "Quit rattling those damned dishes, Louie." His mind had jumped over to

Goodnight and he considered the man in relation to what he knew. There was something inside Virginia's head he didn't quite reach. She wanted to use Goodnight because she was afraid to ask a favor of Boston Bill. That made almost no sense to Carruth in view of what he knew about her. She never had been afraid of anything, never had doubted her ability to handle any situation. When her will was set, she was as single-minded and as tough as any man he had known; and he had known some really tough ones. It had always seemed to him that she had wanted Boston Bill. He had on many an occasion noticed her eyes follow Bill around the yard and he thought she had long ago made up her mind to possess him. It was just a question of getting the man on her own terms. He still thought that.

He backed away and took a sight on the problem from a different angle. Boston Bill wanted the ranch and meant to have it, one way or another. Goodnight's presence angered Bill and the arrogant, big-nosed man had already made up his mind to get rid of Goodnight. Already had tried, Carruth guessed. That was the explanation of the shooting in Sherman City. Well, then, Virginia was spotting one man against the other—for what reason Carruth at least could not explain. But it left Goodnight in a hole.

He sighed and rose from the table and walked into the yard. Tap and Slab sat on the shady side of the bunkhouse. Goodnight had gone on to the corral. Carruth crossed the yard toward him, shaping up a smoke as he traveled. He stopped at the corral, stretching his lips back from his teeth as he inhaled the cigarette smoke.

"Frank," he said, "I'm never a hand to like another man very much. Not my style. But I like you as well as any. Here's my advice, which I wouldn't bother to

160

give anybody else. Get off the ranch."

Goodnight stared beyond Carruth, at the green wave of trees flowing down the hill. He had his eyes almost shut and daylight danced in them. Heat burned down upon the clearing and flashed on the panes of the main house; the air lay thin and dry and the smell of dust and pitch was everywhere. "I know," said Goodnight.

"Doubt if you do."

Goodnight looked down at Carruth. "She's afraid of Boston Bill."

Carruth wanted to say something about that. He saw that she had gotten into Goodnight. The glance she had given him, the picture she had made for him as she stood on the porch, had done the trick. He tried to frame something in his mind that would make it clear to the tall man, but his loyalty stopped him. All he could say was: "You ain't got a high card in your hand."

"Always had luck in the draw. Anyhow, it's too late to leave."

"Why?" asked Carruth. But in a moment he heard the first advance echoes of a parry coming down the hill. He said, "You got good ears," and swung about, waiting. It was Boston Bill's outfit, he guessed, and a big one from the sound it made. A man's "Hyee" came on ahead, quite loud in the heat-stretched air, and a moment later the party broke out of timber into the yard, Boston Bill at the head.

He was always a smart one. His glance swept the yard, saw Tap and Slab, saw Carruth, and came to a full-centered aim on Goodnight. For a moment it appeared he would ride straight on at Goodnight. His expression and the position of his body telegraphed the intention, but in another instant Virginia came to the porch, calling his interest to her. He dropped

161

to the ground, high and confident as he walked to the porch. The two went inside the house.

The rest got down—there were twelve in the bunch—and scattered around the yard, soon dropping into the dusty shade, soon smoking or soon falling back for quick catnaps. Carruth drew out the last smoke of his cigarette and spoke, not looking at Goodnight: "This is it. Too late for you."

Virginia came to the doorway. "Frank," she said, "will you come here please?"

"Showdown," murmured Carruth. "He's made up his mind."

"He made it up the other day," answered Goodnight, and walked over the yard.

He found Virginia standing in a corner of the room when he reached it; he found Boston Bill swung around, waiting for him to come. Boston Bill's fair face showed the brittle scruffing of sunlight and the deeper flush of an anger produced by some previous argument with the girl. He was very watchful, he was on edge, and Goodnight got the clear impression that Boston Bill expected trouble to break. There was a round-topped center table near Bill; he had his left hip against it, the top of his holstered gun rubbing against it, and he had his hand dropped on the table, close by the gun's butt.

Virginia said in her calm, self-certain way: "Bill's been doing some talking. Perhaps you ought to listen to it."

Boston Bill said: "I'm not repeating myself to strangers, Virginia."

"This man," said Virginia, "is foreman of Sun."

"Is he?" murmured Boston Bill. "I don't recognize the title. I'm talking to you, not to him."

"You'll deal with him," she said.

"No," said Boston Bill, "I'll do nothing with him.

162

You're a clever girl, Virginia. You've put him up as a dummy between us. I won't waste my time. You're the one who says yes or no."

"Not unless my foreman agrees," she said. "Talk to my foreman, Bill."

She treated him coolly. She stood away from him, throwing her will against his will. Goodnight had no knowledge of the game being played between them; it went on beneath the surface, the two of them violently struggling for some kind of control. Boston Bill's face showed a growing stubbornness. His cheek muscles grew bunched and his mouth lay tight beneath the spectacular arch of his nose. Goodnight remained still, studying the man, not yet certain of the other's nerve. The scene could end here if Boston Bill had as much brutality in him as he had ambition. All Bill had to do was lift his voice, bring in part of his crew—and the whole thing would be over.

But the man dallied with his thoughts and presently Goodnight noticed the girl's expression shade away into something that looked like triumph. She thought she had Bill beaten.

Boston Bill made up his mind and turned on Goodnight. "I'm not talkin' to you, I'm telling you. My outfit camps here and I'll do what Virginia can't do—which is fight for this place against Harry Ide. There's no room for you. Ride on."

The girl's expression again grew solid and resisting. She put her glance on Goodnight, waiting for him to speak. This was why she had hired him—for just this moment. What was he supposed to do? He turned his head slightly, noticing now that Bob Carruth had come to the door of the room. Goodnight murmured: "Step in and shut the door, Bob."

Carruth moved in and pushed the door behind him. Boston Bill's head lifted and he threw an irri-

163

tated glance at Carruth; the next instant his attention rushed back to Goodnight.

"I notice," said Goodnight, "you're left-handed."

Boston Bill studied the remark, suspicious of it, fast-thinking of it. He nodded slightly.

"It is the second time I have noticed it," said Goodnight.

Boston Bill showed a small, passing puzzlement. He said: "What of it?" But he was keyed up, giving Goodnight the full weight of his thoughts. The man faced him, quietly, expressionlessly—meaning everything or meaning nothing. "No use of this going on," Goodnight said. "You have made up your mind about me. I have done the same about you. This is the place to have it done. Back away from the table and give yourself room to draw."

Boston Bill kept his head still; his eyes rolled aside, catching view of Carruth, and rolled back to meet Goodnight. He said softly: "You've got an extra man."

Goodnight threw an order over his shoulder. "Step outside, Bob."

He listened to the door's opening and its closing. The girl's face was intent, with one small line showing on her forehead. She had changed her attention to Boston Bill; she was watching him with an engrossed interest, without sympathy and without any feeling that Goodnight could observe. She was probably wondering—as he himself still wondered—if Boston Bill's nerves would hold or fail.

Boston Bill smiled a starved, wintery smile. "My outfit's outside. How far do you think you can get?"

"You talk too much," said Goodnight. "Step back and draw."

"I told you before," said Boston Bill, "I pick my fights when I please."

"Better pick this one now," said Goodnight.

164

"Probably," said Boston Bill, very cool, "you can handle a gun faster than I. My impression is you've had more training at it. I'd be foolish to step into that, wouldn't I? I'm not drawing. If you like to shoot your ducks on the ground, go ahead."

"I will," said Goodnight.

"I doubt it," answered Boston Bill. "Your kind never likes to shoot without getting the other man to draw first. It is just a way you justify a shooting — a convention that is supposed to make everything fair and square. I'll not supply you with the excuse."

"You guess wrong," said Goodnight. "That rule applies to men standing equal. It doesn't cover a man that stood on the right side of a hotel window and shot left-handed through the glass at a man asleep on a bed."

The sharp glitter of angry, tight amusement died out of Boston Bill's face. He stood grave and indrawn; he stood like a man hollowed out. He looked at the girl. He said in a queer voice: "You brought this on. Do you like it?" Then he pulled his attention back to Goodnight and strain narrowed his face and he had nothing more to say.

It was the girl who broke the tension by coming forward until she was between the two. She turned to Boston Bill. "He would kill you. Don't you see it on his face?" She swung quickly to Goodnight. "I don't want a shooting."

"Out of your hands," said Goodnight.

"No. Bill will not take charge here. You are still foreman. You see, Frank, I still have one weapon he's afraid of. The hill ranchers are friendly to him, but they are all people who came here with my father. My word would turn them against Bill. He knows that. If he moves into Sun without my authority he'll have no help from the hills."

165

"Nothing to do with the present moment," said Goodnight. "Stand aside. I want this settled."

"I want nothing to happen here," she said.

He considered her and found no answer. She had hired him to protect her against Boston Bill; she was now protecting Boston Bill. It made everything complicated. He had known since daybreak that Boston Bill had shot Niles and that knowledge gave him his clear line of action. This was the time to settle it, for if Boston Bill walked out of the door alive, it would only be to give a signal that would set the rest of the crowd against him. He would be trapped. Still, the girl wanted no shooting. In addition, he no longer knew where she stood.

"There's no necessity of my staying on Sun any longer," he said. "You can use this man for your work."

He backed to the door, noting the change on her face. Disturbance came and unsettled her perfect assurance. "I don't want you to go."

"Then you should not have interfered. I'm riding off the place. But I won't be riding far and I'll make a point of meeting you, my friend." He said the last of it to Boston Bill, opening the door as he talked. The girl shook her head and for the first time he saw helplessness come to her.

"I didn't think," she said, "you'd run."

"You should not have interfered," he repeated. "Or maybe you had better make up your mind what you want." He closed the door as he stepped to the porch. He said to Carruth waiting there, "Stick right here until I reach my horse. I'm leaving."

"He froze you out?" murmured Carruth, not quite believing it.

Goodnight paused and threw him a black glance. "We'll see," he said. He went down the steps, the men

166

of Boston Bill's crowd watching him from their scattered places along the yard. He made no attempt to hurry; he cut behind the bunkhouse to his horse and rose to the saddle and rode back over the yard. They were still watching, and one man had risen and started for the house. He circled the mess hall and faced the trail. As he reached the first edge of timber — the trail rising and curling before him — he heard Boston Bill's voice rush over the yard.

"Come on — come on."

He went up the slope in a slow run, with the scurry and scuff of men and horses coming off the yard, and the murmuring of men's voices growing. He reached a bend of the trail and ran around it, and faced another sharp rise. His horse fell to a walk on this grade but he dug in his spurs and made it go. The trees softened the sounds rising from the lower level.

Boston Bill rushed from the front door, yelling at his outfit; and all of them sprang up from their sleepy reclining and in a moment were gone, leaving behind the slow-settling streamers of dust in the still air. Slab and Tap remained by the bunkhouse, astonished at the unexpected action and not quite certain of what had happened. Bob Carruth was on the porch, caught in the swift play. Virginia had rushed out on the heels of Bill, had run over the yard after him. She had kept calling to him; she had tried to catch his arm as he reached his horse. He had swung around her, his left stirrup grazing her as he rushed on. Virginia, standing in the heavy yellow dust, cursed him until he was out of sight.

Bob Carruth watched her turn and come back to him. He saw the fury that blackened her eyes and pulled the blood from her face until it was dead

167

white. She breathed heavily and she gave him a bitter, killing glance—hating him because he was the only thing near her to receive her temper. He stood still, knowing this girl's willfulness but shocked at the depth of rage she showed. Violence changed her until she was no longer pretty, no longer admirable. He sighed and shook his head.

"You played hell when you brought those two together."

"I should have let Frank shoot him! I should have let that happen!"

"One of 'em," said Carruth, "is damned soon goin' to get shot." She made him sour and embittered. "Comes of you fiddlin' with two men. No sense—no sense at all. You think you're God to make men come together and back up like you want? What in hell did you expect?"

"The dog," she said in a shaking, husky voice. "The dog!"

"Which one you talkin' about now?"

"He was afraid of Goodnight. He smiled and tried to cover it, but he was afraid of his life. I saved him, and then he betrayed me the moment Goodnight left. He's yellow, Carruth, and he's dirty."

"That's something you should of figured before you started this business. Friend Goodnight's goin' to get killed." He drew his lips back from his heavy white teeth. "What you think of that? What you think of your schemin' now?"

She wilted before his eyes. Her shoulders dropped and the life went out of her face. She turned from him and walked over to her horse. She stood a moment beside the horse and he saw that she was crying. He had not seen her cry before and therefore he knew she was hurt, and this pleased him and he silently wished that the hurt would stay on; for by now

168

he had lost all his loyalty to her and saw her as a cold woman whose scheming was about to cause the death of a man. She went up to the saddle and looked at him. "That can't happen," she said. "I won't let it."

"You'll play hell," he told her. She was out in the meadow, running north, and he shouted it at her again. "You'll play hell!"

He kept his eyes on her as he walked back to the bunkhouse. Tap and Slab never said a word; all this had rolled over them like a wave of water and they had not yet pulled clear of it. She was, Carruth decided, going up to Ned Tower's place to have him spread the news to the hill people. Maybe that would work, maybe it would be too late. He turned to Slab. "Take my long-legged buckskin and go down to Sherman City. You tell Rosalia Lind whut's happened."

"Whut'll she do about it?" asked Slab.

"Go on—go on!"

He went into the bunkhouse and found his pipe and he filled it and lighted it and found some comfort in the heavy smoke. He came back to the yard, standing beside Tap. Tap said something but he paid no attention to it, in fact he really never heard it. The point was, he decided, Virginia had found out at the last moment it was Goodnight she wanted, not Boston Bill. She apparently hadn't known it before. She had hauled the two men together so she could compare them, maybe have them ram each other all over the place to prove what they were to her. Then she had got trapped. The wrong man had won and she had just discovered it.

He shook his head, a little bit sick of the thing, and he went over to his own horse and got aboard. As soon as he hit the saddle he felt somewhat more hopeful; he'd follow after Boston Bill and maybe get a line on what was happening; maybe maneuver around so

169

that he could do Goodnight a useful turn in a pinch. Going into the timbered hill trail he remembered Virginia's cursing; that had been a rock-bottom display of what she was. He had never seen a woman so thoroughly turn herself inside out.

"That damned Goodnight," he thought soberly, "thinks she's something particular. If he pulls out of this he might marry her."

Slab was a man neither very thoughtful nor very bright and therefore when he was given an order his small mind closed down upon it and it became the law of his life until he had fulfilled it. He never asked questions and he never stopped to debate the wisdom of what he was told to do. Simply, he took his orders and set forth upon their performance. Had Bob Carruth told him to ride his horse into the middle of the creek and remain there, Slab would have done so in full confidence that Carruth had a good reason for asking it.

So, he set out at full tilt for Sherman City and reached the town with his horse dead-beat and himself pretty well pounded up. He whirled before Rosalia's house, dropped to the ground and ran to the door. When the girl appeared, Slab said, "Carruth told me to tell you that this Goodnight is in a jack pot. He got crosswise of Boston Bill. They had an argument on the ranch. Goodnight got to his horse and jumped for timber with Bill and nine-ten of Bill's bunch after him. They're in the hills now, somewhere."

Rosalia said: "Why did Carruth want me to know that?"

Slab opened his mouth to speak, and found nothing to say. He closed his mouth and he searched him-

170

self for an answer, but the searching produced nothing. He had been told to come here and deliver his message. That was all. Nowhere along the hard ride had he given an instant's thought to the reason behind the message. He spread out his hands before her and he murmured: "Damned if I know. I just told you what I was supposed to tell you." He turned back, got his horse and led it up to the Trail. He stepped inside the saloon and wigwagged for a drink. He took his drink and he murmured, "Ah," and eased himself against the bar. He said aloud: "I bet that's the fastest that trip's ever been rode."

"What for?" asked the barkeep.

"Don't know," confessed Slab. "But it sure was a fast ride."

Rosalia stood on the porch, watching Slab go to the saloon. Gabe drifted from the alley and said: "Anything important?"

"No," she said and went into the house, wondering why Bob Carruth had thought of her. She thought of Carruth for a little while, knowing the man's toughness. She said to herself: "He would never lift a hand to help any man, unless he liked the man well. Therefore he must have come to like Frank. Nor would he have bothered to send a message to me unless Frank was in genuine trouble."

It was a compliment, from Carruth. It was a warning, too, that things had gone bad for Goodnight. She closed the front door and turned and put her shoulders against it. She looked across the room at the wall, grave and deeply troubled. Goodnight was clearly before her; she saw him, the shape of his body and the tone of his voice and the things which tormented him. She thought: "I could help him. I could send men up there to fight for him."

But she came slowly to her painful answer. She had

171

given him more than she had given any other man. The rest of it was up to him. She could not give more. He had gone into the hills of his own free will. He would have to come out of the hills the same way. Perhaps he would never come back; perhaps he had not wanted to come back. If he came back she would be here; if he wanted her, she would be here.

"He went there because he wanted to. He will come back if he wants to. He will live or he will die. If I helped him now he would resent it, or be in debt to me. I will do nothing. It is up to him."

She remained still, inwardly protesting at her own decision, but her will was strong, and held her fast.

TWELVE

DEEP IN THE OWLHORNS

Goodnight had a quarter-mile lead on Boston Bill's men. He heard the sound of their pursuit come steadily behind but at the end of a twenty-minute run he thought he had increased his lead. One horse and one man made better time than a crowd.

He stayed with the main trail upward and it took him presently to one of the many small and narrow meadows creasing these hills; he saw nothing on the meadow and ran across it into farther timber. The main trail continued upward again but at this point he wheeled aside, into the timber, and paralleled the meadow until he had reached its far end. Here, sheltered by the trees, he gave his horse a blow and watched the open area over which he had recently come.

Boston Bill broke over it first, two other men closely behind him. These three crossed and disappeared and it was a full minute before the rest of the group came plugging along. This last group halted and seemed to be talking. Presently one of the men who had been with Boston Bill rode back and said something, whereupon the party moved onward at a jaded walk and entered the trees.

The timber around Goodnight was old first-growth pine, massive at the butt and rising in flawless line toward a mass of top covering which made a solid umbrella against sunlight; there was little underbrush and at certain angles he was able to look a hundred or two hundred yards away. The sound of Bill's men faded in gradually diminishing echoes until the hot silence of the hills lay fast upon everything, until the breathing of his own horse seemed loud. It would be a matter of time, of course, until Bill would backtrack and eventually discover his solitary set of tracks on the spongy humus. Considering it, he set his course steadily east, toward the Owlhorns' heights. Up there the country would be more greatly broken and thus afford better shelter.

He knew none of this land, yet he had no concern. All his days from boyhood onward had been a pattern of hills and desert, of silence and heat and cold, of strange voices speaking out of night's pit and pale far images in the sun glare. He could say of himself that his proper home was wherever night found him, that his accustomed hearth was the rim of a campfire. Never in all his traveling had he felt the need of more than this; and never, when sleeping inside some town upon the trail, had he ceased to wish for the trail.

Far away was one starved echo. Riding, he listened for its repetition and heard no more. The red-barked trees ran solemnly before him and somewhere high above the arch of boughs afternoon blazed; here the air was blue-shadowed and still. He came presently upon the relic of an ancient wagon road, its twin ruts wiggling before him; and later struck the fallen-in wreckage of a log-and-shake cabin. Near it was a square patch of ground enclosed by stakes; and centered in the patch was the mark of a grave, its headboard, once white, lying rotten upon the earth. A pine stood hard by and when he raised his eyes he saw an ax imbedded in the bark. Once, long ago, some man had driven it full into the wood and had walked away, and had never returned.

By degrees the country roughened and the pines turned smaller and ravines began to come down toward him. He held to the crest of the ridges as long as possible, then dropped into the ravines, crossed over and rose to the next ridge. Near sunset the trees momentarily gave way and he faced a creek running quickly over its stones. Beyond the creek the trees again marched toward the heights.

He stayed within shelter, long watching the upper and lower reaches of the creek and the timber beyond it. When he was satisfied he rode to water's edge, let the horse have a long drink, and forded. Twenty yards inside the timber he came to a trail looping stiffly up the side of the mountain and, since there was no other way, he took this.

He rose with the short switchback courses, higher and higher along the edge of the cliff as daylight slowly faded out of the sky. He arrived at last to a leveling-off place, gave the glen below him one last look, and moved over an area roughened by some ancient geological upheaval. He still pointed toward the summits of the Owlhorns, but within fifteen minutes the trail brought him to a complete standstill at the edge of a precipice running three hundred feet or more downward into a canyon whose bottom was now covered by night shadows.

The land was deceptive. He had marched out of one canyon to these heights, and now faced another canyon. He had worked himself to a kind of island of height. Night wind began to flow off the Owlhorn summits, soft but cold, and as he watched the canyon he saw the tide of blackness slowly drown out its bottom. A pathway dropped along the face of the precipice at a breakneck angle, running lower and lower until he could no longer see its course. From the look of it, he judged it had not been recently used and possibly was nothing more than a foothold cut out by deer.

There was undoubtedly a better way of moving off this ridge. One end of it was probably anchored against the Owlhorns, providing him with a level route; but it grew darker and he wished a sheltered spot for his camp. So, not altogether free of doubt, he tipped the horse over the brink of the precipice into the descending ledge.

The cliff was rock and earth, with some vegetation clinging to it; the trail was no more than three or four feet wide, sometimes tightening against the cliff and causing him to foul his leg against the outcrop of rock. The horse was both tired and doubtful and frequently stopped, to be pressed on by a touch of the spurs. The pathway at places pitched downward so steeply that the horse's front feet slid along the loose rubble, and the farther it dropped the blacker it became until there was no view above Goodnight and no view below.

He had gone a hundred feet when the horse stopped and would no longer advance. He bent forward in the saddle and fixed his eyes upon the ground before him until he thought he saw the continuation of the trail, and he urged the horse again; the horse gathered its feet close together and began to wind about, gingerly and slowly in little mincing shifts until it had reversed itself. Then, pointed downward still, it moved on. Looking directly behind him, Goodnight vaguely saw the turn-around; the trail made its switchback at this point.

When he realized his eyes had failed him he felt a twinge of uncertainty. He was now less than halfway down a cliff whose total drop was something like three hundred feet. He grew anxious to have the passage done with but he let the reins remain slack, trusting the horse; and when the horse again stopped he made no effort to push it. He bent again in the saddle, again seeing nothing; for he was now surrounded and pressed upon by the full weight of the inky canyon shadows. He

176

waited for the horse to move; he waited a full two minutes and then, knowing that something stood in the way, he slid carefully to the ground — crowded between horse and canyon wall — and moved forward. He got down on his hands and knees and used his hands for exploring; he felt the slide of rock and soil which, coming from the cliff, blocked the trail entirely. He stood up, running his arm forward, trying to judge the depth of the barrier. Some wet spot in the cliff had given way, coming down in a short slide and landing on this ledge.

It was a new slide, the dirt not yet packed firm. He ran his hands shovel-like into the dirt and moved it; and he crouched, and began to throw the debris below him. He heard the rocks strike long afterwards down on the canyon floor. He was still considerably up in the air. He thought: "If this thing goes very far I'll be here all night," and he sat idle a moment and considered backing the horse to the turn-around and retracing his way to the top of the ridge. He had a good horse and full confidence in him; yet at this hour, with the animal jaded from a hard ride and with the going altogether blind, he discarded the thought, settled on his haunches and began to shovel the slide away with his fingers.

It took him half an hour to clear the barrier and when he got up again, his fingers bruised and raw, he estimated he had scooped aside a pile of dirt five feet long and three feet wide. Catching up the reins, he led the horse cautiously forward. Fifty feet brought him to an uncertain spot and he stopped and crawled on his hands and knees, exploring until he discovered he had reached another turn-around. He let the horse take its time making the swing, and again descended.

There was water flowing at the bottom of the canyon; the cold dampness of it began to rise to him and the sound of it strengthened. He had been on this descent an hour or there-abouts and he felt the strain of it, and thought he heard other echoes above him. He stopped, listening for them through the washing murmur of the water and received nothing satisfactory; but he was dissatisfied and stood longer still, reaching for his tobacco and rolling a cigarette. He had a match in his hand, ready to light, when he caught himself. He put the match away, nursing the dry smoke in his mouth, and moved ahead.

There had been, through all this tedious march of the afternoon and twilight, a memory. It came forward strongly now in this sightless night — the recollection of Virginia Overman, beautifully poised in Sun's ranch house, her eyes upon him, needing his support against Boston Bill and yet too womanly to permit him to draw a gun against Bill. She had not understood how bad a decision she had made in stopping the showdown. At that moment he had been on equal terms with Bill. Afterwards, with the weight of Bill's crew against him, he was against odds. Bill would use those odds against him. She had not understood that, still believing perhaps that Bill was an honorable man. Yet even with that bad decision against her, he remembered her fairness and her need of him — and the soft side of her nature which would not permit a killing. It was a thought that buoyed him on this black, downward grade.

He had been walking with a short forward step, surer of himself as the bottom of the canyon appeared nearer; he took one more step and, without warning, found no trail to meet him and lost his balance and dropped forward into emptiness.

He had been lightly holding the reins. As he lost his balance his grip tightened upon them and as he swung forward, one foot still on the trail, the weight of his fall struck hard on reins and horse; the horse took that pressure with a startled upward fling of its head, hauling Goodnight upward. He whipped himself around,

178

grasping the reins with his free hand and, with this double hold, he swung outward into space and downward. His other foot slid off the trail and he dropped until his breast scraped the edge of the rocks; the horse, alarmed, moved backward, this action dragging Goodnight along the sharp edge of the rocks and sawing at his ribs. He got one elbow hooked over the rim; he let go the reins completely and anchored himself now with both elbows. He hung there, feeling a moment's sharp pain in his chest, his feet digging against the wall of the canyon and finding poor support. He kicked at the wall with his toes; he moved them up and down and found lodgement for one toe. He lifted himself gently, his elbows taking the strain from the insecure foothold, and he gathered his strength, made an upward lunge and crawled back to the trail and rolled and sat upright.

He still had the cigarette in his teeth, the scattered grains of tobacco half down his throat. He strangled on them and his coughing reminded him of the beating he had taken in his chest. He got to his feet. He said: "Coley," calling the horse. He couldn't see the horse and he took a step onward until he brushed its muzzle. He ran a hand back along its neck. He said: "All right — all right. Stand fast." He drew a deep breath and was relieved.

He walked back to the break in the trail, shuffling his feet until he reached the edge; he got down on his knees and stretched his arm outward and touched nothing. He sat back a moment, drawing a long breath, and then he flattened on his belly and inched forward until he teetered on the edge of the break like a balanced board, and reached out again, and again touched nothing. That was a three-foot stretch; the gap was wider.

He found a couple of small rocks on the trail and threw one of them a distance which he judged to be slightly more than three feet; it fell short of its mark, dropping in little bouncing strikes all the way to the

179

canyon floor. He threw the second rock a farther distance and heard it land on the trail. That made it somewhere between five and eight feet.

He sat back, defeated and full of exasperation. He drew in a huge breath and let it go. He got another handful of small rocks and dropped them one by one over the edge of the trail, listening to the strike they made against the canyon bottom. He tried to visualize the distance but had no great luck. As a final resort he pulled out a match, struck it and cupped his hands so that the light would shine upon the break in the trail.

It was better than a ten-foot gap. But he saw something else which gave him heart: the break had taken away the outer half of the pathway, leaving an inner shelf of about two feet or so in width snuggled against the cliff's face. He had walked along the middle of the trail and had come upon the break; had he been tight against the cliff face he would have remained upon firm ground.

The light died out, leaving him hopeful in one respect: he himself could cross over. What troubled him was the situation of the horse. He doubted if it would stand on this narrow ledge all during the night without attempting to turn and so come to disaster. That meant a try at the ledge. He figured the girth of the horse against the width of the ledge and came to the conclusion that, with some luck, the passage might be accomplished.

He rose and tackled the ledge, testing it for footing. He walked back, running his hands along the face. He struck an outstanding rock and stopped and dug it out and threw it into the pit; he crawled back to the horse, removed the saddle and carried it over the break, there dumping it, and came back again to catch up the reins. He paused a moment, thinking of the depth below. It seemed to be a full fifty-foot fall. "Well, Coley," he said, "this is the jack pot." He led the horse forward, holding to the extreme end of the reins. He got halfway out upon the ledge, and pulled.

Coley was a sure-footed brute, made wary by his experiences. He came up to the break and stopped there. Goodnight stepped against Coley's head, using pressure to shift the horse nearer the wall; he pulled again, moving Coley tentatively on. Coley's foot struck the edge and slipped and he drew back and emitted a blast of air. He stood fast. Goodnight came up to him and laid a hand on his neck. "Coley," he said, "you got to gamble once in a while. Don't be a damned fool." He backed onto the ledge, hauling suggestively at the reins. He pulled on them, let the pressure go, and pulled again.

Coley took another step and hit firm footing and came forward. Goodnight held the reins tight until he figured Coley's hind feet had reached the ledge. Then he let them sag so that the horse might drop its head and see the trail. Coley thrust his muzzle downward, breathing against the ground. He placed a forefoot ahead like a weary old man unsure of his bones, and advanced the other front foot. Goodnight heard Coley's flanks drag along the rock face and he spoke gently, to check Coley from panic. "You're halfway. Stretch out your neck and you're across." Suddenly Coley's near hind foot, too near the edge, slid downward and the horse made a lunge that carried it all the way across to firm ground. The surge caught Goodnight off balance. He jumped away, stumbled and fell. He got up again and went forward. Coley had stopped and was trembling.

"You think you're the only one?" said Goodnight.

He found the saddle and slapped it on and made a loose tie. Wind scoured down the canyon, its coldness beginning to reach him. But his face was sticky and when he took off his hat sweat dropped over his face and left its salt on his lips. He led the horse downward, taking his steps with caution. Hunger rolled around his belly, growling, and he was very tired. Somewhere in the night new sounds lifted and fell away and lifted again, barely clearing the increasing rush of the river. He halted, waiting and listening. Somewhere men were talking and as he swung his head the sound came clearest from above him. He could see nothing, but the murmur broke and ran on in idle fragments, and presently died.

He thought: "Echoes from the river," and moved cautiously downgrade again.

The trail played out through gravel and chunks of rock to the river's edge. The river's surface had a thin glow. The gravel churned under his feet and his horse stumbled and stopped, dead-beat. He pulled it on, coming to better footing. Here he unsaddled again, put hobbles on the horse and rolled up in the saddle blanket. He felt a continuing ache in his chest, but he was almost instantly asleep.

Not more than five minutes after he crossed the small creek in the earlier afternoon, Jack Babb and Monroe Mullans came up the creek on a scout, having been sent out by Boston Bill. They cut the fresh damp tracks of Goodnight's horse on the trail. Babb said: "I'll wait here. You go back and bring 'em up."

Boston Bill arrived with the main party an hour afterwards and immediately pushed uptrail, following Goodnight's clear prints. Darkness caught them on the switchback, whereupon Babb suggested retreating to better ground for night camp.

"We'll over-ride the place where he turns off and smear up his tracks with ours."

Boston Bill got down from his horse and led it forward. "He started up the switchback," he said. "There's no place for him to turn aside, therefore he followed this trail to the top of the ridge." He went on. When he reached the summit he stopped to think it out, Babb again suggesting camp.

"Everybody's tired. So's the horses. No supper and no breakfast in sight."

Boston Bill got down on the ground and lighted a match. He rose and walked forward until the match went out, and came back to his horse. "He's still going straight ahead. He doesn't know the country and he's pushing for the summit."

"He might break off the trail," said Babb. "Remember, he did it below at the meadow."

"Break off where?" asked Boston Bill. "You couldn't buck through this stuff anywhere else. He's in a hurry. He'll take the shortest way."

He led them forward and at occasional intervals he dismounted and tried another match; and so came, late at night, to the rim of the canyon. He lighted a match here and found Goodnight's prints, and snapped out the match at once. "Down there. Come ahead."

"The hell we do," said Babb. "That's the old Glory Mine's pack path. They used burros. But it's been ten years ago. You get halfway down and find a block and how you goin' to get back up?"

"He went down," said Boston Bill.

"By daylight."

"Couldn't have," said somebody else. "He ain't more than two hours ahead of us, and it's been dark longer than that. He had to take it in dark."

"You see?" pointed out Bill. "Come ahead."

"I've seen that thing by daylight," objected Babb. "In fact I got caught on it last year. There's a break, fifty or sixty feet from the bottom. It is nothin' to fool with. I'm not tryin' it."

"He's there," said Boston Bill impatiently.

"Then he'll be there in the mornin'."

"No," contradicted Bill, "he'll get away from us."

183

"I don't guess you know this part of the country," stated Babb. "That canyon has got damned steep sides. He can't find a way out by dark. Except by goin' down-grade with the creek. But that's tough too. If he's there, which I do doubt, he's sleepin' off a bad day. We'll catch up with him in the mornin'."

Boston Bill was dissatisfied. "Where else could he be?"

"I think he came here, saw the trouble in front of him, and backtracked. Maybe on this ridge. There ain't nothin' here except dog-wallopin' big chunk of up-and-down land, hard to ride in. He couldn't do much at night with it. He ain't far away. May even be near enough to hear us. Wait for daylight."

Boston Bill stood silent, unwilling to let go his hopes for a quick capture. The desire drove him badly and it was with poor grace that he surrendered. "All right. Camp here. But I want somebody to go back down-grade and cut over to close the mouth of the canyon. You do that, Jack. Take Mullans."

"Oh, my Godfrey," said Babb. He wanted to refuse it and would have refused if Boston Bill had not suddenly cut in with his biting voice: "I shouldn't think you'd worry about him that much. He's just one man."

Babb grumbled, "Come on, Monroe," and turned away with Mullans, over the rough top of the ridge and down the switchback. When they got to better ground Babb halted. "This is far enough. We can make the canyon in an hour, soon as it gets light." The pair made cold camp.

What woke Goodnight around midnight was a stone grinding in his back. He rolled away from it and slept again, but the memory of it stayed with him so that he was never quite asleep, and woke again to find he had other stones beneath him. He rose and carried his blanket to better ground. Deep in the chilly black he rolled a cigarette and smoked it through, and tried to rest.

Then he got to thinking of the sound which had been like the sound of voices on the top of the rim, and so he watchfully awaited the first dismal streaks of light seeping into the canyon. He sat up, looking for the horse, and found it strayed upstream in pursuit of grass. Beyond the horse was a black, loose outline which, as the shadows began to grow lighter, turned into some kind of building. He rose and went forward to have a look at it. He passed through a doorway into a loose board building and he found the remains of bunk frames around the walls. He thought disgustedly of the poor sleeping he had had on the gravel, and turned out of the house to bring up his horse. It was gray dawn then and he heard a clean, distinct shout, hollowly echoing. Looking upward he discovered a man standing at the lip of the trail, four hundred feet away. The man brought a rifle sharply to his shoulder and fired, the bullet striking wide of Goodnight's position.

The horse was twenty feet from him at the moment, now flinging up its head at the sound. Goodnight made a run for it, unsnapped the hobbles and led it back toward the house. A bullet broke ground ahead of him, and a third one splintered the side of the house wall as he jumped through the doorway, leading the horse inside. He made one more run to seize up his saddle and blanket.

THIRTEEN

THE HAUNTS OF LITTLE MEN

Goodnight hauled the horse well inside the shack and swiftly saddled it. The marksman on the rim pumped his shots methodically down. He laid a pattern around the outside edge of the door, and then began firing through the roof. Lead came through the shakes with small, gusty snorts and crashed into the floor close by. Goodnight backed away, watching the holes spring up in the floor, marching toward him. He caught the horse and moved through the shanty; he reached another door at the far end of the place and stood there, fast-thinking.

The firing ceased for a moment. The marksman would be taking time out to reload, to improve his position, and meanwhile the day brightened and the shadows in the canyon grew paler. If he stayed here a chance shot would sooner or later reach him or cripple the horse. He noticed, from the pattern of bullet holes on the floor, that the marksman had set about his job with a design—to cover the shanty from one end to the other—and had gotten about fifteen feet along the floor. Goodnight caught the horse and moved it back near the door through which he had entered, making a guess that the marksman, having covered the area, would spot his next shots farther on.

He stepped to a side window and tried to catch an upward glance at the rim, and found his field of vision too limited; he walked to the door, took off his hat, and pushed his head around the door's edge. The marksman's gun was at the moment dipping down at him, ready to try again, and at the same time he saw other men standing along the rim's edge, poised to fire.

He ducked back and caught up the horse. He pulled it the full length of the shanty and stood a moment at the door. Boston Bill's outfit had crossed his trail and now were above him; and presently this shanty would be riddled like a sieve.

A volley crashed down, cracking through the roof and raising the floor's long-collected dust. He caught the reins in his left hand, slapped the horse out through the door and went up into the saddle. He was twenty feet from the shanty, rushing up a small meadow beside the river, when the party's firing swung over and began to reach for him.

The distance was four hundred feet and most of the firing was from revolvers, which were not meant for long-range work. But there were some rifles searching him out and coming close upon him. He veered in until he scraped the edge of the cliff and looked back and up and saw one man leaning out from the rim, trying to land an accurate shot; that bullet missed him by three or four yards, scutting the gravel at the water's edge. He ran along the meadow, and turned with the cliff's gradual bend, and when he again looked back he found himself sheltered.

He stopped and studied his situation and looked about him. The canyon made a long slow turn into darker country. The right-hand wall remained sheer as far as he could see it; across the river the rough shoulders of a ridge came down in heavy folds of timber and rock. It was a rough slope but a passable one, once he crossed the river.

The river itself, freshly born in these hills, was small and shallow and fast; he put the horse over the meadow and into the water, and at once heard the renewal of gunfire. He pointed Coley upstream for better footing and felt the current break hard against the animal's legs; at the halfway point the water began to push against Coley's barrel and chest and a bullet struck the stream close by with a gurgling echo. Coley struggled with the slippery rocks, came to a full pause to gain his balance, and moved on again, working through the shallows to dry land. Across a narrow beach stood the foot of the ridge, with its timber. Toward it Goodnight rushed. Gaining the shelter of pines he stopped and swung about.

Boston Bill's party was against the side of the cliff, coming single-file and slowly down the reverse pitches of the trail. He counted eight men, spaced out and moving with caution; and although it was at a considerable distance, he recognized the high shape of Bill in the lead. But the firing of the rifle continued, slugging around the base of the timber behind which Goodnight stood; and when he lifted his glance he noticed that one man remained on the rim, guarding the party as it descended.

He pulled his rifle from its boot and crouched down, steadying the gun beside a pine trunk. He made a guess as to distance and elevation and drew a thoughtful sight on the marksman. He waited, and took up the trigger's slack, and waited until he had the marksman's shoulders in the notch of his sights; and let go. He missed, but he saw the marksman roll back out of sight.

Boston Bill had turned the second reverse of the trail and had paused at the break. The rest of the party drifted on until the horses stood tail and nose, crowded together; and some nervous man in the center of the party began to complain. Goodnight heard the murmur of it above the rattle of the river, and he knew what fear the man had begun to feel, trapped on a ledge that permitted no turning. He lowered his rifle on Boston Bill, having that target plainly enough in view, and he took up the trigger's slack, and held it, realizing what his shot would do. At least one of those horses would lose its head, rear back and try to turn, and go over the cliff in a fifty-foot fall. Panic would raise hell with the rest of them.

He took his finger from the trigger and sat in debate with himself. In another five minutes the outfit would be at the bottom of the canyon, hard after him; and this was a way of crippling that pursuit. He knew Boston Bill would remain stubbornly on his trail, giving him no rest, and he knew also that Bill would show him no mercy. "My turn now," he said, remembering Niles, and lifted the rifle again, watching Boston Bill as the latter swung in the saddle. Bill had reached the gap and was warning the outfit — and the man at the tail end suddenly grew afraid and backed his horse slowly toward the turn-around behind him. Bill yelled at him and waved an arm, but the man kept retreating. Bill yelled again, quite loud, and then the rear man's horse lost its footing and went over the edge of the trail. It fell with its front legs stiff-legged and its hind legs crooked up, and the man in the saddle began to tip sidewise, crying full voice. Horse and rider struck at the same time, and bounced and rolled, and ceased to move. Goodnight pulled down his rifle and went back to his horse. He put away the gun and stepped to the saddle, turning to the rough hill. He found a kind of footing and moved forward until outcrop stopped him; and found another short

189

passable vista and pushed forward. In this manner he worked himself two or three hundred feet up the side of the ridge before stopping. Now looking below him he caught sight of Boston Bill and the party at the mine house. They had halted.

He fought his way over some of the roughest footing he had ever seen. He had to dismount and lead the horse, breaking through vine undergrowth, circling great masses of fallen rock and soil, skirting logs lying breast high before him. The horse came patiently after, now taking a slope with a lunge that pushed Goodnight out of the way, now balancing himself on a grade so steep that only Goodnight's added weight on the bridle kept the horse from sliding downgrade.

This was the way of it for half an hour. Presently some kind of glen made a wrinkle in the ravine's side, forming a long chute; Goodnight took to it and made better time, and eventually came upon an area of bald, worn rock. He passed around chunks of rock two stories high and discovered a trail winding between worn walls of like rock. Turning the corner of such a rock he came upon a small campfire burning.

He stopped at once and looked about him and saw nothing, but he knew that somewhere around one corner or another of this massive boulder patch a man stood and held a gun against him. He knew that because of the frying pan beside the fire and the blackened can with hot coffee steaming in it. He stood still in front of his horse, feeling his danger. He said in his easy voice: "All right."

He heard a scrape behind him, he heard boots slide forward over the solid-rock floor. A man went by him, slowly swinging—a young man with a sharp, pointed face pinched sharp with the shadow of hunting and being hunted. He had a gun in his arm but a moment later, considering Goodnight closely, he put the gun back in his holster. He pointed at the fire. "Those fish are ready to eat. Go ahead and eat 'em."

"A drink of coffee is all I've got time for," said Goodnight.

"Oh, hell," said the young man, "that outfit won't ever get up this way. If they try it, you'll hear 'em a long time before they arrive."

"You heard them?"

The young man pointed above him. "From the top of that rock I can catch the canyon a mile either direction. So I heard the racket and went up for a look. What kept you from shootin' at the lads when they came down the trail? It would of been like knockin' duck off a wire."

"That's right—it would have been," agreed Goodnight.

The young man served him with a keen survey. "Well, hell," he said, "they'll do you in if they find you, won't they?"

"Yes."

"Then you were a big fool. Go ahead and eat my breakfast. I been livin' easy for the last month. I ain't hungry."

Goodnight walked to the fire and squatted before it. He dragged the coffee can aside, saw another can near by, and poured himself a drink. He took it down in noisy swallows, hot as it was. He looked at the fish and bacon lying crisp in the pan and he pulled out his pocket knife and went to work. The young man crouched across the fire from him, watching with amusement. "I remember when I was that hungry. But I found this spot and I been livin' fine ever since. Fish in the river, venison for the lookin'. Rabbit any old time. I never lived so well in my life. That fish taste all right?"

191

"Fine," said Goodnight.

"Yeah," said the young man. "You can't beat this place. It is a funny thing. A man gets in trouble. All wound around with grief and disaster. Hunted like a dog. Can't ride without watchin', can't sleep without one eye open. Can't walk down a street. So he says if he ever gets to a place where he can just relax and never worry, then he'll be happy and never move again. Yeah. This is the place. I can hear anything come, half a mile away. Don't suppose more than four men have ever found this spot in couple hundred years. Why, it's perfect."

"Should be wonderful," said Goodnight.

"Wonderful," said the young man absent-mindedly. He bent forward and poured more coffee into Goodnight's drinking can. "Want me to fry up more bacon?"

"Had enough," said Goodnight. He sat back to roll a cigarette; he relished the smoke and the food sent its warmth and its energy through him. Sunlight moved overhead. Presently heat would pour full down into this rocky cup. "The place gets hot, doesn't it?"

"Around ten o'clock," said the young man, "I move up to my parlor in the trees. Cool there. I sleep here at night. Sleep there durin' the day. Never found anything like it. Man could live to be a hundred and ten right here. Sure is wonderful."

He rose and vanished around the corner of a rock. Goodnight, lying back relaxed, heard him scuffle around the top of the rock, thirty feet above; and heard his voice. "They on your trail serious?"

"That's right."

"They ain't in much of a hurry," said the young man. "Well, here comes a couple more men from the lower end of the canyon. They're talking. You know, this is a wonderful spot. I can see everything—hear

192

everything. I'll just watch those fellows a while."

Goodnight threw the rest of the coffee on the fire, killing the flame. He dropped on his shoulders and drew a hat over his face, grateful for the rest and for the chance to do a little thinking. So far he had been on the run to clear himself of the weight Boston Bill could bring against him, well knowing he could not buck the man's whole outfit. All he wished was a straight chance at Bill, an even encounter. He wanted nothing more, and would have nothing less. It was another obligation in his life, like the obligation to satisfy his sister's memory.

He turned slightly on the ground, that memory bringing its ache again and he thought to himself: "When will it grow softer, when can I think of her without that feeling?" And bitterness came up and the old hatred of the world and its insolence, the old distrust, the old savage desire to set himself against men, without mercy or tolerance; to lay his hand against cruelty, to make them cry, to grind into their brutal souls the knowledge of fear and misery, to pay back in kind every bitter thing they had done to him and to those he loved. If the world was cruel, then he would abide those rules and make the cruel suffer with their own kinds of torture until pride and manhood was bled out of them and until they cried for a mercy they had never given.

He sat up, bringing his big fists together slowly, ridden by his feeling, and he remembered that he had had his chance only a half hour before; he could have shot Bill's party off the cliff. He could have stampeded those men. "Why didn't I do that?" he asked himself, and was puzzled.

He brought his mind back to Bill. He thought: "I've got to get at him. I have run far enough." He drew idle patterns along the dusty rock with his forefinger.

He was clear of Bill now, on even terms with the man in this tangle of country. As he was hunted, so he could hunt. It was fifty-fifty. Maybe Bill didn't know that yet.

The young man came off the rock, into sight. He squatted on his heels, made cheerful by this break in a long day. "They've started up the canyon. It'll be two-three hours before they get out of it. Ain't a decent trail short of five miles from here."

"Where will the trail lead them?"

The young man swung his arm to the east. "Up there is an old Indian trail over the summit. They'll come up the canyon and strike it. Then they can either go over the mountains, or turn and follow the trail back to the main road, ten miles off. That's another way of going over the mountains. Or of going back to Roselle and Sherman City." He dropped on an elbow, content with the day. "But they won't ever find a way of gettin' here. There ain't any way." He gave Goodnight a hopeful look. "How'd you like beans and biscuits for supper — with a side dish of fried rabbit?"

Goodnight rose. He walked to his horse and tried the cinch, and tightened it. "I am obliged," he said. "And I wish you luck."

The young man's face dropped. He got to his feet. He said: "Anything excitin'? Maybe I can get in on this."

"Thought this place pleased you," said Goodnight.

The young man drew a heavy breath. He lost his cheerfulness. "It's a wonderful place. But I'm sick of it. If I got to stay here and talk to myself any longer I'll go crazy."

"Safe here," Goodnight reminded him. "No worries."

"I know — I know," grumbled the young man. "But I guess I'd rather die by a bullet. This is what I sure prayed for, couple months ago, when I was one jump

194

ahead of hell. Well I got my prayer and it was all right for a while. But it ain't now."

Goodnight laid his hands over the saddle; he looked across the saddle at the young man, judging him to be neither better nor worse than the average. A break one way had made him do a foolish thing; another break in the same direction would send him to the wild bunch for the rest of his life. But a break toward the right would make a respectable citizen out of him. The lad was young; that was the only thing wrong with him. Young and swayed too easily. He thought about it and was troubled; the young man's future, at this moment, lay in his hands and the burden oppressed him.

"You did something wrong," he reflected in a quiet, soft way. "Then you got chased out. You couldn't ride like other men. You took side trails and you ate small and slept cold, always lookin' over your shoulder. Then you found this spot and it was a safe spot. You quit lookin' over your shoulder. But you still can't do what other men can do. You can't ride by daylight down the middle of any road that pleases you."

"I'll take care of myself," said the young man.

"A man," said Goodnight, "was meant to be free. If he isn't free he isn't anything. You have taken away your own freedom. You have put yourself in your own jail and the sentence is entirely up to you."

"You're in trouble, ain't you?" said the young man. "You could use help, it looks like. Take me along."

"I could use help," agreed Goodnight. "But I won't take you. If you came with me you'd be slammin' the door on your cell for good. You want a life of this business? You think it's fun?"

"I'll do all right," said the young man.

"Like now?" said Goodnight, and watched the young man's eyes show uncertainty. He stepped into the saddle, looking down. "The finest thing I know of," he said, pressing home his point, "is for a man to be able to ride into a strange town, go inside a restaurant and sit down with his back to the door, drinking his coffee without worrying what's behind him. How long you been in this hole?"

"Twenty-four days, at seven o'clock tonight."

"Twenty-four days of misery. If you're smart you'll ride over the hill and a long way from here. You'll find an outfit and you'll stick there until the smell of smoke wears off. Then you'll be out of prison for good."

He rode over the rock floor of the bowl, turned a corner and put the young man behind him. Once in some past age there had been a river flowing here, washing its way down to solid rock; through this old bed he traveled, the rock walls to either side and little islands of rock before him. At the first convenient spot he left the depression, made a way through the trees and came eventually to a point from which he viewed the canyon. Far upgrade in the canyon, even then passing around a bend, moved Boston Bill's party.

He backtracked and began anew the labor of finding a route through the timber and broken land. He wished to keep close to the rim so that he might watch Bill's party, and therefore he made frequent wide detours where the rim broke away. Near midmorning he made another survey of the canyon and discovered Bill's party turning up the side of the ridge; he stood by, watching the party go out of sight in the timber, reappear at a higher elevation, and go out of sight again. When he was certain of Bill's direction, he moved ahead until he reached a point near which he believed the outfit would come; and dismounted to wait. In his own mind there was but one thing now to do — keep within reaching distance of Bill's group, to follow and to wait until he had an even break with the man. Sooner or later the group would split into smaller bunches.

He thought of his talk with the young man, and suddenly worry came strongly back to him. The kid was teetering and maybe one more word, one more picture would have turned the trick. He reviewed what he had said, figuring how he might have made it stronger, or better. He had wanted to say: "An outlaw is a man alone—and no man alone is free." But you couldn't say a thing like that; it was something you had to learn. It had to be ground into you. By sitting alone at a campfire night upon night and watching the stars and seeing beauty there, and feeling wonders in the wind, and tasting the greatness of the earth—and having no living soul to share these discoveries with.

He had been slouched back against a tree. He straightened, astonished with these things marching so clear, so logical through his head. He said, aloud, "What the hell am I thinking about? Where did I get those notions?"

The sound of a voice came out of the timber, thinned and short, and afterwards he heard the rattling of brush. All this was ahead of him somewhere, beyond sight; but he got into his saddle and waited, not sure how near the outfit would come. The noise of brush ceased for a while, the voices continuing—so that he guessed the party had stopped for a breathing spell. The sun stood straight overhead, heat beginning to pile up on the earth.

Later both voices and sound of travel came to him, fading somewhat; whereby he knew the outfit had swung away from him. He moved on and presently reached the trail Bill's men left behind them. Then he dropped back until he caught only an occasional echo, and patiently followed.

Their way was upgrade for a mile or more, with the land gradually growing less rough; afterwards the trail made a sharp turn to the left and paralleled the higher summit points of the Owlhorns. Two hours of this kind of pursuit brought Goodnight to a trail—the old Indian trail mentioned by the young man—and this trail Bill's party had taken. Something had hurried Bill at this point, the hoof prints showing a deeper bite in the earth.

Goodnight paused a moment to debate the proposition. If he delayed he lost them. If he took to the trail he ran the risk of being ambushed. It was one of those quick decisions, ended immediately. He turned into the trail and set his horse to a canter along a series of little curves and up-and-down pitches.

He had his mind entirely on this business and still, from time to time, the thought of the young man came back to him, to worry him; and then other thoughts moved through his head in rapid succession, of Niles, of McSween, of his sister, of older days that had been pleasant. Of Virginia Overman. That thought with its recollection of her face and her voice and her quiet smile stayed longest. It was still with him when, rounding a bend, he came upon a horse and a man dismounted and sitting with his back to a tree.

He pulled up to avoid a collision with the horse, and as he pulled up he saw the seated man make a halfhearted effort toward his gun, touch the butt and then drop his hand away. Goodnight waited, not bothering to draw; for he noticed the sick set of the man's face and the purple coloring of his lips. This, he remembered, was one of Bill's men. He recognized the face.

"What's up?"

The man shook his head. He pressed a hand against his heart and a distinct fear came to his eyes. "Too much for me. Too much climbin'. Never happened before."

"They left you here?"

"I guess," said the man, "they're in a hurry."

"A hurry for what?"

The man looked up at him, once his enemy, once pressing him for the kill. This man looked up at him, wiped clean of the desire by the slow ticking of his heart, too sick to feel hatred. He had reached for his gun and then, as a gesture of something no longer important, he had dropped his arm. It was a strange thing, this change, this helplessness, this lack of interest. It was as though the man had been jerked by strings, his actions not of his own will; and then the strings broke and he had collapsed and was nothing.

"To swing around and box you in," said the man.

Goodnight said: "Where's a good way to Roselle?"

The man motioned along the trail. "It comes into the Roselle road." He stopped speaking and again put a hand over his heart, and fright showed on him clearly. He struggled through it and murmured, "Whut you think I can do for this?"

"Fall back and rest—and sleep," said Goodnight. "And hope you wake." He crowded by the man's horse, intending to go on. But he stopped and got down and unsaddled the other horse and took off the blanket. He laid out the blanket on the ground; he took the man by the armpits and shifted him to the blanket. "Lie back," he said, and hauled off the man's boots. "If I had some water I'd leave it. Good luck."

"Don't go," said the man, fear full in his voice. "Don't go." Then he shook his head and said dully, "Never mind."

Goodnight returned to his horse. From the saddle

he looked back. The man's eyes were on him; the man held them open, as though afraid that if he closed them he would die. The man held on, bitterly afraid. He shook his head. "Funny thing. You're the same as any other man. Why was I in the pack that chased you?"

"I'll send somebody back, when I reach a ranch."

The man gave Goodnight a bleak look. "Who'd come?" he asked. "Who'd give a damn?" He turned his head away and his voice echoed the futile feeling, the faith that was gone, the wreckage that could never be repaired. "You're the first man to give me a hand in many years. I'm older than you, ain't I?"

"Yes."

"This is no good," said the man. "This business you and me are in. Look at me and see what it comes to. We're livin' like dogs and this is a dog's end. Take a look at me. It'll happen to you. Better get out."

"So-long," said Goodnight, and rode on.

For this little while he had forgotten Boston Bill and he had forgotten his own situation. The nearness of one man in trouble had taken it out of his mind; now it returned, to remind him that Boston Bill was somewhere ahead.

He had lost time and now went along the trail with less caution. Occasionally, the trail's turnings took him near the edge of timber, through which he saw one or another of the upper mountain meadows and, beyond them, the rocky summit reefs lying black in the afternoon sun. The trail grew broader and better; and presently fell into a road which came upgrade and passed before him on its way over the Owlhorns. It was, he believed, the same road which touched Roselle and Sun Ranch on its way down to Sherman City. Boston Bill's party had swung into it, going downgrade.

That outfit was by now a quarter hour ahead of him and presumably still in motion; and since he had no other plan than to keep within sound or sight of Bill, he set out upon the road, following Bill's tracks. The sun had swung low and the timber was taking on its early shadows, its first night stillness. The air coming from the summit began to cut the forest heat. He meanwhile noted that the dust lying disturbed along the ground—made by the passage of Boston Bill's outfit—had largely disappeared, so that he had only the smell of the last particles still hanging unseen in the air. Bill had pulled away.

He had watched the margins of the timber, never trusting this nearness of shelter, he had looked on through the loose screen of pines into the deeper mass of forest, he had searched the presented vistas. He had seen nothing. Yet quite suddenly out of the timber, hard by him, he heard a voice—a woman's voice—speak to him in soft urgence:—

"Frank. Turn and come here. Hurry."

He looked directly to his left, from which direction the voice had come, and saw nothing. He wheeled and ran in, swinging right and left around the pines. The root system of a capsized pine made a bulwark before him, and when he turned it he discovered Virginia Overman waiting there on her horse.

FOURTEEN

THE TASTE OF A WOMAN'S LIPS

"Bill's just ahead of you," she said.

"I know that."

She looked at him with a swift, sharpened interest. She turned her head. She called: "Ned," and waited. Goodnight heard an echo break behind him, and swung about to see the long, black-whiskered Ned Tower move into sight, walking. Tower gave him a short-sizing up, not speaking. The girl said to Goodnight, "Did you see his outfit?"

"Yes."

"How many did he have with him?"

"Ten or so."

"He passed here with nine," she said.

"He's got more men than that scattered around," said Tower. He paused, and placed his suspecting glance back on Goodnight. "If he was chasin' you," commented Tower, "how you come to be chasin' him now?"

Goodnight gave the man a stiff glance; the preceding twenty-four hours had wearied him and he was hungry and in no tractable frame of mind. He rolled himself a smoke, making no answer. The girl, meanwhile, had been debating something in her own mind, and now said to Tower: "Better drift down towards

202

Roselle. I think he'll stop there to eat." She started to say something else, checked it, and later added: "Keep an eye on them, Ned."

He nodded and moved away. Before disappearing, he swung, speaking again to Goodnight. "You comin' along?"

The girl quickly spoke for Goodnight. "We'll follow later." She watched Tower go; she turned and looked at Goodnight with a full, light expression. She smiled and the smile went warm into him. She kept her eyes on him, open and silently promising. She was beautiful to him, a poised and deep woman slow to awake and slow to give; but once awake and once willing to give, she glowed and was beautiful.

"I have not slept at all, thinking of you. I have been through the hills, setting a dozen men on your trail. Then we came back here, hoping. I guess we felt the same thing Bill did—that you'd come here to eat."

There was movement around him, in the farther reaches of the forest. He heard horses traveling. "Who's here?"

"Ned's got a few men with him. We'll go toward Roselle later. You come with me."

She swung away, heading into the forest with confidence. At a short distance she picked up a trail and went with it, downgrade across a creek and upgrade over a small ridge. The sun had dropped and the shadows turned steadily blacker and the visibility lessened until he saw only the shape of the girl and her horse before him. In a general way it seemed to him they were dropping from the high point of the hills; and presently they reached a meadow and crossed it and came upon a cabin. She said: "One of Sun's line cabins," and got down and went inside.

He remained in the saddle, looking back at the

meadow's edges. She had lighted a lantern and he heard her rattle the lid of the cabin's stove. The lantern's light came through the doorway, touching him; he pulled aside, so long on the alert that he was dissatisfied now. Smoke lifted from the chimney, its smell curling through the night. She came out, curious at his delay.

"Nobody will come this way," she said. Her voice had a ring to it. He listened to its sureness, its confidence. He thought, "She is used to authority, she is used to being obeyed." But he was suddenly tired into his bones and he dropped from the saddle and moved inside the house. The fire had caught hold and added heat to the small room. There was a dirt floor and a double-decked bunk against one side of the cabin; there was a soapbox on the wall and some supplies in it. This line cabin, he judged, was in use through the season. He saw an empty bucket and he said: "Where's the water?"

"Lie down and sleep until I call you."

He obeyed her. The night and the day had caught up with him and when he lay back on the bunk — on its lumpy, straw-filled tick — he shut his eyes and thought of the man up on the trail, dying or now dead. The memory troubled him and he thought: "I've got to tell somebody about that." He heard the girl lift the bucket and he heard her leave the cabin. He meant to rise and do that chore for her but he thought, "I'll do it in a minute."

He heard his name called and called again. He felt a hand flat on his chest and he opened his eyes and found her standing above him, bent over, her eyes and her mouth close to him. "Supper's ready."

He said, "Fell asleep," and rose and was ashamed. She had walked somewhere for the water. She had cooked a meal. He sat down at the table before biscuits and fried potatoes and bacon back and coffee. He drank the coffee first, badly in need of it. She refilled his cup and then sat opposite him, her chin cupped in her hands, her elbows propped on the table, her smile steady on him and her glance sharp in its survey.

"You slept hard. The print of the straw is on your face. I should have let you sleep longer. Didn't you get any rest last night?"

"Not much."

"Where were you?"

"Bottom of a canyon. By a little river. By the bunkhouse of an old mine."

"The Glory Mine," she said. "Was Bill following?"

"Yes," he said. "He followed."

"Were you shot at?"

"They were poor shots," he said.

Her eyes hardened. "I made a mistake, Frank. I should have let you alone when you had your chance with him on Sun. I should not have interfered. When he started after you with his outfit I knew what I had done. I'm sorry."

"The time will come again," he said.

She had a strong jaw for a woman. He saw it set, and wondered about that. But presently her face softened. She dropped her eyes, gravely speaking. "The last hours have been the worst in my life. I never ceased to think about you. I have missed you."

He looked at her, surprised at the change. He said: "I'm the same man you said was just another candidate for the wild bunch."

She shook her head. "I know I said it. And I felt it. I do not feel it now. How can I tell you when the change happened? I do not know."

He said, "What have you got started now? What's this Ned Tower doing?"

205

"By now he's waiting outside Roselle, keeping watch."

He said: "I thought Bill was the man you needed to help you against Harry Ide."

"I once thought that, too."

"How many men with Tower?"

She paused on the edge of her answer. She watched him closely for a moment, then turned back to the stove to catch the coffee pot. She filled his tin cup. "I don't know how many he got together."

He said: "I'll drift down there and lend a hand."

"Ned will have enough," she said evenly.

He listened to the answer and found it strange. "I don't make this out. What does Tower figure to do?"

"Break up Bill's bunch. Once and for all, and forever."

"My understanding was," he said, "that these hill ranchers got along well enough with Bill. What's made them turn righteous, after he's supplied them with prairie cattle for a year or two?"

She said: "They were his friends as long as he knew where to stay. When he forgot that, they turned against him."

She was offering him nothing. She answered his questions in her even, short manner, explaining nothing extra. He sat before her, watching the strength of her face, its resolution and its will. It seemed to him that she gave him what he wanted to know only as a favor and not as a right; that even then she questioned his right to ask. But her small smile remained.

"Who got them started against him?"

"I did," she said. "As soon as he left Sun, following you." She added, very softly: "I changed my mind about him, Frank, because of you."

"This was the man," he said, "you depended on to keep Harry Ide away."

206

She drew a breath, a deep breath, and let it fall. Her smile pinched out and he realized she was impatient with him. "Listen to me," she said. "He has his ambitions. If he helped me against Harry Ide, he wished payment. There's only one way of paying him—to marry him and give him Sun. He would take nothing less; and he would at least take Sun if I refused to marry him." She paused, showing her small irritation at the need of this explanation. But she went on. "To be honest with you, I once thought of marrying him. I once saw admirable things in him. You changed that. When you faced him, he broke before my eyes. In that room. When you offered to fight. I stepped between you two to stop a killing not for any love. He had changed to a poorer man, with less in him, in that moment."

"You're takin' a chance of a killing now," he pointed out. "How do you think it will go at Roselle when they begin to shoot?"

She looked at him with her resolution showing around her mouth. "He went after you and meant to kill you. I would no longer try to save him. He must be driven out. Otherwise he'll stay by and hunt you again."

He had his own irritation, and rose. "I'll take care of my personal quarrels," he said.

She stood up with him, closely watching as he moved over the room; she was inwardly angry with him, and not all her carefulness held it entirely away. "You are rather proud," she observed. "I apologized for interfering the other day. Do I have to apologize again?"

"You like to run your own affairs," he said. "So do I."

Her mouth came tight. Her cheeks reddened and she lowered her head, looking down at the floor with a

207

small-lipped repression. Her hands came together, palm tightly pressing palm. She struggled with herself, she argued with her pride and her will, and at last she lifted her head and drew her shoulders straight. "I'm sorry, Frank," and held out a hand to him.

They had come close to quarreling and for a little while she had hated the crossing of his will against her own: but she had stepped aside with a woman's gracious gesture, and the gesture made her lovely before his eyes. He moved to her, he took her arm and held it a moment. Her eyes widened on him; they held him. She wasn't smiling but her lips were drawn apart in a voiceless expression and when she tipped her head he saw the light shining on her throat, and all this broke something in him which long needed the breaking and he brought her forward and kissed her. He felt her lips meet him, willing and readily answering. He felt her body sway and go soft.

And then she was still and the receptiveness went out of her; she had ceased to answer him and he drew back his head and saw that she had opened her eyes and was watching him, all cool and quiet. He felt embarrassed and stepped away.

"Sorry," he said.

"Why?"

He didn't know why. But he was still embarrassed and reached for his tobacco as a gesture. For a little while it had been as he had hoped, a giving and a receiving, warmth for warmth and a hard long call from one heart to another. This was a thing for which no word existed. It lived in a man and in a woman, compelling but silent, until that man and woman met. The answer came then, still wordless, and there was never any need of words. It had been this way between them when he first touched her; she had given.

Then she had withdrawn and had left him alone with his kiss, permitting his touch but not answering—and she had afterwards watched him with her speculative glance. He grew red and awkwardness came to his fingers.

"Why?" she repeated in her quiet, curious voice.

"Don't ask me something I don't know," he said.

She made a gesture with her hands, with her shoulders. "I thought I knew the ways of most men, but you are strange. I never know you. What is it you want?"

He shook his head. "No use talking about it."

It turned her dark and disappointed, and in turn made her awkward. "What did I do wrong? Shouldn't I have let you kiss me?"

"Time to ride on," he said. "How will you get back to Sun?"

"You'll take me," she said.

"I'm going to Roselle."

"Nothing will happen until you get back there," she said. But she had never ceased to watch him with her strained expression. She had failed, she had touched him only for a moment; and when he lighted his cigarette and looked at her he discovered she seemed ready to cry. The expression was on her, and that expression softened and made her beautiful again, so that everything he thought about her returned in full flood, and he desired her as he had before. He told himself: "I'm the biggest fool alive. I want her." But he said aloud: "Let's get started."

When they left the cabin she turned to the left, which seemed wrong to him. He said: "Better take the Roselle road until we reach town, then circle it. But keep on the road."

"I know a shorter trail," she told him, and led away.

Boston Bill and his seven men rode into Roselle at

sunset and put up before the saloon. Bill said: "He left Sun without any supplies. A night and a day will starve him out. He won't go back to Sun because he'll be afraid of running into us. Sherman City is too long a haul for a hungry man, and he'll be too suspicious of the hill ranches to drop in at one of them. He'll come here." He started to leave the saddle, and then changed his mind. "If we leave the horses here he'll spot 'em and know we're waiting for him."

He led the group around to the back side of the empty building—that same building in which Goodnight and McSween had had their fight. He rode into the building with his outfit. "Good place," he said and left his horse and walked to the saloon.

The bunch stood around the saloon, drinking up a sharp thirst, and later crowded into the back room for supper. It was dark then and Boston Bill thought about setting out a guard. "He'll scout the town very carefully before he comes in. We'll have to lay low. Rex, you go out and keep an eye peeled."

Afterwards the rest of the bunch returned to the front part of the saloon. Boston Bill's attention was caught by the side window which had no curtain. He said to the barkeep, "Cover that with something."

Some of the group started a poker game while the others sat idly by. Jem Soders laid himself out on the floor and fell immediately asleep. The barkeep came back with a blanket and nailed it across the window. He stood by the poker game, looking on. He said, idly and to nobody in particular, "Who's payin' for the meals?"

One of the poker players looked up at him. "What meals?"

The barkeep moved back to the bar. He stood behind it, without expression. He looked at Boston Bill who supported himself at the end of the

210

bar. "You payin' for the meals?"

"You can stand a night's charity," said Boston Bill. "You have been sticking us for years. Lay up a couple bottles on the bar. The treat's on you."

The barkeep had a round and soft face in which no great amount of character resided, and eyes of some kind of blue. He dropped his glance from Boston Bill. He backed away from the bar, but kept his hands on it. He cleared his throat and was morosely idle for a moment. Pretty soon he reached around for the whisky bottles, placed them before Bill and walked into the back room.

The echo of other riders came on in dull rhythm and presently four new men of Bill's outfit arrived. He said: "Put your horses across the street in that empty building," and watched them go out. He rested the small of his back against the corner of the bar, looking at the card game. One of the men began to sing to himself, making an odd noise. Bill said sharply, "Cut it out. You can be heard outside." He turned and placed his elbows on the bar and supported his chin in his hands. He watched the light shining on the dark top of the bar, his face pulled together unreadably. He dropped one hand on the bar and began to drum with his fingers.

All this bored him and in a little while he walked into the back room, and on through it to the kitchen. The barkeep was at the moment saying something to his wife, a heavy woman now standing over the stove, her face red and rough. He cut off his talk a moment, and went on by saying, "Couple more steaks, I guess," and looked at Bill.

Bill grinned ironically. "You weren't talking about steaks." He got a cup off the kitchen table and poured himself coffee out of the big pot on the stove. The red-faced woman kept her eyes on the stove, her mouth hard-closed. Bill wandered around the kitchen with his coffee, still grinning; he stopped in front of a lithograph hung to the wall by a single nail. It was a winter scene with two horses drawing a sleigh across the snow toward a farmhouse. The horses were stepping high and a woman on the porch had her hand lifted in welcome. A big red barn, with its silo, stood back of the house.

"New York State," murmured Boston Bill to himself. He stared at it a long while, the smile dying. He said: "Where'd you get this?"

The barkeep had gone back to the front room. It was his wife who spoke over her shoulder, grudging the talk. "Somebody left it here."

"Somebody who came from there, I suppose," said Boston Bill, again talking to himself. "Another traveler far from home. Damned odd how it sticks to you." He walked into the small dining room, listening to the growing racket in the front; he sat down at the table and lounged back in the chair sipping at his cup of coffee. The air in New York State in winter was clear and cold and the apples in the storehouse had the sharpest possible flavor. He remembered them and he remembered the smell of the storehouse. As a boy he had been afraid to go into the place because of its darkness, because of the fear of snakes; once his father had found a copperhead there, had plunged his hands into a bin of potatoes, touching the copperhead. But he remembered the smell of the storehouse, and the smell took him back and a thousand other memories came hard and sudden before him; and then, as always happened when these memories arrived, he had a longing to be what he once had been, and his mistakes gave him cruel pain, and he hated himself for what he was.

He hated not only himself, but the men around

212

him, despising their ignorance and their vulgarity, and sometimes he was inexpressibly lonely—and that loneliness always revived his memory of better days. One by one he knew the precise moments when he had made his mistakes, when he had turned the wrong way; they stood before him with terrible clarity, and somewhere out of that past a voice seemed to say: "You might have been—you might have been."

He had come West to escape all that, to start anew, and for a while his hope had been great. But once more the turns had been the wrong turns until he knew at last that the fault was in himself; he would always turn wrong because there was something in him which would never let him be wholly right. He finished his coffee and put down the cup and rose from the chair. He faced the empty wall and he looked at it and through it, seeing many things, seeing nothing; he turned back into the kitchen and went to the lithograph and pulled it from the wall. He rolled it up, feeling the eyes of the barkeep's wife on him.

"They sold these for fifty cents apiece," he told her. "Back East. I'll give your husband a dollar. I'll—"

The sound of voices in the saloon quarters dropped away, warning him. He heard a man walk over the floor and speak. "Which way this road go?"

He had rolled the lithograph; he carried it into the little dining room and opened it again, looking at it; he laid it on the table and folded it until it was small enough for a pocket, and put it into his pocket, and walked into the saloon room. The newcomer stood at the bar, drinking; a small man with a dry face and a pair of badly sprung legs. He laid down the glass and he paid for his drink. He felt the silence around him, and he looked around him with a kind of casual interest and turned back to the barkeep, who stood heavy and still.

"Which way this road go?"

"Which way you travelin'?"

"That way," said the man and pointed upward to the Owlhorn summits.

"It just keeps going," said the bartender, "over the mountain."

"What's over the mountain?"

"Same kind of country you came out of."

"How do you know what I came out of?" said the newcomer.

The barkeep shrugged his shoulders. "Looks like you been drinkin' desert water."

"You got rooms here?"

The barkeep punched a thumb upward. "Take the outside stairway and pick a bunk. Four-bits now."

The newcomer tried a second drink and bowed his head, thinking. He stirred a little and paid for the whisky; he said, "You got a pound of bacon to sell and some bakin' powder?"

"No."

The little man shrugged his shoulders. Boston Bill looked down on him with a kind of unsympathetic amusement. "You're in safe company, brother."

"Am I?" said the newcomer and thought about that. He took off his hat and scratched his head; he shook his head. "That would be somethin' new," he murmured and turned, walking out of the saloon.

The barkeep picked up bottle and glass and set them away; he ran a rag indifferently over the bar top and took a patient, dismal stand, looking at the men in the room wearily. Boston Bill poured himself a drink and held the glass between his hands. He was thinking then of Rosalia, growing warm from the thought of her. He drank the whisky at one swallow. He said irritably to the barkeep: "Nothing as rotten as this." More of his crowd had drifted in during the last

214

fifteen minutes, so that the room was comfortably full. Some of the late-comers went by him, into the little dining room. Jem Soders was sound asleep and snoring. Làne Brazee, who was the most alert of this outfit, looked up from the poker game.

"No use all of us waitin'. I'm goin' to turn in. We stay here?"

"We stay until he comes."

"Ed ought to be limpin' in pretty soon."

Ed was the one fallen back on the trail with the bad heart. Boston Bill shook his head. "That lad's dead by now. I've seen that happen before. His mouth looked funny."

"Maybe somebody ought to go back."

"He's better off dead," said Boston Bill.

Suddenly one of the crowd—a huge, big-shouldered one at the bar—made a full half turn. "I've seen that fellow before."

"What fellow?"

"One that just walked in and walked out."

"Said he was new here," stated Lane.

"He didn't say it outright," pointed out the other. "I've seen him before."

"Where?"

The big rider searched his mind and found no answer, and shook his head. Boston Bill drew partially out of his distant thoughts and looked at the barkeep. The barkeep hadn't changed his attitude in five minutes; he was a gloomy statue supported by the bar. Nothing disturbed the tired, disillusioned mask of his face. "You know him?" asked Bill.

"Am I supposed to know everybody that comes through?" said the barkeep.

"You see them all."

"Some of them stop and some go on. Them that stop either pay or don't pay. All kinds of people."

"You still worrying about your money?"

"You lads are tough on a man just gettin' by."

"Fix it up tomorrow," said Bill. "We'll sleep here to-night."

"Don't make a lot of noise," said the barkeep. "My wife's got a bad tooth."

Some other man in the crowd turned with interest. "Why didn't you say so? I can pull it. I used to—" He went no further. He looked at Bill and walked to the far end of the room.

"Don't be bashful," said Boston Bill, his irony coming out again. "There's men here who have more to hide than you do. Lane, you better go out and relieve Rex. I think—"

He looked at the open doorway and saw a man walk slowly across it and disappear. "I think Good-night will crawl in before much longer. I'm going to stay up."

The passage of the first man had not caught his attention, for he had thought it one of his own. But another man came into the doorway's square and turned and stopped and looked at the crowd a moment; and that man said, "Hello, Bill," and whipped out his gun and fired.

Boston Bill whirled aside from the bar as the bullet struck. He saw Harry Ide back away from the doorway into the blackness and he shouted to his own men, "Get away from that lamp," and watched them rise and swing in immediate confusion. He drew and killed the lamp with a shot; and at the same moment a full volley crashed in through the doorway, and somebody yelled in the darkness, and the whole side of the house shook as another blast of gunfire tore through the window that had been covered with the blanket. He called: "Drop!" The crowd rushed against him, toward the back room and the back door, and

216

the pressure of the stampede swung him around and slammed him against the bar, and somebody's elbow hit him a hard blow across the face as he whirled and dropped behind the bar.

FIFTEEN

ACTION AT ROSELLE

Boston Bill dropped full length on the floor behind the bar and heard the splintering of the wood above him as the bullets of Harry Ide's party crashed into the saloon room, through the front doorway and through the side window. The glass of the window shattered and dropped, chairs and tables went down in the violence of his own outfit rushing for the back room and for the rear door. All these men were near the bar's end, trying to get into the small room and slugging and cursing one another as they jammed together. He heard one of his men die, he heard death come as a rough tearing impact of lead through clothes and bone and flesh, followed by a grunt and a sigh. The man fell against the bar and slid around it, falling across Boston Bill's legs.

He had a creepy feeling about it and a small moment of panic that made him roll and jerk his feet away; he kicked at the man, feeling the soft, dull flesh give and roll back. He crawled farther along the bar, keeping well down, using his forearms to drag himself. Harry Ide, he thought, had traveled fast and with great secrecy; otherwise he could not have gotten this far without being spotted by one of his own men—Bill's men. Bill prided himself on his scout system and now he thought that he had been betrayed and even in this bedlam he remembered the men of his outfit who were not here, and suspected them all.

The firing swung around. It seemed no longer to be pouring through the front doorway; it seemed to be smashing against the back end of the house, toward which his outfit fought their way. The thing was terrible. It was a savage destruction that shook him to the very roots of his courage. Lead flailed through wall and room, making a sieve of the house; he heard more men yell and drop, he heard them race back from the rear, run over the saloon room and jump through the front doorway—and he heard them cry as they were hit. Nothing in all his imagination was like this. He lay flat, not so much frightened as cowed by the inhuman execution of an idea. He said to himself distantly: "Nobody could do a thing like this. Nobody."

Every muscle in him was so tight that he began to ache; the big leg muscles of his front thigh were cramped. His mind was very clear, very sharp; he heard every sound in magnified importance. He followed the fight and the shifting of Harry Ide's attack with his ears and he thought now of one thing alone, his own survival. Ide intended to wipe out the wild bunch, but Ide wanted him more than he wanted the others. Ide would search every corner of Roselle, break down every door, pour lead into every black corner in search of him. He thought: "Why should he do it? There was room for both of us. We could have gotten along."

The barkeep had been behind the bar at the commencement of shooting, but had apparently slipped away. That made Boston Bill think of this room

219

quite carefully, visualizing it, and then he remembered there was another doorway leading from the far end of the bar directly into the kitchen. The main weight of fire seemed to press against the back of the house, so that for the moment no more slugs beat through the bar. Boston Bill rose to his hands and knees and crawled on.

One palm came full and flat down upon a ragged splinter of glass and the weight of his shoulders plunged the splinter deep into his hand. He sat back, gritting his teeth together, and seized the end of the splinter and pulled it out. Blood gushed warmly into his palm; he untied his neckpiece and wrapped it around his palm, closing his fingers on it, and got to his feet and moved forward. His hands found the door frame; the door stood open before him.

He dropped again, crawling into the kitchen. He heard somebody breathing heavily, not far away; he heard two people breathing—the barkeep and his wife, he supposed. He crawled on, listening to some of Harry Ide's men run fast and clumsy beside the outer wall of the house, toward the front. He heard voices sharp-calling out on the street, and once again the shooting boiled up on that side. He crawled over the floor, striking a table and going around it. He reached a wall, noting the dull patch of a window above him. He explored the wall with his hand until he found a door's knob. Opening the door, he drew back and waited.

Nothing happened. He stood up, flattened to the wall, and waited again. Nobody seemed to be watching the door and in a moment he put his head through it, seeing nothing at all in the curdled shadows of the small alley running between the sa-

220

loon and the adjoining house. Drawing his breath, he stepped through, crossed the alley and put his back to the wall of the other house. He had left the most dangerous spot in town; he had gotten away from it into the loose darkness. He let his breath fall away, and rush freely in and fall away again.

The shouting went on, running at random through Roselle; it reminded him of nothing so much as the howl of a wolf pack. The firing broke out first at one spot and then another, each burst telling him of another of his own men trapped. He stood helpless, surrounded and desperate. Ide's men raced here and there, and then a shout brought them rushing together and their firing rose in smothering racket.

He crept to the rear end of the alley, stopped to listen at the roundabout darkness, and moved farther from the saloon. He passed four houses sitting side by side, rounded the last one and stepped to the road which formed Roselle's main street. All the town seemed in complete darkness, no light anywhere showing, and at the moment the activity boiled somewhere behind the saloon. A man came out of the blackness directly across from Boston Bill and ran down toward the saloon, breathing in snorted gasps. At that same moment Boston Bill crossed the street, ducked behind the buildings and ran toward the old brick building which housed the horses.

He wanted one thing only, which was to escape; the weight against him was too great and his chances too slim. Back in his head was the knowledge that he had been badly caught off guard and his reputation as a leader partly destroyed; his own outfit would never again ride solid behind him unless at

221

last he brought some kind of order out of this defeat. They threshed headless around the town, hunted and running, no doubt cursing him for his carelessness. If he could get at Ide—He put the impossible idea behind him. It was better to run, and to try again some other time, even if it lost him his command over the wild bunch.

He came to the back doorway of the brick building and paused there, listening in for the shuffle of waiting horses, for the crunch of teeth against bit, for the small tinkle of bit chains. He listened and heard nothing, and stepped inside to move softly over the hardpacked dirt. He circled the inside wall, one hand well before him, suspecting the presence of an Ide man. He was half around the big room when his foot touched the yielding bulk of something on the floor and stopped him. He drew away and he waited, and suddenly bent and laid his hand on a horse. He turned back and pointed directly for the outline of the rear door through which he had come. He stumbled over two other horses before he got outside. He went straight into the darkness fifty feet and sat down, sick and trembling at what he knew. Not even the death of his own men disturbed him so much as this new information: Ide had shot all the horses to prevent his escape. That told him more clearly than any other thing of Ide's frame of mind.

He sat there several minutes, like a man exhausted beyond the ability to move. His mind would not work and his nerve had gone. He said to himself, time after time: "I have got to get out of here," and then the question would come, "Where'll I go?" From his position he saw the corner of the saloon and noticed a light burning in it. Ide's men were moving rapidly down the street from house to house,

222

a shot now and then breaking the quiet.

He got up and walked the length of the houses, circling to the road well below town. When he reached the road he moved toward Sun, not sure of his intentions or his destination; and before he had quite pulled himself together he bumped straight into a bunch of horses gathered on the road and a man guarding them.

He had no warning and when he stopped he had nothing to say at all. He stood still, watching the man's shape move in the dark. The man said: —

"Harry ready for me to come in with the horses?"

"Yes," said Boston Bill.

"All right. I can't lead 'em all. You take some."

"Sure," said Bill. He moved around the man and reached a horse. He stood still while the man waited. His mind began to work. He went on from horse to horse, then he said, "This is mine," and stepped into the saddle.

"You take that back bunch," said the man.

"All right," said Boston Bill, and drifted away. He was fifty feet removed when the horse holder called after him. "Where the hell you goin'?" He looked back and realized he was sheltered by the dark. Digging in the spurs he raced down the road toward Sun with a single bullet following him.

Goodnight heard the sound of distant firing and stopped at once. He sat still on the saddle, listening to the full-out vigor of the shooting. The girl had been ahead of him and now turned and waited in silence beside him. The sound was straight to the north.

"That Roselle direction?"

223

"Yes."

"How many men did Tower have with him?"

"Ten or twelve."

"That's not enough against Bill. You know these trails. Lead off. We'll go there."

She didn't say anything. She struck into the darkness, going north, and came to a meadow over which they passed. The trail thereafter wound dogleg fashion through the timber with no light anywhere. It dropped into a shallow draw, crossed a creek, and went up the bare side of a hill. On top of the hill, half an hour later, he saw the top of Roselle's houses and one lantern bobbing along the road. It took another ten minutes to come up against the back side of Roselle. He stopped here hearing no more gunfire. "Over with, one way or another. I'll ease up and see."

"Frank," she said, softly, "there's no need to bother. Ned had enough to handle the wild bunch."

"A dozen's not enough."

"Might have been more than that," she said and went ahead of him.

Her assurance puzzled him, and her lack of honesty with him seemed strange. He went with her, rounding the corner of the saloon at the same time the man with the lantern swung up. It was Ned Tower. Presently somebody lighted the lamps in the saloon, that glow springing out of the door. Ned Tower looked taciturnly at Virginia. "You ought to have been careful comin' in here."

"When the shooting stopped," she said, "I knew the trouble was over."

"So it was," he agreed. "But you shouldn't of been certain as to who was doin' the shootin' and who came out on top."

224

"You had enough men to do it, Ned."

"So we did," he said. "But we never got the chance."

"Speak so I can understand you," she said impatiently.

"We been coolin' our heels in the brush, listenin' to all this. It wasn't us that did any fightin'."

"Then who was it?"

"Harry Ide," said Ned Tower. "I never saw anything like it, and I hope I never do again. We were in the brush, about ready to move in, when Ide hit town. He must of been scoutin' these hills for a week. He must of had a hell of a crew on Bill's trail." Ned Tower paused and rubbed his chin. He added, dry and glum: "He did the job."

Virginia Overman sat thoroughly still, looking down upon Ned Tower. The lantern light and the glow from the saloon played upon her so that Goodnight, turning his attention to her, noticed the strictness of her face. She was hard as iron at the moment yet her voice came out quite small, quite uncertain: "Bill?"

Tower shook his head. "He got away."

Goodnight watched her features with a growing alertness. She let her lips loosen, she drew a breath, and then she became aware of his glance and made an effort to hide her feelings. Her whole frame of mind at the moment was odd to him; it left him uneasy and troubled.

Tower said: "But he's had his teeth pulled. The wild bunch is busted up. You got nothin' to fear from Boston Bill any more."

"No," she murmured. "I see that."

"Should please you," said Tower, his black, brilliant eyes fastened to her.

225

"It does," she answered, cold and distant.

"You show your pleasure in a damned queer fashion."

"Perhaps."

The barkeep came out of the door and stood in the night. His face was round and dismal and gray. He ran a hand over his face, squeezing out the oil film shining on his skin. He said in a groggy voice: "I could of warned him. I knew it when the little fellow came in for a drink. I knew the little fellow. I knew he was Ide's man. But that's what happens when a man won't pay his bills. I never lifted a hand. Awful close night. No wind, no air."

Virginia said, "I thought it was chilly," and looked at him. Then she got down from saddle and moved toward the saloon's door. Tower said in a sharp voice. "Don't go in there," and the barkeep reached out with his arm to bar her way. She knocked his arm aside with a sudden willful gesture and opened the door. She stopped on the threshold and looked in a moment. She turned and came back to the horse, and mounted. She stared at the ground, her mouth closing into an unpleasant line.

Tower said irritably: "Couldn't you take my word for it?" He shook his head. "That Harry Ide. It was a massacre and it will stink up the mountain for fifty years."

"I'm thinking about him," she said. "He's probably camping on Sun now with his outfit."

"I wouldn't worry about Harry Ide," said Tower.

"Why not?" she asked. "What's to stop him?"

Ned Tower turned about and walked thirty feet down the street, his lantern bobbing. He halted and he said, "This is what stopped him."

Virginia and Goodnight rode forward. Ned Tower

226

turned the lantern slightly so that the yellow beams slanted downward upon the man lying in the dust, face upward, his legs spraddled and his hat rolled away. This was Harry Ide, his black hair stained by dust, his face bleached of its color. One little spot of black-red stood against his shirt to indicate what had killed him. "I got an idea," said Tower, "he was hit by one of his own men, unbeknownst."

"Which way," asked Goodnight, now thinking of something else, "did the rest of his outfit ride?"

"Back toward Sherman City."

"Where'd Bill's men ride?"

Tower gave him a gray look. "Them that got out of this slaughter house probably scattered any direction. They walked—they didn't ride. Ide killed all their horses first thing to pin them down."

"Kind of tough," said Goodnight.

"Tough enough," said Tower.

A man moved out of an alley into the lantern light. It was Bob Carruth with a day's whiskers on his stout face, turned tough and cranky by steady riding. He stared at Virginia in a way that irritated Goodnight. It was a plain show of malice, of stiff and settled dislike. His voice also echoed it.

"Well, Virginia," he said, "you got it all your way. Bill won't be big enough to bother you no more and the desert crowd got a broken back when Harry Ide was killed. It all came out your way."

Virginia turned to Goodnight. "Let's ride back to Sun," she said, and moved on with her horse. Goodnight came abreast of her and presently Bob Carruth swung up to them and these three rode the black highway homeward, each one wrapped in silence. Coming down the narrow meadow which faced Sun, Goodnight saw bunkhouse lights burning,

227

and lifted his voice by way of warning. "Tap—Slab."

A shape showed momentarily at the bunkhouse door and slid on into the dark. "Who's there?"

"All right—all right," called Bob Carruth.

The three rode into the yard. Tap and Slab came up. Carruth said, "Anybody been here?"

"Boston Bill came by and stopped to eat. He went on. There was a hell of a bust of riding around here afterwards. Small jags of men comin' down from Roselle. They didn't stop here. What happened?"

"World fell down," said Carruth crankily. "I'm goin' to tell the cook to get somethin' on the table." He went away, leaving Goodnight and the girl. She looked a moment at Goodnight, the shadows covering whatever her face held. She dropped to the ground. She said, "Put away my horse, Frank." Then her voice sank to a lower tone, softer and warmer. "I'll be in the big room when you come."

He took her horse to the corral, stripped off the gear and lugged it back to the front porch. He dropped it there. She had left the front door open as an invitation; she had gone to some other part of the house. He looked into the front room for a moment and turned away, crossing back to the bunkhouse. He had his own blanket on the bed and his own traveling kit in the condensed-milk box tacked up near the bunk. He took his shaving material and walked to the kitchen. He got himself some hot water and shaved in front of the back-door mirror; he washed up and he went into the dining room, finding Carruth there. He sat down with Carruth, waiting for the Chinaman to bring supper in.

Carruth stared at Goodnight's face. "Saturday night already?" Then he got to thinking about it. "No, this is Thursday. Time's all gummed up. Did

228

you take a look into that saloon?"

"No."

"It was bad," said Carruth.

The Chinaman came in with coffee and ham and eggs. He said: "What's matter you not come when right time is to eat? All-time I cook. I damn tired. Come and go, come and go. No good. This no hotel."

Carruth reached for an extra cup on the table. He balanced it and threw it and missed the Chinaman. The cup broke against the wall and the Chinaman, once in the kitchen, began to curse. They ate and they rolled up their smokes. Carruth said: "Well, she came out on top."

"You said that before."

Carruth flicked his glance across Goodnight's face. He said: "Where'd Bill chase you?"

"Up into a canyon. Old mining operation there."

"Glory Mine. Where'd you go then?"

"A trail took me to the main road over the mountains. I met Virginia when I was riding toward Roselle. She had Tower and a few men there, watching for Bill."

"A few men?" said Carruth. He shook his head. "You know how many she had lined up? Close to thirty. She was waiting for Bill to collect his outfit. If Harry Ide hadn't cleaned out that bunch, she would have done it."

Goodnight said nothing. The information puzzled him. Virginia might have told him this in the beginning, and had not. He could not understand the reason for her secrecy except perhaps that it was a part of her complete independence, her dislike to share her affairs or her power with others. Maybe she was like her father. He scowled over the cigarette smoke tracing aimless outlines on the table with the thick hard edge of his thumbnail. Bob Carruth studied him with a good deal of care, with a secret liking for him, with a wish for his well-being that he would never openly have expressed. This young man, Carruth had already decided, was meant for the straight road and never any other. He was a man meant for riding in the sunlight. He had sharp edges to him, a sound mind untouched by the sly and evil and spongy thoughts of the wild bunch. He was the kind of a man who needed to laugh and find fun in the world. It had been a long time, Carruth guessed, since he'd either laughed or been completely at ease. There was a weight on him and a darkness, and he struggled with some tough problem that would not let him alone, with some feeling that had him bound in its thousand thin strands.

"Frank," said Carruth, "these hills are too damned full of shadows for a man of your sort. Get back into the desert and ride until you feel like you ought to feel."

Goodnight gave him a surprised, open look. "Where'd you pick that up?"

"I can read what I see in front of me," said Carruth.

"A man," said Goodnight thoughtfully, "can never go back."

"A man can never do the same piece of the trail over again. But he can always turn into the one he ought to be on."

"What trail?" asked Goodnight. He was interested. He watched Carruth, asking a question he badly needed answered.

Carruth thought it out in his head over a long silence. He searched himself, anxious to find something that would bite into the young man's mind and strike response in his heart; at last he shook his head. "I never was much for talk. I can't tell you." Then with a mild sort of desperation he pointed toward the big house. "But I can tell you one thing. The trail don't lay through that door. Get your roll on your horse and get off the place before it is too late."

"You don't like her," said Goodnight coolly. "I have noticed that."

"I worked on this place twelve years," pointed out Carruth. "I got my rights to like or dislike."

"Then why do you stay?"

"This," said Carruth, "is my last meal here."

"Why?" asked Goodnight.

He got no answer to that. Carruth simply closed his heavy jaws, rose and left the room. Goodnight tapered up a second cigarette and lighted it and sat still, drumming his knuckles on the table. He had the sensation of being afloat, of being carried downstream against his will. He had muscles to use and a mind and a will, and these lay idle and nothing good was done, and he sat sour and restless, close by some one thing he needed but could not find. He shrugged his shoulders. He thought: "I can do what I started out to do. I can follow Boston Bill." It was like that with him now; he had to have a chore, and this was his chore. He rose and left the mess hall, moving idly across the yard toward his horse. He stopped in the middle of the yard, looking at the open door of the big house, and a breeze of interest suddenly blew through him and he had a light and eager feeling that moved him to the house.

When he got inside he found Virginia waiting for him. She said, "Shut the door," and watched him lay his big hand backward against it. She had combed her hair, so that it lay soft and neat along her head; she had changed her clothes and wore now a green dress with faint threads of gold in it. Against it, her breasts and her shoulders lay firm, and vitality came out of her, and in her steady smiling was a warmth that fell generously upon him, with its open invitation, its promise. She faced him with her calm waiting, proud of herself and sure of what she wanted him to have.

He came toward her, wanting all of it. He put his hand on her arm, watching her eyes widen. They were soft gray and light danced upon them, making her spirit gay; he saw her lips lengthen and begin to draw apart and he guessed she was thinking of him in the same violently desiring way he thought of her. He took her in and kissed her, his mouth bearing down hard and heavy upon her. He felt her wishes come up to him, he felt her give and he thought at that moment he had reached the end of the road.

It was only a momentary thought. Deep in the thundering rush of feeling, the chill of some strange and darkly unknown mystery came in harsh countercurrent. He felt the wonder slip away, he felt this woman retreat from him, he felt himself recoil. He stepped back from her and he dropped his arms, looking at her and hating the change with all his heart. The warmth of her lips had died in that single instant; they had turned lifeless and unpleasant.

She knew it as well. Her eyes were wide and watchful; they mirrored the oddest expression he had seen, cool and tragically calm. She let her hands drop and her shoulders fell down and then, to cover the blank, stony emptiness of what had happened, she began to talk in a light, hurried way.

"You're all tired out. Why don't you turn in and get a long night's sleep?"

"That will come," he said.

"Frank," she said, "those bunkhouse beds are hard. Use the extra bedroom tonight."

"That would look odd."

"Does it matter?"

"Better not," he said.

She drew a short, swift breath. She looked closely at him, trying to read the immediate things in his mind. "My father," she said, "would have been happy. For the first time in twenty years Sun has no strong enemies to worry over. Harry Ide hated us so much. He made all the trouble. The rest of them won't."

"Fine," he said, "fine," and found himself struggling with a leaden conviction. He had to leave here.

"Frank," she said, "I meant what I said the other day. You're foreman." She watched him with a greater and greater closeness, noting the stolidness coming to his face. He started to speak. She stopped him by the quick onrush of her words. "How can I say what I mean, Frank? Sun is as much yours as it is mine — if you wish it that way. Or was I wrong in thinking you wanted me when you kissed me?"

She made it harder and harder for him. Each word she spoke built a fence around him, binding his sense of honor. In a little while the fence would be too high.

"I'm pulling out, Virginia."

"But why?"

It was like a cry, spoken rapidly and at the top of her voice, full of dammed-up wonder and defeat and misery. The calmness went away, the pride went away. She stood before him, stripped of aloofness, turned naked to him by her defeat; in that terrible instant he saw the glory go out of her and never afterwards did he forget the moment. He shook his head. "I don't know why, Virginia. Never any answer to a thing like that."

"I'm not enough, am I?" she asked him, holding herself together. "Oh, don't bother to be nice to me. I want the truth. I'm not enough. I've known it for a long while. I've known it ever since I was a girl. I've looked in the mirror and seen it. I've gone to bed and thought, through the hours, that there was something I didn't have—never would have. What is it? Please—what is it?"

"There's a man for you," he said. "For that man you've got everything."

"Oh, no," she said, dull and bitterly sure. "No, I'll never have it for any man. I can tell. By the way they look at me. For a while, when you looked at me, I thought everything was all right. You're the first one. I would have killed Bill for you, Frank, because of the way you looked at me. Then you kissed me—and you knew. Just as the others knew without kissing me."

The talk hurt him worse than a beating. It slashed his sympathy; it broke through him in a thousand ways until he could no longer keep his glance on her.

"Well," she said in a quiet, resigned tone, "put Sun Ranch with me. Isn't that enough?"

"No," he said, more and more embarrassed.

"No," she whispered, "of course not. It would do for Bill. But not for you." She made a little gesture with her hands, resigned and saddened. "It would be nice to have the love of a man, so close, so strong, so deep. But I have other things and I suppose I must be content."

He nodded and turned away. He reached the door when her voice stopped and turned him. She came forward, managing a smile. She took both his hands and held them a moment and the strange change occurred once more in her, making her sweet. She wanted nothing of him then, nor wanted to put her will upon him; and in this way she was beautiful. "Good-by," she murmured, and kissed him and turned away.

He moved over to the bunkhouse, past Carruth and Tap and Slab. He rolled his blanket and came out and tied it behind the saddle. The three men watched him as he swung up. Carruth smiled at him. He lifted a hand at them and rode into the dark, toward Sherman City.

"Ah," said Carruth in a soft, pleased tone. Tap and Slab presently moved into the bunkhouse, leaving him to his reflections. He was still there, fifteen minutes later, when Virginia came out of the house to him. She stood near him. She murmured: "I'm lonely, Bob."

"You didn't have your way," he said.

"Is that it? Is that the thing—"

"I remember when you were a girl," he said. "A damned sweet girl until somethin' went against you. Then you cried and busted things, and everybody gave in. You always got your way."

"The things I wanted," she said, "were always right."

"It all led to this," he said. "Then this must be right, you losin' this man. Therefore you should be glad, because it's right. I'll be leavin', too. I have been ashamed of you."

235

She stared at him. She wheeled, looking wildly around her. There was a chopping block near the door, with a small ax sunk into it. She seized the ax and whirled with it, striking out at him, roused to a rage that could not be controlled. He ducked as the ax grazed his shoulder, and he turned and seized it and flung it away. She came at him, her breath hard and heavy; she scratched his face deeply and she slapped him and doubled her fists and hit him like a man would hit. He caught her and pinned her arms to her sides. He spoke through the strong draw of his breathing: —

"You didn't get your way."

She ceased to fight, she fell against him. He pushed her away and went around the bunkhouse. He got his horse out of the corral and threw on the gear and led it back. He went inside and rolled up his belongings and came out and lashed them down. She stood dumb in the shadows, watching him, her eyes round and unwinking. He had started off when she called to him: —

"Bob, don't go. I've got nothing left."

"You'll get somebody."

"No," she said. "Nobody'll stay. You're the only one. You're like my father, you go back to the beginning. You put up with me. Nobody else ever would. I'll be good. Don't go."

He was fifty feet away when he stopped. He heard her crying in a small, helpless fashion and the sound went through him and got at him. He knew the meanness in her, he knew the punishment he would take from her in the future; but he remembered how she had been, far back, as a small girl depending upon him and admiring him. It was a tie that he couldn't break. He thought: "Well, Goodnight got

236

away. I guess one's enough. I guess I stay." He rode back to her and got down. "All right," he said. "You can stop cryin' now. You got your way."

"Can I borrow your horse?"

"Where you goin'?"

"To Sherman City. I don't want him to meet Bill. He's still got his mind on killing Bill. If I can stop it, that will be a good thing I've done, won't it?"

"You can try it," he said grudgingly. Then, as she moved away, he called after her: "Leave Goodnight alone."

"It would do no good to see him again, Bob."

He settled back against the wall, smoking out a fresh cigarette. He thought: "I suppose the next twelve years will be as bad as the last twelve," and felt unhappy at his own weakness. Still, somebody had to be by her. Somebody who knew her and could understand the sweetness so interwoven with the badness. Then he thought: "I wonder if she figures to get Boston Bill now, as the best of a bad bargain?" The idea both alarmed and intrigued him. It would be like her.

SIXTEEN

THE LAST DECISION

Boston Bill reached Sherman City at midnight and circled to the back side of a small house at the lower end of town; this was scarcely more than a comfortable shed belonging to Mack Honnicut, a prospector, who used it only as headquarters when he came in from the hills. Bill moved into the place, lighted a lamp and pulled down the blinds on the two windows. It appeared Honnicut had recently been to town. The table was occupied with empty whisky bottles, the blankets on the bed were all in a disheveled state and a frying pan sat on the cold stove with its scum of bacon grease. Bill found part of a drink in one of the bottles and sat on the bed a moment to consider his position.

Harry Ide had missed him and would let no grass grow under his feet to hit him again. Too much had happened to let it rest as it was. Ide would be coming back through town shortly and no doubt put up for the night, and soon enough would know that he, Bill, was here. It was too small a town to hide in; too many eyes were always watching. He needed a fresh horse, a meal and some supplies, and then he needed to fade out.

He considered where he would go. His crowd was

238

broken up. He had no idea how many had died, and he refused to guess; that whole scene in Roselle was too grisly a thing to face. As for those who had escaped, they would no doubt be hiding in the hills. They would not, for fear of Ide's further vengeance, go back to the headquarters ranch and they would not stay too long in the Owlhorns. He knew them too well to expect they would form again and make a stand. They were outlaws, men on the run, brave when cornered and fighting for their own particular lives or when the weight of numbers gave them a feeling of safety. But once attacked and defeated, they would run. They were that kind.

Even if they remained, Bill realized he could not go back to them. He had lost his leadership over them. The plans he had so long nourished were dashed down, his dreams of power were done. He got up and hunted for another drink, and found it, and he had a good look at himself as he stood solitary in the room; and he silently said: "Everything I touch goes bad. It has always been that way. I was never born to be lucky or successful. Not in the stars."

It was hard to know why that should be. He had a better mind, a bolder and more fertile mind than any man in the hills. He saw what other men did not see. He had no illusions to blind him and very few scruples to halt him. He was a free man, possessing power and ambition and logic. He could drive toward anything he wished and be anything he wished, while lesser men threshed around without energy, handcuffed by their stupidities or bound by a code of morals meant for the common and the timid. Traveling thus, he could travel far; for the world was the prize of the man who dared. Then why had he not traveled far?

Somewhere his logic was at fault and somewhere he had failed himself, and he looked at himself in the furtive and fearful way of a man who knows the fault and will not face it, and he said to himself, softly and with self-pity, "I was born without luck. Damn the world for cheating me of what is mine."

He remembered how near he had been to victory when, surprising Ide on the latter's ranch, he held the whole key to his fortunes in his hand. That had been the turning point; that had been the moment of success and the moment of disaster. He reviewed it, morbidly seeing it, desperately wishing that it might have been different. Goodnight had turned it into disaster.

"I should," he thought, "have faced him then. I was too easy." Why had he not challenged him at that instant? Why had he not, when other chances came, faced it out with Goodnight? Somehow he had let his opportunities slip through his fingers. He reviewed those moments one by one, seeking the key to his own failure, and in each instance his sharp mind came back to something within himself that he suspected and distantly knew, but would not openly look upon.

"I've got to get away," he told himself, and left the house by the rear door. He continued with the back line, going toward the hotel with the intention of entering the kitchen for something to eat and something to carry away. He came to the small yard behind Rosalia's house and he saw the light shining through the window, and hurried as he was, the light caught him like a magnet and drew him to the door. He tapped on the door and opened it before he heard her answer, sliding through and closing the door behind. Standing in the kitchen, he saw her come tall and grave out of her bedroom. She had her hair braided down for the night and she wore a long blue robe, and she faced

240

him in a way that made his defeat indescribably the worse. This was the woman to whom he wished to bring his victories; this was the woman he wanted to sway, to seize. As in so many other events of his life, he realized he had once come near to capturing her. Once she had looked upon him with a different expression, interested and undecided. He had reached for her and he had tried to command her, and had failed. Why had he failed? It was the old question haunting him again.

"Rosalia," he said, and heard horsemen beating through town. "What are you dreaming about?"

"Where have you been?"

"In the hills."

He noticed concern come to her face and he wondered at it. She reached up, drawing the edges of her robe more tightly around her throat. "What happened?"

"Harry Ide caught my party at Roselle. It was tough."

"Is that all?" she asked.

"I expect he's still on my trail. I'm leaving."

"What else?"

He said, "Isn't that enough?"

There was a shouting in town, the quick hark of voice answering voice. Horses wheeled in the center of town and afterwards came hard by this house, running down toward the desert.

She said: "Didn't Goodnight find you?"

"I didn't find him," he said. "I let him slip through my fingers."

He saw the loosening of her body beneath the robe. He thought, "All that beauty stirring at the mention of one man's name. All that round, full surface responding to the thought of him. Why isn't it mine?"

241

"Bill," she said, "you'd better go. Ide or Goodnight, one or the other, will watch for you and trap you on some road, in some canyon, down some dark alley."

"Do you care?" he asked and felt a small stir of hope.

"No," she said, "not for you. You deserve to die. Of all the men I know, you are the one who best understood the things you were doing. Every step of the way you knew good from evil, and knew you were doing evil. Other men have done these same things, never knowing better, or doing them because they felt they could do nothing else. You did them because you wanted to, even as your judgment warned you."

"Then why worry about me?" he said, short and sullen.

"I don't want another killing on Goodnight's record."

"That is the man, isn't it?"

She closed up and looked at him with her dark judgment. What she felt was close and treasured and she would not cheaply share it. He watched expression play over her expressive face; he saw the generosity of her mouth, the glow of her eyes — and he would have sold all his remaining hopes of life to have possessed the wonder he saw at that moment in her. For he was a man keenly aware of beauty, tortured by its nearness that never came nearer. He drew a long breath.

"I've been a sinner. Who hasn't been? I am my own worst enemy, but who is not? There has never been a day I have not thought of you. Never a campfire I have not seen your face within. Would it help if I told you heaven for me is in your eyes? Through all the evil sounds of this world, I hear your voice. In the worst of misery I feel the touch of your hand. Don't you suppose I know what I miss when you hold your tenderness away from me? Don't you think I realize you would be, for me, the greatest thing in my life? Standing this near to you, I know I'm as close to goodness as I shall ever be. I know. There is a part of me you could lift up until the worst of me would die out. I know what I am, Rosalia. I know what I have lost."

She shook her head and she was sorry for him. Pity came out of her in a warm wave, changing her lips as she stood so solemn and straight before him. She murmured: "It is strange, and sad."

"The strangeness is," he said in a changed and sulky voice, "that I'd go down on my knees and bind myself in chains for something you'll give away to Goodnight without any promise at all."

"Perhaps," she said.

A hand tapped the back door. Rosalia went by Bill, to the door. She stood there, listening to a man's soft voice, and she came back to face Bill again. She studied him with another expression, turned still and sure; and it came to him then as a queer thought that his recent life had been thrown against two women poles apart except for one common thing: they both had strong wills, they both had iron in them. He had suffered defeat at the hands of both of them because of it. Looking at Rosalia now, her silent resolution, her calmness that weighed him and decided upon him, it was as though Virginia stood in her place. They were both stronger than he was; in one terribly candid moment he admitted it.

"You need a fresh horse," said Rosalia, "and some food to pack with you. Rex—"

The man had apparently been outside the door all this while. He said, "Yeah."

"Take Bill's horse over to the stable and swap his gear to a fresh horse. Stop in at the hotel kitchen and find him some food he can carry along." She looked at Bill. She said: "Your horse will be at the stable. Goodby, Bill."

He sensed a change, he suspected it. "What's up?"

She watched him, knowing him and not wholly trusting him; and there was a shadow of trouble upon her. "Harry Ide was killed at Roselle. Didn't you know?"

"No," he said. "No." But a black pleasure sprang through him and he said, "That pays back some of it." He stood still, running this new information through his head. It made a difference. It took away the haste and the fear, so that the old illusion of personal greatness came again, and he had his swift hope of retrieving glory out of disaster. Everything changed that rapidly. He looked at her and smiled.

"There's no hurry about the horse."

"Goodnight is still after you, Bill."

"No," he said. "I'm after Goodnight. Do you think I'll let him go? He was the beginning of this trouble."

"You'll go," she said, iron-calm again.

He understood what was in her mind and it made him a little vengeful. "You're afraid he'll die."

"I don't want him to kill another man," she said.

"He won't," said Bill.

"And I will not have you standing in a dark alley waiting for him."

The blacker side of his temper came up. "Let him fight his own fight. If he's worth as much as you think, let him prove it. I won't run from him."

She lifted her voice. "Rex," she said, and waited until Rex stepped to the door. He had heard this talk; he had his gun half lifted, half ready. "Rex," she said, "if this man isn't out of Sherman City within fifteen minutes I shall blame you."

Bill stared at her, trying to face her down, to shame the streak of cruelty she used on him; but she held his glance, stronger than he was, simpler and braver and more primitive. He saw that she had one great resolve, which was that Goodnight should not suffer; and for that she would let nothing stand in her way. He shook his head when he was certain of it and his last vague hope of winning her died. He bowed his head. "You know," he said conversationally, "I never really understood the people in this land. I never belonged here."

"No," she said, "you don't. You will always be hunting a land better than the one you're in. You will always fail. Good-by, Bill."

He nodded and passed out, feeling the poorness of his showing. He was bitter at her and bitter at himself and he went down the alley with self-mockery in his heart and sly schemes half awake in his head. Rex tramped behind him, all the way to the corral. Tex called into the corral. "Jap. This man can have the big sorrel with the star." He turned to Bill, dead-set and positive, a dangerous man handling a man he believed to be less dangerous. "You stay here while I go get your horse."

Bill watched him turn the corner of the saloon; he heard his steps tramp steadily along the walk, that sound breaking into the night stillness. The lights of town had been turned out when he first had entered. Now they were on again, glowing from doorway and window, and he knew men stood in the shadows watching him. On the high side of town the sound of a horse came along rapid and loose—the slightly ragged pace of a tired horse being pushed. Bill drew

245

back into the stable's arch, waiting.

The rider broke into view at the head of the street, shadowed and unknown. The beams of house-light flickered vaguely on him as he crossed them, swung at the corner and came straight for the stable. Bill stood still, drawn half inside the stable's wide doorway, turned keen as the rider moved through the stable, dropped down and stepped aside from the horse. The man came to the mouth of the doorway and paused there to build a smoke. He stood, bent slightly forward, a gray and not wholly distinct shadow, and he remained this way until he had finished his smoke. Boston Bill heard the man's hands scrape along his trousers and his coat, searching for a match, and then he heard the sound stop and he saw the shadow grow still. Presently the man made a slow quarter turn toward Bill. He had sensed Bill. In a little while his prying eyes located Bill's shadow at the edge of the doorway. He waited, cautious and silent, not sure of what was before him. He let the silence drag, and grew weary of it, and challenged: —

"You got a match?"

It was Goodnight's voice.

Boston Bill started to answer and then his throat stopped up and he remained still. He wanted to answer, he wanted to warn this man he so thoroughly hated, this man at whose door he laid so large a part of his recent misfortunes. He wanted to call his own name and identify himself and then draw and have an end to it all.

But even as he wished to do this — wholly honorable and face to face, without evasion or trickery as he had once said he would — that streak within him which was sly and untrustworthy got complete possession of him and would not let him speak. All his words of bravery

246

and all his wishing for a great life fell down at a moment like this. The foundation of his nature was that unstable. For a moment he faced the truth and was bitterly ashamed; and then as he had done so many times before, be ignored his shame and pretended it did not exist, and he stepped deeper into the shadows. Thus he had Goodnight more clearly framed against the open arch of the stable.

Goodnight said: "What the hell you fiddling around there for? Stand still. Who are you?"

Boston Bill moved steadily backward. He touched the end of a stall, he grazed the tail of a horse; he swung rapidly aside as the horse, spooked by the unexpected contact, struck out with its foot. Goodnight said: "Stand fast or I'll fire," and at the same moment he drew out of the arch, into the more solid blackness of the barn.

Boston Bill cursed himself for his lost chance. He drew and he waited. He stopped, listening for the sound of Goodnight, and heard nothing. He thought: "If I cross over and stand against the stalls on that side I'll catch him against the light again." He moved out, very softly and without any sound in the spongy dirt. He was half over when a bullet's explosion battered the silence and cracked against the sides and roof of the building. The breath of it touched him; he heard the spent slug slap against a far board as he jumped against the edge of a stall. He said aloud: "Damn you, I'll outguess you."

"Bill," said Goodnight and remained silent a considerable time. Then he said: "I came down here to wind up this deal. Step out to the street."

"This is good enough," said Bill.

Goodnight listened to the voice carefully. He placed its source somewhere along his own side of the stable halfway toward the rear. He swung a little, watching for Bill to expose himself once more by crossing against the pale hole of the rear entrance. He guessed that Bill, in attempting to maneuver him against the front entrance, had forgotten about the rear doorway. He waited, and as he waited he remembered Niles Brand smiling at him and he turned cold and hatred came to him again as it had so often before. He felt it pour through him, changing him, chilling him. Patience made rock out of him so that he could have waited forever. It was waiting that would break Bill down, as it had broken McSween.

He heard at last a sigh come out of Boston Bill. It was a sudden need for air which betrayed Bill and he seemed to know it, for he began to fire with a pure recklessness, raking the corner of the stable. Goodnight stepped inside an empty stall. He heard a horse begin to thresh, and stumble and drop; he heard all the horses fiddle in their stalls. He counted three shots and knew Boston Bill could not have more than two more, counting the one bullet already spent. Probably he had only one left. A man seldom rode with his hammer lying on the sixth cartridge.

He called: "I'm comin' forward, Bill," and moved out of the stall on soft feet. He meant to make his man back away toward the rear door and thus come against the dull patch of light. He crawled past a horse and halted at the edge of another stall; he slid into it and repeated, "I'm comin' forward," and stepped on. He felt a bridle hanging near by; he reached up, softly unhooked it from its peg, and balanced it in his hand. He let a full half minute pile up, and then threw the bridle across the stable. It struck with a short echo, and drew Bill's fifth bullet.

"You wasted that one," said Goodnight. "I'm not there."

He made out the scrape of Bill's body against a wall and when he heard it he drew up his gun and laid it on the vague patch of light at the end of the stable and waited. It wasn't a long wait. This man had less pure nerve than McSween—and McSween had broken. Therefore he wasn't surprised when he saw Boston Bill's shape creep out from the complete blackness and take shape against the rear opening. Goodnight laid his gun against the shape and he held it there to catch a good aim.

But he did a thing that he had not intended doing. Just before he fired he dropped the gun's muzzle slightly and sent two bullets low at Bill. One of them struck. Bill gave out a heavy grunt and his shadow weaved and collapsed on the ground. He heard Bill's breath quicken and draw deeper.

"You're hit?" said Goodnight.

"Yes."

"Throw away your gun. Throw it this way."

Bill was out of sight on the ground. He was sighing, he seemed to be speaking to himself. The better part of a minute passed before Goodnight heard the gun drop on the ground. He stepped into the middle of the runway, moving forward. He saw Bill's shoulders rear up and plain caution made him spring aside, and so miss the last bullet Bill flung at him. It was one of those tricks. He came at Bill, his revolver sagging on the target that lay as a dull lump directly before him on the ground. He said: "You played that one too close, Bill."

"You broke my leg," said Bill, grinding his words between his teeth. "I'm in bad shape. Light a match. You hit me in the knee. You've crippled me. Light a match."

"No use botherin'."

"You wouldn't do it," Bill said. "I'm through. You wouldn't shoot now."

"Think of Niles Brand," prompted Goodnight.

There was a part of a crowd on the street. He heard men's voices out here. He heard a woman's voice, sounding like Virginia's. Bill heard it too. Bill said to him in a more confident voice: "No, you wouldn't." He called out in a suddenly anxious, high tone: "Virginia—come here."

Goodnight swung back through the stable. The girl passed him in the darkness, walking rapidly, and men came into the stable after her. When he got to the sidewalk, he saw Syd there. Syd said: "A bad job of it?"

"I suppose so," said Goodnight.

"Poor light for shootin'."

"Yes," said Goodnight. He moved to the Texican and stood by its wall. He got to thinking about himself and he said: "Why'd I turn down a fair chance? Why did I fire low?" He was puzzled about it and searched for some kind of answer. Three men walked out of the stable, carrying Bill by him. Light struck from the saloon and ran over Bill's face. Bill had his eyes shut and his skin was pale and he held his fists together on his chest, his fingers tight. Virginia walked behind. She saw Goodnight and stared at him as she went by. She didn't stop, but the stare lingered with him. It was as though he were far away from her, a stranger looked at without recognition; and all this piled up on him until he crossed to the Trail and signaled for a drink. He stood with his elbows on the bar and he thought to himself: "Why did I fire low?"

He was disappointed in himself and the memory of

Niles Brand reproached him for a job poorly done; and still the drive was out of him and he felt no more desire in the matter. He felt no triumph, no regret. He was like a long-abandoned water-barrel on the desert, empty, its staves warped, capable of holding nothing. That emptiness was the only feeling he had. "Why," he asked himself again, "did I fire low?"

Virginia stood in the lobby, waiting. They had taken Boston Bill to the back room at the hotel, that same back room in which Niles Brand had died. She heard him lift his voice to a desperate shout: "Get me off this bed!" She heard Syd say in his even, unsympathetic voice: "Be damned if we spend the time to lug you upstairs. What's the matter with this bed?"

"Get me out of this room."

"The bed sheets have been changed," said Syd. "They ain't the same ones Niles Brand was lyin' in. That's fair enough, ain't it?"

She watched Doc Teeter come in and go down the hall to the room. She waited, her face sharp and set. She heard Bill groaning steadily; she heard him cry out and curse as Teeter — whose fingers had grown rough from handling so many men like Bill — made his examination. She sighed a little, but not for Bill. She had a problem in her mind and it engaged all of her attention. Teeter came down the hall, the day's heat flushing his face. He said: —

"I'm goin' to get some chloroform. I'll need you. You can go in there and wait. Settle him down."

"What's wrong, Doc?"

"Goodnight's bullet smashed his kneecap. I got to clean that out. Go in there. I've seen men take it a lot better than he is. Tell him he ain't doin' his reputation any good."

She walked down the hall, into the room. Syd and two other men stood back, looking on with disinterest. They weren't enjoying Bill's pain; they were simply calloused to it, watching his weakness with some contempt. They expected better of him. Bill lay under a sheet, he had his hands clenched together on the edge of the sheet; he had torn it, and gripped another section, and torn that. He kept turning on his shoulders and his face was gray, and glistened damply. He stared at Virginia, the pupils of his eyes large and black.

She said to the other men: "Go on out," and waited while they went. She stood at the bed's side, looking down on Bill.

"Get me out of this room," he said.

"What's wrong with it?" she said.

He looked at her, and said nothing. It was Syd, just leaving, who turned to answer her. "This was the room Niles Brand was in," he said, and went on.

She watched Bill, knowing him better then than she had before. Her face took on its cool expression and he saw it at once.

"What are you thinking of now?" he said. "What are you going to do?"

"Stay by you, Bill."

"I can see something. Some scheme. Something up your sleeve."

"No, Bill," she said. "I'm staying by you. You need me." He was, she realized, a far weaker man than she had guessed. He was tricky and he was dishonest. Even through his charm she had long ago discerned that fact. But what she now knew was that he lacked iron. He could be harnessed and he could be managed. As soon as she knew it, she understood how it would be. This man was hers.

Doc Teeter came in with a small can, and a little coneshaped frame. He put these on a table; and presently the hotel man came in with a pan of water that had been boiling. Doc Teeter took off his coat and rolled up his sleeves; he opened the can and dripped some of the liquid on the gauze which lay over the cone frame. The first smell of chloroform brought a dead, dark expression to Bill's face.

"What are you going to do?"

"Get a bullet out of you."

"Let it stay."

"Sit on the edge of the bed, Virginia. You'll hold this over his face."

Bill squirmed. He stared at Virginia. "Be careful with that thing."

Teeter put the cone over Bill's face. Bill moved his face aside, whereupon Teeter cursed him, and added: "Don't make trouble."

Bill's voice came out from the cone, muffled and touched with panic. "Don't let him do anything drastic, Virginia. Look out for me, will you? There's nobody else I can trust—"

"I'll look out for you," she said, and watched him slowly fall asleep.

"This going to bother you?" asked Doc Teeter.

"No," said Virginia. "Nothing like that bothers me." She watched Teeter pull back the sheet, exposing Bill's smashed leg, from which the trouser leg had been cut. She said: "Will it cripple him?"

"He'll be lame," said Teeter. "But he don't have as much grit as I figured."

"He'll do," said Virginia.

Teeter lifted the cone and looked at Bill's eyes and face. He pinched Bill's skin. He gave Virginia an old,

253

shrewd glance. "Your man?"

"Yes," said Virginia.

"You're takin' a chance. You know what he is."

"I can manage him," said Virginia. She watched Teeter set about his work with an unconcerned method. She watched the instrument drop into the bullet hole, but it made no effect on her. She was thinking, "He'll be satisfied with the bargain. I know him that well. He'll never love me very much, but neither will I love him. Not at all. And I can hold him down. I know it." She thought of Goodnight with a sharp start of longing. And then, to console herself, she thought: "I could never have made him do as I wished. But Bill will mind me. It is best that way."

Goodnight, having had one drink, moved out of the Trail, turned the corner and walked in idleness toward the foot of the street — toward that shed where he had met Niles days before. He went all the way to the shed and stopped there, looking into the farther shadows. He thought of Niles, and he thought of his sister, and those two people were far away from him, and he was alone and without anything to hold him. He turned and cruised back. When he got before Rosalia's house he saw her on the porch, standing beside the doorway's light. He came to her steps and he stopped and looked at her. He sat down on the steps, and rolled himself a cigarette. She was behind him.

"When does it rain in this country?"

"October."

He lighted the cigarette. He folded his hands together looking out upon the shadows.

She said: "You're through now?"

"Yes."

"Where are you going?"

"Wish I knew."

She said: "Bob Carruth sent Slab down here to tell me you were in trouble. I might have helped you. But I didn't come. You went up there of your own will and you were old enough to take care of yourself."

"That's all right," he said.

"You could have stayed on Sun, couldn't you?"

"I could have stayed."

"But you wouldn't," she murmured. "It is too late. You need to ride, and be in trouble."

"No," he said, thinking it over. "I had a fair shot at Bill. And I was thinkin' of Niles when I leveled the gun on him. Still, before I fired I dropped the muzzle and shot him in the legs. I do not know why."

"Frank," she said.

He rose and turned to her. He saw her round, stilled face. He saw the shape of her shoulders and the shining of her black hair; and he remembered the great wave of warmth that had come from her lips, surrounding him with comfort and rushing its sweetness and its discontent through him. She said: "The wish to kill him wasn't in you."

"No," he said, "it wasn't. I must be—" He stopped to consider it and his thoughts took him back. He stood in front of her a full minute before he thought he had any kind of answer. "It must be that I remembered McSween. Nothing came out of that—nothing good. It didn't end anything. I don't regret it, but it didn't make the memory of my sister any better. I suppose a man learns these things pretty slow."

"You could have had Virginia, too," she said.

He ignored the question. He said: "It is hell to reach the end of one road and not know where the next one goes."

"Why didn't you take her?" she asked.

He threw away the cigarette. Her presence came strongly against him. He recalled her first kiss; and he recalled the last scene with Virginia. Then he knew why he had not taken Virginia. He said: "Because I kissed you first and there never was anything like it afterwards."

He saw her face lift a little. He said, "Why, of course. I am an ignorant man for not knowin' it before." He came forward and touched her with his arms. "Is it that way with you—as it is with me?"

She didn't answer him. She didn't move away at the pressure of his hands; she didn't move forward. He pulled her to him, looking down at her face as it came up. He saw her lips tremble a little, and wait—and it was like a great burst of heat when he kissed her and felt again that rush of inexpressible things through him. He thought: "This is what has been troubling me," and he stepped back. She was smiling at him; and now she held him.

"Frank," she said, "it was hard not to come to you. But I could follow you no farther. I had to wait while you found your own wishes."

"It takes a long time and a lot of misery," he said, "for a man to come to what is right and to what is good."

"Now that you are here," she said, "I'll follow you wherever you wish. I told you that in the beginning."

He thought about that and he said: "These hills are good. I want to stay in them. I want to stay where I found you. I want—"

The way he said it struck her powerfully, so that she could not wait for all that he said. The pressure of her hands drew his head down and he met her lips again.